Also by Graham Swift

Ever After

Ever After

by Graham Swift

Alfred A. Knopf

New York

1992

This Is a Borzoi Book
Published by Alfred A. Knopf, Inc.

———————

Copyright © 1992 by Graham Swift, Ltd.
All rights reserved under International
and Pan-American Copyright Conventions.
Published in the United States by
Alfred A. Knopf, Inc., New York.
Distributed by Random House, Inc., New York.
Originally published in Great Britain
in 1992 by Picador.

Library of Congress Cataloging-in-Publication Data
Swift, Graham [date]
Ever after / Graham Swift.—1st American ed.
p.   cm.
ISBN 0-679-40954-8
I. Title.
PR6069.W47E9 1992
823'.914—dc20   91-57917   CIP

Manufactured in the United States of America
First American Edition

For my mother and father

. . . et mentem mortalia tangunt

Aeneid, I

Ever After

1

These are, I should warn you, the words of a dead man.

Or they are at least—the warning stands—nothing more than the ramblings of a prematurely aged one. I have been in this place now barely a year, but I am fully aware from the inside, as I think the public is from the outside, of its effect of induced senescence. There are, these days, those sexy young studs of academe who attempt to go against the grain. But even they, it can be observed, when they reach a certain age—roughly my age, a little past fifty—begin to settle rather quickly into the lean and slippered pantaloon. They look about them at their venerable surroundings, at the privileges they possess, they take stock of their no longer galloping careers, and they decide, consciously or not, that true donhood, like the quality of fine wine, is inseparable from age.

It is something in the air here. Before they are sixty, they are emulating one of the many varieties: the crusty and cantankerous; the bald and bumbling; the silver-haired exquisite; the bespectacled and tousled distrait; the free-wheeling eccentric; the wide-eyed, latter-day infant, helpless in all mundane matters but possessed of a profound understanding of Sanskrit. By seventy or eighty—and there is no reason, given the pampering they get, why they shouldn't go on for decades—they are convinced they have reached their true flowering and that, whatever their status in their particular fields (though eminence may be assumed), they are, in themselves, rare birds, exceptional cases, worthy of living enshrinement.

(Potter, by the way, is pushing forty-eight.)

We are, of course, an endangered and thus protected species. If natural selection had had its nasty way, we should have been wiped out long ago, a fragile, etiolated experiment (I have slipped into the insidious "we"). Once, no doubt, when we stepped, blinking, out of our cloisters, the newfangled foibles of the modern city, not to say of the world beyond, would have seemed specious and temporary; our ancient walls would have seemed the true, real, permanent thing. But now it is those ancient walls which have become artificial and implausible, like a painstakingly contrived film set. It is everything beyond that is real. If hardly reliable. Out there, we are given to believe (twelve months, did I say? It feels like twelve years), the world is falling apart; its social fabric is in tatters, its eco-system is near collapse. Real: that is, flimsy, perishing, stricken, doomed. Whereas here . . .

But shouldn't we dodos understand this?

The University naturally takes its own shrewd steps, as it has always done, to ensure its survival. But survival of the fittest? A few dubiously nimble brains in a few desiccated, enfeebled bodies? I had hardly been here a few weeks when I began to have a dream which I am sure all my fellow Fellows dream. Out there in the dark, in the "real world," is a prowling, snarling lout, all tattoos and bared teeth. He too, like us, is social scrap, but without our preservation order. No privileges, no prospects, no pride, no compunction. Like many who do not have those things, he has plenty of brawn and spite, and one day, with a horde of his brethren, he is going to break through our precious, time-honoured walls and beat our estimable brains out.

4

But this vision does not trouble me so much now. Not now. If the Vandals are coming, the Vandals are coming. Death in such a fashion, deserved or undeserved, would of course be appalling. But death itself is another matter. The deaths of others have lately punctuated—shattered, overturned—my life. No less than three—I shall come to them all—in eighteen months. But only very recently, despite this forced familiarity, have I looked the beast itself hard in the face. Not just looked it in the face but wanted it to devour me. I am talking of that experience, given to few, of being returned to life from almost-death. I am talking, in my case, of attempted self-slaughter.

This is the real reason why I say I am prematurely decrepit. My recipe, you see, was at fault. These things (I know from example) can be well executed or hopelessly botched. I was found. They rushed me away, pumped me, thumped me, jump-started me, wired me to the latest gadgets. And the net result of all this was that I opened again these eyes which I thought to have closed for ever and began breathing and thinking for myself (though that phrase begs questions) once more.

But you can imagine the shock to the system. It is not as though my hair has turned white or I have been reduced to a haggard and wasted spectre. I recognise the face in the mirror. Or rather, I recognise that I have never truly recognised it. But I have certainly slowed down a bit. I certainly need to take it easy. I have, for the time being at least, the pitiful gait, the sad posture and the low reserves of an old man. I look more *like* a don. But, more to the point, I feel as though I have *moved on*, in some critical but indefinable way, from what I was before. I have left my former self, whatever that was, behind. I am changed.

What I do not feel is pain—I mean spiritual pain. I do not groan and weep to be restored again to the consciousness I had hoped to forfeit, I do not regard the failure of my attempt as a twist of ineffable cruelty. I simply feel as though I have become someone else. And I am not sure if I accept or resent the process. One part of me seems to have occupied a place of serene detachment. I feel like the ghost of Troilus at the end of Chaucer's poem, which, ascending through the spheres of heaven (no, I did not have that famed experience of rising out of my own body and surveying it from the ceiling), looked down with dispassionate equanimity on the former scene of all his joy and sorrow. While another part of me—hence these ramblings—feels the forlorn urge to find and meet my former self again, secretly wondering, as it does so, whether the meeting will be happy or disastrous.

I am not me. Therefore was I ever me? That is the gist of it. A proof of all this lies before your very eyes. Or at least before mine, since you have no means of comparison and only my word to go on. But that is the point: these *words*, or rather the tone, the pitch, the style of them and consequently of the thoughts that underly them, are not mine. I have penned in my time—long ago—a thesis and an academic paper or two, but I have never begun to write anything as—personal—as this. Yet this way in which I write is surely not *me*. What would you call it? A little crabbed and sardonic? A little wry? A tendency to the flippant and cynical? Underneath it all, something careless, heartless? Is this how I am?

But these are minor matters, you say. What is important, what you are dying (excuse the phrase) to know, is what brought me to the pitch of staging my own death in the first place. I could get out of this by saying that since I am a different person now from what I was then (only three weeks ago), how can I possibly tell you? But it is not as simple as that. Perhaps these pages will eventually explain.

6

Perhaps they will give *me* an explanation. I will only say, for the time being, that for a large part of my life, ever since my old English master, Tubby Baxter, made us read the play, I have imagined myself—surreptitiously, presumptuously, appropriately, perversely—as Hamlet. And you all know one of his tendencies.

Fifty-two, you will say, is a little old to be playing Hamlet, but the fads of adolescence die hard. If you knew me better, you might suppose that for much of my time, despite being for some years (things have come full circle) a professional exponent of English literature and having also a privileged link with the theatre, I would have had no use for this skulking, brooding figure. This is a roundabout way of saying that if happy men exist, I was for many years, for the best years of my life, a happy man. Yes, a happy man. But perhaps the pensive prince was always there, lurking in some morbid toy-box, a foil to the brightness of my days. And when the lights suddenly went out, less than two years ago, he popped up again with a vengeance— vengeance being another of his preoccupations.

It is strange that I never told Ruth about this secret affinity. After all, she more than once played Ophelia— the last time, you might say, for real. I don't like to think I had secrets from Ruth. But perhaps it was because she was an actress that I never confessed: she would have taken my fixation as the pretension of a would-be actor. And it was she, in any case, who made the image absurd. It was she who made me happy.

I shouldn't blame Tubby Baxter. Rather, I owe him infinite thanks for introducing me to Literature, which despite its failure to save lives, including, I suppose I must say, my own, and despite its being, in a place like this, for ever chopped up and flung into preservatives as if it were a subject for an autopsy, I still believe in. I still believe it is the speech, the voice of the heart. (Say things like that round here and see what happens.) Tubby Baxter was not to blame for the doleful but charismatic Renaissance protagonist who has somehow got under all our skins. Nor was he to blame for the circumstances which induced in me a particularly acute rapport.

Hamlet is actuated, or immobilized, by two questions: (1) is there or is there not any point to it all? (2) Shall I kill Claudius? Or to put it another way: shall I kill Claudius or shall I kill myself? It was the vengeance theme that grabbed me from the start, just as much as the distraught meditations on the meaning of life, though I understood, even aged thirteen-and-a-half, that the two questions were not inseparable.

For Claudius, read Sam Ellison. "Uncle Sam," as he was inevitably known, since he hailed from Cleveland, Ohio. Otherwise my stepfather, and founding father of Ellison Plastics (UK). For forty years of my life I have conducted a theoretical vendetta against Sam, though I do not think real killing was ever on the cards. And the odd thing is I have always liked him. I have never been able to help liking him.

Now he is dead; and revenge is pre-empted, or has been satisfied. Or, if revenge is a two-sided game, it is Sam who in a posthumous but canny fashion has got his revenge on me. I rather think, in fact, that Sam's death, which occurred only six weeks ago, may not have been unconnected with my own averted one. It is not the huge, primary things that push you over (I suppose I can speak now as an authority) but the odd, secondary things. He died, and I always really liked him. Furthermore, Ruth being already dead, his death removed—I have to admit it, absurd as it seems—one of the main shaping factors, one of the plots of my life.

———

What was left? Potter? Katherine? The strange, stray notebooks of an unknown man—another latter-day fixation—who lived over a century ago? But I will come to all this.

The manner of his death—death number three, chronologically speaking—was also significant, though to me it was neither as surprising nor as scandalous as it might be to a number of people who do not know about it or as it is to a number of people who are conspiring to hush it up. (I could get my posthumous revenge that way, but it would be cheap, low-down revenge.) He died of a heart attack in a Frankfurt hotel room, aged sixty-seven. His death was reported by the call-girl he was with at the time, who, to give her her due, might simply have fled the scene. At the fatal moment, either Sam was on top of her or she was on top of Sam. At any rate, it seems they were intimately connected when death occurred. An unsavoury business. But then if we could choose our deaths—and I tried to choose mine—I am not so sure that this wasn't exactly the kind of death Sam might have preferred. (You see what this new me is like.)

Under certain circumstances, generosity is one of the most effective and perhaps one of the sweetest means of revenge. If it were not for Sam, I would not be enjoying the mixed blessings of my present situation—I mean the sanctuary of these ancient walls, not my recent resurrection. I will come to this too in a moment. There is the more immediate question of Sam's will and my prominent inclusion in it. I must reveal that I find myself a rich man, and that had my attempted demise been successful, I would have immediately made the taxman the chief beneficiary of my short-lived wealth. I am a plastics heir, you might say, in the way that people talk of cocoa heirs, or rubber barons.

But it is not just a question of the money. Is a plastic cup less real than a china one? Nylon stockings less real than silk? More to the point, is plastic any more fraudulent than a stage performance? Or a poem? Yet long ago when my former self refused my stepfather's offer of a future in plastic, it did so in the conviction that the real stuff of life lay elsewhere. And I am not alone, perhaps, in regarding plastic as the epitome of the false. Sam never saw it that way. In those days when it seemed to me that his goal was nothing less than the polymerization of the world (this is when the spirit of Hamlet breathed newly and fiercely in me), his argument would have been roughly thus: "You gotta accept it, pal" (he called me pal, when he did not call me "kid" or, scathingly, "professor"), "the real stuff is running out, it's used up, it's blown away, or it costs too much. You gotta have *substitoots*."

Yet, as Ellison Plastics went from strength to strength (without my assistance), it would have been clear to anyone that Sam's appetite for the "real stuff" developed in proportion to his capacity, with the money he made from substitutes, to purchase it: the new mansion in Berkshire —*real* Tudor (with a swimming-pool), as opposed to the mock Tudor in which I was raised; the affectation of fine tailoring and choice antiques; in its ultimate form, the apotheosis of Sam, a New World clone, into a Real English Gentleman. A plan preposterously conceived, doomed from the start by his indelible Cleveland accent, but earnestly and perseveringly undertaken: the genealogical investigations (why should these things have mattered to *him*?); the wondrous discovery, not that he had come over with the Normans or was of *Mayflower* stock, but that a former Ellison, John Elyson (d. 1623), had been a senior Fellow of this College, this place where I am now myself an inmate. Which gave him an hereditary stake in the hallowed ancient walls; and gave him the nerve, in his sixty-seventh year, to boost the college finances by a handsome endowment, the one (secret) condition of this munificent gesture being that it should provide for a new college fellowship, the Ellison Fellowship, whose first incumbent, whatever the outward form of selection, should be me.

And this is the Sam who once mocked and refused to fund my former yen to be a scholar.

Without knowing the full story—give me time—you may sniff here the bitter scent of retaliation. It was his way of coming to my rescue after Ruth's death. There was the question of my income. One way or another, as he tenderly reminded me, I had lived off Ruth's earnings. And there was the question of my seemingly incurable paralysis in the face of Ruth's absence. Better to be somewhere where paralysis was generally accommodated. In other words, it was his way also of humiliating me and, after lifelong resistance, rendering me entirely dependent upon him. The cloister was my real home all along, wasn't it? So much for my fugitive dream of a life with performers, show people. Back to your books, professor.

The trouble was I really liked him, and the trouble was I was desolate and he was being kind. In the event, anxious not to forgo its windfall, the College did not raise a squeak at the dubiousness of my candidature (a ten-year career, abandoned some fifteen years ago, as an unillustrious university lecturer). The embarrassments and resentments came later. Nor did the College seem to mind its revered fabric being underpinned by plastic.

Sam's death, leaving me in this utterly bogus position, with the duty of being a living testimony to his noble public gesture, was like the closing of a trap. "One day, pal, you'll get the money, I'll see that you get the money!" This was how he threatened me when I went my own proud, penniless way, years ago—as if money were a penalty, an inescapable second-best.

You see, I think I found the real stuff, the true, real stuff. Now it seems, in this new life, I am turned to plastic. I am born again in plastic.

Four o'clock. Chimes float gently over the soft, historic air. What benign incarceration! What beguiling obsolescence! What agreeable trappings in which not to know who you are. The contemplative life! Sometimes even the most disgruntled inmate or sceptical visitor will be touched by a sentiment that is more than just picturesque nostalgia. Twilights full of bells and the pad of feet on old stones. Lights in study windows. Arches and towers. The whole absurd but cherished edifice rising like some fantastical lantern out of the miasmal Fens and out of the darkness of dark ages. The illusion of the illusion. It is civilization that we are talking about, that we are saving, we dotty dons.

Here, in our exclusive asylum.

When I emerged from the hospital, a fully reconditioned if fragile specimen, a period of convalescence was ordained. What better convalescent home than the old College itself? With its immured peace, its quiet lawns and its long experience of catering to the frailties and follies of learning. It was the long vacation. The long vacation, indeed. I was considerately and spitefully relieved of my scant college duties. A mere charge to its budget. A mere token of a Fellow.

And so I sit in these college gardens, under the shade of an Indian bean tree (a fine, mature example), trying to recover my substance. The weather is warm and settled. All the tranquil delights of a lovingly tended garden in high summer greet my eyes. The gardeners give me a wide, respectful berth. It is not quite a case of the Bath chair and the plaid rug. I can make my own way here from my rooms. On my knees is an inverted wooden tray and on it this notepad.

The gardens lie separate from the college buildings, across the river and, happily, some distance from it. At this time of the year, in weather like this, the river is a mêlée of mismanaged punts, splashes and squeals, with all the gentle charm of a wet T-shirt competition. Even here, in my arbour, the occasional scream or cackle of laughter reaches me; and more adventurous tourists, taking the path from the bridge, through the avenue of limes, and stopping at the gap in the high hedge and the little gate with its discreet, white-on-black sign, "Fellows Only," might even be able to observe me, across the lawn. Look, they must think, like visitors at a zoo, pausing by some cage of shy rarities, there is one of *them*. And no doubt, seeing me scribble at this notepad, they take me to be immersed in some unfathomable and abstruse research.

But aren't I?

Why should I resent my situation? I am restored to life. The sun shines through a punkah of green, tender leaves. Life! Life! Does it matter, so long as you breathe, who the hell you are? Or where you are? Or what you remember? Or what you miss? Why should I hate the man—who is dead anyway, and whom I *liked*—who has provided me with all this? Who has taken away from me—good God, how life can change, how everything can change in the space of less than two years—all worldly cares? But I have not told you yet the nub of my hatred, the nub of my forty years' vicarious habitation of Elsinore as my second home. There is nothing worse than Revenge Refuted. You see, I thought Sam killed my father. So to speak. But now I know he didn't. My father killed my father. And this in more ways than one.

2

When I try to remember the glorious, the marvellous, the lost and luminous city of Paris, I find it hard to separate the city that exists in the mind, that existed even then, perhaps, mainly in my mind, from the actual city whose streets I once trod and which is now older by some forty years. I have never gone back. I never went there with Ruth—because of the memories—though I went to most places with Ruth, and all couples, they say, should go to Paris. Perhaps now I should return—now I am this free, this disengaged man, and now I know, in any case, that certain things were not as they once seemed.

We see what we choose to see, we see what we think we see. In Paris my mother first took me to the opera. A matinée of *La Bohème*—a Parisian tale. And there, in Act One, behind Rodolfo's garret window, and again, in Act Four, as poor Mimi lay melodiously dying, was a painted vista of Paris rooftops just like any you could actually see, and perhaps still can, around Sacré Coeur or Montparnasse. It had never struck me before that Reality and Romance could so poignantly collude with each other; so that ever afterwards I saw Paris as a palpable network of "scenes," down to the subtle lighting of a smoky-blue winter's morning or the blush of a spring evening, the incarnation of something already imagined. It scarcely occurred to me—my imagination did not go in this simpler direction—that this same Paris which we came to in November 1945 had been occupied not so long ago by Hitler's soldiery and that our very apartment in the Rue de Belle-chasse, in the heart of the ministerial quarter, had perhaps been the temporary home—as it was our temporary home—of some official of the Reich.

My mother (whom I would definitely not, in the final analysis, call Romantic) must have been moved by the same ambiguous, uncanny reality as I, because I can recall her, only days after our arrival, saying in a rapturous if half-startled voice, "Look, darling, this is Paris, darling" (I knew it was Paris, we were in Paris, we were strolling down the Champs Élysées), "isn't it divine?" And that word, through the refining filter of Paris, is all I need to conjure up my mother. My mother that was (death number two): as she flung the Armstrong-Siddeley through the flashing, leafy lanes of Berkshire (me, a gaping, gleeful, infant passenger beside her); as she licked from her lips the residue of some oozing cream cake (a sweet tooth which only slowly taxed her figure); as she held up to herself, like some flimsy, snatched-up dancing partner, a newly bought frock: "Divine, darling! Isn't it just *divine*?"

I cannot summon my father so easily. I have no touch-stone. Perhaps because of what happened. Perhaps because, in any case (sons need time—they truly need time—to get to know their fathers), he was always a distant and sombre figure, outshone, first to his delight, then to his consternation, by my mother's heedless brightness. Yet I remember him once attempting to draw near—or so I think was his intention. It was in that same Paris apart-ment, on a cold, windy evening, with winter still at war with spring, the lights on outside and a fire burning heart-eningly in the massive, grey marble fireplace. He was standing by the fire, one elbow on the mantelpiece, in full evening rig, waiting for my mother before they left for another of his official functions.

"The thing is," he suddenly said, slowly, with an air of weighed wisdom and of speaking aloud some uncontainable thought, "when you are out on an adventure, you want to be at home by the fire, and when you are at home by the fire, you want to be out on an adventure."

I wish I knew what it was I had said—if anything—that elicited that unusual pithiness. And I wish I had known then, while the fire flickered and the wind scraped at the window, what should have been the proper response. I was nine. There he was, in all his pride, fifty-five years old— some twenty years older than my mother, medals on chest, cigar lit, Scotch and soda—a large one—poured. Some question of mine? Or some impulse in his own mind that seemed to raise the whole, daunting phenomenon of his soldierly past and his mysterious present duties, his aura of belonging to a world of great, glorious (but peculiarly awkward) things?

He seemed surprised at his own words, as if he had not known they were stored inside him. He looked self-consciously at his watch.

"Whatever can your mother be up to?"

Perhaps it was on that same evening—but this surely would have been sooner after our arrival—that I had asked him, point-blank, what were we doing, what was *he* doing, here in Paris? And he'd replied, with a sort of jocular, self-effacing gravity, "Oh—sorting out the world. You know, that sort of thing."

Only once can I remember his attempting to show me the sights of Paris. We had scarcely set out—our first port of call was Napoleon's tomb—when an icy shower caught us, the first of a series which would turn our jaunt into a stoical exercise. I could not help feeling how I would much rather have been with my mother. How she would have turned a change in the weather into a positive pleasure.

Wrestling, laughing, with an umbrella. Scurrying into the aromatic warmth of a café and ordering, in an Anglo-French that was infinitely more convincing if no more proficient than his, "*Un crème, un jus d'orange*," and, falling back into expressive English, "and two of those wicked little tarts!"

Seeing the sights of Paris with my mother! Shopping sprees with my mother in Paris! From her I learnt to see the world as a scintillating shopwindow, a confection, a display of tempting frippery. From her I learnt the delights of ogling and coveting and—by proxy and complicity—spending. I would go with her to spend money. To buy hats, necklaces, gloves, shoes, dresses, cakes. I would wait, perched on a velvet-backed chair, smiled at by the attentive *vendeuse*, while, behind drawn plush curtains, things slithered, rustled, snapped, to an accompaniment of sighs and hums. In the city of perfume we bought perfume. In the city of lingerie we pondered over lascivious creations of silk and lace. If they were meant expressly for his eyes, it only made his noble loftiness the more impressive; but I suspected—I knew—they were not. And in all this I was the adjudicator, the referee, the scapegoat. The oyster-grey or the rose-pink? "Oh, you decide, sweetie. No, you can't? *Bien, tous les deux, s'il vous plaît, Madame.*" "*Tous les deux, Madame? Ah oui, d'accord. Le petit est bon juge, n'est-ce pas?*"

Coming out with her booty, she would hug me ardently, as if it were I who had enabled her so successfully to succumb. In the same way, prior to such purchases, when her eyes fell on anything particularly delicious and desirable in a window, she would squeeze me fiercely, conspiratorially, giving an Ooh! or an Aah! as if it were I alone who could tilt the balance between mere looking and rushing headlong into the shop. "But isn't it just *heavenly*, darling?" I could have lived for, lived in that squeeze. Until I grew up and realised it was almost entirely selfish. She might as well have been hugging herself, or a handy cushion or spaniel.

Sorting out the world! He should have sorted out himself and his own jeopardized household. Did he know—but he must have done from the very beginning, he must have known what she was "up to"—that while he was busy sorting out the world and "talking with the Allies" (another cryptic phrase, which made me think of some gossipy, over-neighbourly family) and I was busy at the little *école* for foreigners they found for me, "*Maman*," as I'd begun precociously to call her, was busy entertaining or being entertained by Uncle Sam, or plain Sam Ellison as he then was, who had his own recipe for sorting out the world, expressible in one single, vulgar word: plastics? In *Maman*'s defence, it could be said that she too was engaged with the Allies, Sam being American. And in Sam's defence, it could be said that, fuelled as it was by rank commercialism, he too had a sense of mission.

"It's the stuff that's gonna mould the future. I mean, literally. Anything from a coffee cup to an artificial leg, to the sock that goes on it."

"And then there's plastic surgery."

"No, that's kinda different, sweetheart."

(As my mother, an expert at lash-fluttering *fausse-naïveté*, well knew.)

He must have known. If I could sniff these matters out, even in their early, covert stages, then he— But then I was a virtual accomplice. When I emerged from my *école* in the afternoon to see Sam just dropping *Maman* off from a taxi, or made my own way home to find her in a distinct state of having hastily bathed and dressed, I would receive not guilty looks but one of her swift, smothering, implicating hugs—essentially no different from her shopping hugs. Thank you for letting me buy that dress—isn't it gorgeous? Thank you for letting me fuck Sam—isn't he *divine*? And, yes, that word had only to spring from her lips and I believed it to be so. I thought Sam—six feet of hard-muscled American avarice—was divine, and I thought *crêpe suzette* and *tarte tatin* were divine, and I thought oyster-grey silk cami-knickers were divine, and I thought my mother's laughter, the sheer, vicious gaiety in her eyes, was divine.

"Do up my buttons, sweetie, would you? There's an angel."

A whole world existed in which men did up the backs of women's dresses at four o'clock in the afternoon.

I can see it now, that apartment above the Rue de Belle-chasse. Its ponderous furnishings, its tarnished chandeliers, its diplomatic decorum under perpetual threat from my mother's chatter and laughter, from her gusty scurryings from room to room, and—but this was hardly a threat—from her magic snatches of song. I learnt never to ask, never to prompt, never to wait. Only to recognise the likely moments: in the evenings when the traffic outside began to toot in a distinctly perkier fashion; after one of her unspecified "lunch engagements"; in moments of lingering and meaningful *déshabillé*. Lights coming on in the streets. Wafts of scent. The gurgle of bath water running and, above it, lilting, throbbing: "*Dove so-ono i bei mome-enti . . .*"

And what world was he sorting out? Some new, rebuilt world which would one day be unveiled to the dazzlement and shame of such backsliders as Mother and me? Or some old, dream-world restored, in which implacable British sergeant-majors bawled for ever over far-flung parade grounds and men followed well-trodden paths to glory and knighthoods?

He was fifty-five. And I had the insight of an infant. But it seems, now, that I could have told him then: that world was gone. An axe had dropped on it.

And yet— Paris was still Paris. Even the Paris that a year ago had emerged from four years of occupation. The chestnuts kept their ranks; café tables spawned; a thousand mansarded roofs glinted in the autumn sunshine, without a bomb-site among them. By the following spring, Paris had the air of something simply resumed. It was only winter, not a world war, that had passed: shutters flung open; awnings lowered; bed linen hanging from upper windows; merchandise once more filling the shops, to be pillaged by my mother.

Paris. April in Paris. I had never seen Paris before, and yet even at nine years old I had this recurring sensation of encountering a vision made fact. If the *trompe-l'œil* Paris of *La Bohème* was an illusion, then on my journeys on foot between our apartment and the *école*, journeys which took a meandering form and had something to do, I suppose now, with a sense of having lost the right path with my parents, I daily disproved the illusion: Paris was the living, breathing rendition of itself.

"*. . . di dolce-ezza e di piacer . . . ?*"

Somewhere on those wanderings to and from school, in the crisp, rimy breath of a January morning, I looked up from the pavement through a tall, lighted window and saw —a true vision. Three—four, five—ballerinas, dressed in leotards and tights, swathed in woollen leg-warmers, dipping, stretching, balancing, raising one leg, extending one arm in that curving way ballet-dancers do, while clinging with the other to a wall bar. I stood transfixed, entranced.

How many times did I pass that window again? How many times was the blind cruelly drawn? Once—but this must have been at a later time of day and I must have been by then a fully-fledged truant, *flâneur, voyeur*—I passed a café at the further end of the same street, and there, sitting at an outside table, even in that midwinter chill (warm and pink from exercise), were my ballerinas. But no longer poised, living sculptures. They were little chattering *mesdemoiselles*-about-town, crossing their legs, nestling their chins into their scarves, responding boldly to the *badinage* of the waiter, blowing at the steamy froth on their *chocolats chauds*. I drew close, feigning interest in an adjacent shopfront. Glowing faces. A sound of female glee. Two eyes, in particular, beneath a dark fringe, which momentarily turned on me. Two pink lips, a flicking tongue adorned with the flakes of a croissant.

A crude case of my mother's shop-window lusts? But I knew it was more than that. What enthralled me was the pathos, the dignity, the ardour of *rehearsal*. The sublime fact that in a world so in need of being sorted out, young girls of sixteen and seventeen (but, of course, to me, then, they were Women) could devote themselves so strenuously to becoming sugar-plum fairies.

Lift the axe! I wish I could have taken him, gripped his hand, as he gripped mine, suddenly, on that wet, chilly day as we emerged from the gloom of Les Invalides, stood him before that secret window and said: There, it's for that that you are sorting out the world. I wish he could have gripped my hand more firmly still, come closer to me out of his remoteness; told me, warned me.

Paris first bred in me the notion that the highest aim of civilization is the loving perfection of the useless: ballerinas, café chatter, Puccini operas, Elizabethan sonnets, silk

22

underwear, *parfumerie, patisserie*, chandeliers, the magic hush when the lights go down in an auditorium . . .

"*Mimi! Mimi! Mimi!*"

. . . and Romantic Love.

She actually cried, she actually wept in the seat beside me, dabbing her eyes and clutching my hand, while her lips mimed the arias.

Lift the axe! A Paris morning, in April. Perhaps that very morning I had peeped at my ballerinas. Morning turning to midday. Sunshine; pigeons; the smell of food. She is waiting beyond the gates of the *école*, though by now I am used to making my own way home. She is alone and some-how purposeful, fixed in her own space. She opens her arms and gives me an engulfing hug, as if I have returned from somewhere far away. But she is not smiling (or crying). She is composed and authoritative; the hug is like some solemn ceremony.

"Your daddy has had an accident, at his office."

"An accident?"

"Your daddy has had an accident. And died."

The second part of this statement, uttered unemphati-cally, almost perfunctorily, scarcely registered at first. Cer-tain announcements take time to reach the brain.

"An accident with a gun."

With a gun? With a *gun*? What was he doing, in his office, in Paris, in the seventh *arrondissement*, in the centre of civilization, with a gun? A sudden, racing fantasy, a whole alternative life for my father, who was now dead, bloomed in my head. He was a spy, an undercover agent, he was on some hush-hush mission. It explained his dis-tance, his absences, his resonant words about "adventure." He bore the constant burden of secrecy and danger. For a while the delusion was so strong that it turned into a pang of regret: I had discovered this source of excitement too late—I could never, now, have access to it.

And perhaps it was this sense of deprivation, rather than the simple fact that my father was dead, that made tears rush to my eyes.

"Yes, my darling, you cry. Cry. Cry."

And, opening her arms again, stooping, but unweeping, she crushed me against that warm, ready bosom, where Sam, by now, must already have been crushed many times.

She never used the word "suicide." Perhaps I would not have known what it meant. Perhaps I guessed and only wanted, as she did, to gloss over the fact. It was Sam, in any case, who confirmed my suspicions. He and I were alone in the apartment. She had become a busy woman. I knew nothing about inquest proceedings, let alone in foreign cities. This must have been before she and I went back, the first time, with the body, to Berkshire.

I said, "He meant to do it, didn't he?"

A bold, grown-up, not-to-be-evaded question.

"Yes, pal. I guess so."

Later, it occurred to me that Sam might have been briefed to deal with this very point. But his brief, or his aptitude for it, only went so far. I was nine, he was twenty-four. Twenty-four seems now such a slender age—not so far from nine—but there was no doubt that during that time in Paris those fifteen years between Sam and me could be a wide gap to leap. Not so wide, it's true, as the forty-six years between me and my father. Which gave Sam a distinct advantage in winning me over—along with the ability to slide into a boyish, big-brotherly familiarity quite beyond my father. But I always thought this was just a knack, an act for my benefit.

———

That morning, days after my father's death, was the first time that it occurred to me, from the vantage of my own unlooked-for access of experience, that Sam really was, perhaps, just a kid. The fact that almost as big a gap of years existed between him and my mother as between him and me did not escape me. Once, on one of those tumultuous afternoons that seemed now to belong to another age, I had heard my mother simper, beyond closed, impassive doors, "Come on, Sammy, come to Mummy. . . ." I recalled it now, not recognising one of the least exceptional idioms of love. It was as though at the very point when Sam was most culpable, I both saw he was most innocent and discovered a new cause for enmity.

He took out a cigarette and I saw that his hand, his strong, young man's hand, was shaking. He must have known I'd seen it.

"Why?" I said. The inevitable follow-up.

But "why" was not one of Sam's words, the scrutiny of motives was not his strong point.

"I guess you'll have to ask your mother that, pal." He managed to light the cigarette and took a deep, steadying draw.

"I guess I'll have to be looking after your mother now," he added with a kind of feeble cheerfulness, as if the statement were half a question; as if he were watching his youth melt away.

I asked my mother. She was ready to be asked. I suppose there must have been some confabulation between them, a two-stage strategy. It was the moment, of course, for her to have broken down, wept, begged my forgiveness, confessed that her shamelessness had driven a man to his death. The things that happen in opera, they happen in life too. But she didn't. She spoke calmly, almost dreamily.

————

"Perhaps there was something he knew that we shall never know."

Which was, of course, a twisting round of the truth. It was we who had known something which he hadn't known; or which he had known all along and could no longer pretend not to know. Her eyes hardened into a sort of warning whose meaning was clear: Don't play the innocent, sweetie. If I'm to blame, then so are you. You were a party to this. You allowed it, didn't you? You let it happen.

It was true: I might have gone to him at any time, like a true, a dutiful, a worthy son. Spilled the beans.

Then suddenly she smiled tenderly and took me in her arms. "Poor darling," she said, as if I had fallen and grazed my knee; as if at the same time she thought this whole line of thinking was unnecessarily morbid. We were alive; my father was dead. She had taken Sam into her life. She had known what she was doing; she had made her choice. The fierceness, the frankness, of her will to live! She told me, many years later, with complete equanimity, how she had gone to see him in the mortuary. How his head was swathed in bandages, save his face. How they had even put a sticking-plaster over the hole in his temple. She had no squeamishness. No pity, no mercy. I think she even despised him for his death, which, for all its drastic convenience, was nonetheless cowardly, stupid, messy, extreme. She despised this man she had married, exploited, cheated—destroyed.

And it was true: if I had an allegiance, it was to her, not to him. The image of my father rose before me, as inscrutable, as open to interpretation as it was deserving of belated loyalty. He must have known for weeks about the two of them. And even if the penny had dropped only late in the day, did suicide truly answer the circumstances? A former soldier, a man of action. If a bullet was to be involved, it should surely have been placed neatly between Sam Ellison's eyes.

A recurring dream—the very emblem of my addled adolescence: Sam with a fresh, damson-coloured hole (and no sticking-plaster) in his forehead.

But perhaps Sam and Mother were only the last, ill-timed straw. I underestimated the dimensions of the man, this man who had left my life. During those strange, transitional months, as we moved from Paris back to Berkshire, as Mother married Sam and I reached my tenth birthday, the awesome realisation offered itself to me that my father had tried but had simply not been able to sort out the world. People die when their world will no longer sustain them. Duty, ambition and even, now, his wife had let him down. He was fifty-five years old. I can see him feeling the cool weight of the pistol. The "honourable way out"; a soldier's solution. When you are out on an adventure . . . Suddenly death, not the vivid, vaunted death of the battlefield, but the image of himself as a duped nonentity, stared him in the face—and he rushed to meet it.

Lift the axe! Put the pistol back! Carry me back to that world of boulevards and ballerinas. To that songful, mirthful, deceitful apartment. Carry me back even to the innocence of that moment of icy, naked shock—I had never felt it before—round which my mother, by the *école* gates, cast her cloaking embrace. There was a space in the world occupied by my father, which would never be occupied by him again. The spring sun falling on Parisian shutters, Parisian cobbles, was gentle, kindly, beyond reproach. It fell on the fur collar of my mother's coat and picked out of its filaments little pinpoints of gold. All that day I seemed to see that the sunshine was made up of countless particles of irreducible, indestructible, eternal gold.

3

And when she died, when my mother died, I was rushed back to that moment over forty years ago.

The last time I visited her, which I instinctively knew would be the last time I would see her alive, was one exceptionally warm, radiant evening late last September. The curtains, a pale salmon colour, were drawn in her private room, which gave it a ruddy, subdued glow, but here and there a chink let in a shaft of more golden light, in which specks twirled and twinkled. In a hospital (I thought) there should be no specks. But always, in any beam of light, there are these tiny, sparkling shoals. And in a flash I was transported back to that April day in Paris, to the memory of those little flecks of fire in her fur collar, to the memory of my face crushed in that fur collar, its smell and her smell, and the shapely strength of her body beneath her coat, of which her body now was a sad, prostrated parody.

The windows were open behind the curtains and, as her wing of the hospital overlooked a park, there floated in the smell of cut grass, the occasional ricochet of playful voices and the gentle *pok-pok* of a tennis game in progress. It was as though she had expressly arranged the circumstances of her death so that they might seem the least fearsome, the least inimical to life.

She had already displayed, even as her days became numbered, her contempt for the fear of death and her disdain for those who fell prey to it—who lived their lives, as she put it, as if they deserved "a special pass." It was an impressive and impressively timed demonstration. Never before had I heard her enlarge so much on her family, my forebears, about whom, so it would seem, a mixture of shame and scorn had hitherto kept her quiet. It was as if, now the end was near, she was driven reluctantly back to the other extremity of her life, to her origins and ancestry.

She had scoffed at Sam's recent researches in this area, his absurd pedigree-hunting, but also humoured him, as she always humoured Sam, as you might indulge a child. But then Sam, for all his businessman's bravado and native robustness, had a different attitude to death from my mother, as both she and I knew well from times gone by. If I had wanted to confirm it (and gain a little more cheap revenge), I need only have stepped out of that hospital room and along the corridor, as indeed I did later, to where Sam was waiting (I was first, he was next), an expression on his face, despite the mellow warmth of that evening, as if he were sitting in a room made of ice.

I'm glad death took him quickly and unannounced and, as it were, *in flagrante*.

For all her vocal powers, for all her capacity to chatter, squeal and, sometimes, shriek, my mother was never an eager *raconteuse*. I think she regarded reminiscence and tale-telling as a kind of weakness, an avoidance of the central issue of life, which was to wring the most out of the present. I never received from her, any more than I did from my father—perhaps this is why I became such a bookworm—my due dose of bedtime stories. Yet at the very end I was suddenly treated to a final and, so it seemed, irrepressible bedtime story—me, this time, at the bedside—of her remembered sires. And though the story had its moral, though she seemed to summon these ghosts only to arraign them for their folly (rather than to say she would soon be joining them), I wish she hadn't left it so late. I never knew they were such a colourful bunch.

There was, first of all, my grandfather on my mother's side, George Rawlinson, who died before I was born and of whom I knew only that he had been a medical man and, guessing from my mother's silence, that some misfortune best not talked about had befallen him. He was in fact a surgeon at Guy's Hospital, before whom had once lain a brilliant career in the then still-infant neurological branch of his profession. A pioneer brain surgeon, no less.

Who has heard of George Rawlinson? Who has heard of the Rawlinson Forceps, to which George, vainly wooing posterity, gave his name and on whose subcranial purpose I would rather not dwell (though my mother did not shrink from describing it). My grandfather's path to eminence had seemed altogether assured until one day in 1923, when either his sound judgement or his sure fingers failed him just once. In came a sick but restorable young man; out came a permanent vegetable—who just happened to be the darling son of a Lord. Result, by stages: scandal, divorce, penury.

Then there was George's older brother, my great-uncle, Rupert Rawlinson: Major, formerly Colonel Rawlinson; "Ratty" Rawlinson, as he was apparently known to his intimates—"Uncle Ratty" as he was known to my mother. It was in some lesser-known campaign of the Great War —Macedonia? Mesopotamia?—that his military career, likewise seemingly destined for stardom, took its calamitous turn. The wrong decision at the wrong time, an order given or not given that should not or should have been given. An inglorious, unglorifiable blunder. Result: court martial, demotion, ignominy.

My great-uncle did his best to outlive this disgrace, at

least in the strictly numerical sense, since he died aged eighty-one and was still lingering on shortly before I was born. Yet according to my mother—and I am repeating now what she told me, brazenly enough, when her own death-warrant had effectively been signed—it was craven fear of oblivion, the desire to cheat death by the vain quest for distinction, that was the root of the matter, as much with Ratty as with George.

You would have thought that two brothers following the not unrelated trades of soldier and surgeon would not have been so affected. Both would have had fairly naked experience of mortality. But this, my mother claimed, was just the point. They chose professions that brought them close to death, in the empty hope that this would guard them against it. My great-uncle, who was no coward by a soldier's standards and seems to have suffered, on that fateful day, an excess of valour over sense, hoped that his officer's sword and his shining record in the Sudan and elsewhere would confer on him both renown and a kind of personal invulnerability. Likewise, George, as he audaciously probed what some have held to be the very seat of the Soul, might have felt himself privileged above ordinary beings, and might have foreseen his fame outlasting his forceps.

With Rupert, she insisted, the real trouble only began one snowy morning in the winter of 1920, when, a sound but dishonoured sixty-five, he took a nasty tumble down the front steps, cracking his head badly on the way, and for a day or so lay in a parlous condition.

"The man panicked, sweetie. He went to pieces. He thought his hour had come, with his shame still fresh upon him."

How she could have been so sure of this, I don't know.

She was only nine at the time. But then I was only nine when my father—

In any case, it was this incident, in her view, that exposed the true tenor of the man and turned him for the rest of his life into an incurable and exasperating eccentric. The immediate "panic" had taken a specific form. In the midst of his fever and ill-founded terror, Rupert was apparently heard repeatedly to remonstrate that his younger brother was not to come near him, was not going to poke about in *his* skull with his fiendish instruments. George not only did come near him but, with little more than a cursory examination and no recourse to incision, pronounced that Rupert was making a big fuss about nothing and would recover in a day or so. The second humiliation of Uncle Ratty's life.

My great-uncle was revenged, of course, when George took his own irremediable tumble only three years later. But, not satisfied with this, Rupert, as the senior member of the family and chief possessor of its fortunes, proceeded to play a vindictive, teasing game with my grandfather and his children (my mother and her brother, James), taunting them in their reduced circumstances with the meanness of his hand-outs and his own obstructive longevity.

But by this time, it seems, he was no longer entirely in possession of his faculties. That knock on the head, perhaps—just to spite his brother—had had its effect after all. He now devoted his time to perfecting in himself the caricature of a cranky, retired army officer, exaggerating or inventing past honours, while time softened his disgrace; and, when this didn't work, looking for borrowed glory in the family archives. In his last years, this antiquarian urge (I admit it: the spirit of Uncle Ratty lives in me, as it lived even, for a while, in Sam) took an all-consuming form.

33

Namely to prove that since his name, Rawlinson, denoted "son of Rawling," in turn a palpable corruption of "son of Rawley" or "Ralegh," his lineage might be traced, with much labour and subterfuge, to the great Elizabethan worthy himself, he of the pointed beard, muddied cloak and imperishable fame . . .

And then, going back a generation on my grandmother's side, there was the Devon branch of the family—the right region for Sir Walter if the wrong name—who had made and lost their fortune in local copper and tin, neither of which seemed to have been as steady a bet as plastic. . . .

And then (did Uncle Ratty feel moved to pause here, I wonder? Did he peruse the Notebooks? But what did he want with *another* scandal and a lot of wordy mumbo-jumbo, and another non-Rawlinson?) there was Matthew Pearce—my mother's great-grandfather—of Burlford.

All this she told me in the early stages of her illness—not, if I have given that impression, on that final, gilded evening. By then she could not have said anything more, because she had lost the mechanism of speech. Those last visits were to a silent, staring woman, her throat and neck packed around with all kinds of surgical junk, so that she could still breathe, and all verbal communication restricted to what she could write with a marker-pen on a special, wipe-clean clipboard. I think the sudden bout of disclosures, if it expressed in her peculiar way her own readiness to accept death, was also a recognition of the anticipated fact: that before loss of life would come loss of voice; that if she had things to say, she had better speak away. Though when silence struck, I could not help wondering—I still wonder—whether she had quite got round to saying all she intended.

———

I blamed her, silently, and she knew this, for the timing of her death, coming so soon, or at least announcing itself so soon, after Ruth's. Perhaps Ruth's death had immunized me, so that I could face the distress of my mother's with a sort of foggy, battered steadiness. But then she *was* seventy-eight. And, of course, this worked the other way round. I was witnessing in my mother the sort of horrors that Ruth had—avoided. My mother's unrebelling submission to them was a kind of declaration that she was made of tougher stuff than Ruth, as she was made of tougher stuff than my father. (Oh, she was tough, all right.) And I could not help thinking that her merciless appraisal of her family, her parables on mortal dread and the vanity of ambition, were her indirect way of delivering, at last, her jealous judgement on her daughter-in-law.

Why did she have to do it? To die then? To be so cruel? To block, to steal, Ruth's afterlight? But then it struck me that perhaps all of this could be turned round yet another way again, and that, amazing as it was to conceive, there might have been in the cruelty a shred of unbelievable kindness: she was using her death to shake me out of my stupor of grief. ("Buck up, darling, it's not the end of the world.") There was a moment when my grasp of this possibility must have shown in my eyes; and her eyes had glittered back: you see, I am really a mother, after all, not such a selfish bitch—I give myself up for my son. . . .

It was an irony that went unmentioned that death came for her in the form of cancer of the throat, of the larynx. A punishment for having already, in one sense, forsaken her voice? You cannot help these thoughts. But I do not think she was cowed by superstition, any more than she was cowed by death.

———

Her voice! Her singing! Her ringing soprano. It is significant that in her lecture on the lure of fame she did not cite her own once budding musical career. But then she had abandoned it long ago: the point was made. And in any case, in her opinion, her singing voice was just a "gift," she owed it no special duty; and the reason she always gave for her early dedication to it was simple economic necessity in the face of Uncle Ratty's stinginess: "You have to use what you've got, darling—but only when you need to." Was it her fault that some possessive music mistress had "discovered" her? Or that her ailing father, who had once thought of himself as a "gifted" surgeon, took some solace in his final days from his daughter's accomplishment (the tableau is perfect: the humbled dissector of the brain; that ineffable virtuosity)?

The word "gift" troubles me. Is a gift something that belongs to us or not? If it is simply something we have rather than receive, why do we use the strange word "gift"? And if a gift is a true gift, then surely my mother was right—it comes unconditionally; you can take it or leave it, cherish or renounce it. But Ruth would not have held this view. Ruth would have said, I think, though she never said it in so many words, that we must serve our gifts.

I have always thought of myself as one of the great ungifted, so who am I to judge? My mother died, of throat cancer, because she neglected her gift. Ruth died of lung cancer, because she served her gift and was rewarded for it—and fate strikes quickest at the gifted and successful. There is no consistency or justice in superstition—but you have these thoughts. Easier to say that Ruth died of lung cancer because she smoked a lot. But then, we all know, some people smoke and live to be ninety. I like a cigarette myself. (Neither my wife's death nor my own foiled one has cured me of the habit.) A gift is a gift: to treasure or disdain, to use or abuse, keep or reject. Including our bodies? Including our lives? Including our selves?

And, truly, my mother's gift, as I remember it, was like something that didn't belong to her. When she sang, it was as though some other creature was born inside her. A spasm of breast and throat, an upward parturition, a songbird hatching in her bosom—and out of this woman, so unscrupulous, so indolent, so heartless, my mother, would come a sound so sweet and miraculous, it was impossible not to yield.

"Who is Sil-via? What is she-e . . . ?"

It must have softened even the rancorous heart of Uncle Ratty, disturbed in his dusty studies by those clear notes rinsing through the house. It must have bewitched the audience at concert halls and recital rooms in Reading and Maidenhead and Windsor. Among the debris that came into my possession after her death (along with Matthew Pearce's testament) was a yellowed newspaper cutting recording my mother's solo début (arias by Handel, Gluck and Purcell) at a concert in Reading in March 1929, in which the reviewer, Hugo Duval, saving his barbs for the orchestra, singles out "Miss Rawlinson" for her "exceptional promise" and "exquisite charm and purity." Charm and purity! Charm, yes. How much was Hugo's enthusiasm elicited by my mother's vocal talents alone?

A career lay before her (she might have thrown away that cutting; she kept it). She might—who knows?—have trod the opera stage. And yet when she married my father, she abandoned the prospect and sang thenceforth—as if simply for the pleasure of it—only those intoxicating snatches I remember. And when my father died—it took time for me to realise, time for the truth of it to sink in—

she gave up even that. Her throat never quivered, the song-bird never took flight again.

And it is curious that in that catalogue of family failures, in that roll-call of doomed, obscurity-dreading, honour-hunting attention-seekers, she did not mention my father. She avoided my father altogether.

How were they ever joined together? Why, with her merciless view of masculine pretension—though perhaps it was unformed then, perhaps it only *came* with my father—did my mother marry my father? A man over twenty years her senior and, superficially at least, of precisely the same mould as Uncle Ratty: Colonel Unwin (a full and true colonel this time), formerly of the regular army, latterly of some ill-defined, semi-civilian sphere of duty between the military and the diplomatic services. Another careerist, another star-chaser.

One answer is simple and perhaps all-sufficient. He was a good catch. He rescued her; she bagged him. In 1935, when the marriage took place, he was forty-five years old, to her twenty-four. He came of what might have been called then "good Berkshire stock"; had "distinguished himself," with no unfortunate Rattyesque blots, in the Dardanelles and Palestine; had served in India, where—this was about all I learnt from his own lips—he "shot tigers," and where he was married, briefly, the first time around: one of those pathetic, semi-arranged marriages involving a shipped-out bride and ending in tropical fever. My mother told me her name was Vanessa. I see a creature compounded of white tulle and pale, sacrificial skin. . . .

When he returned to England in '33, he was a seasoned officer in his middle years, conditioned by matrimonial disappointment to a life of service and duty, young enough still to nurse ambitions, possessed of a patrimony he had not yet had the chance to squander—and a perfect target for my mother's charm. I don't blame her for fortune-hunting. Now that her father, the hapless surgeon, was dead, how long was she to go on waiting for Uncle Rupert either to die too or to make some provision for her and her younger brother? Yet Ratty, with all his dread of the Great Leveller, lived on, steadily growing more crankish and steadily exhausting what was left of the Rawlinson riches.

It was just possible that the motive of which I know so much—revenge—entered my mother's calculations. An army officer. With a clean and honourable record. And enjoying, at that time, just that rank of major to which Ratty had *fallen*. The mockery of it. The gall of it. Uncle Rupert could not prevent the marriage, but if he ever swore it should take place only over his dead body, he almost proved himself correct, for within a year of the wedding he at last gave up the ghost. Whether he had achieved by then, to his own satisfaction, the ultimate and redeeming goal of his life—certain proof of his kinship with Sir Walter Ralegh—no one can say.

My mother being excluded, or in any case now provided for by marriage, Uncle Ratty's dwindled estate passed to her brother. Who did not have long to enjoy it. For, in reaction, perhaps, to the family tinge of khaki, he joined the Navy in 1939 and was killed in the earliest months of the war, not in action but in some miserable and obscure collision at sea—another instance, I suppose, of Rawlinson ignominy.

I was three years old at the time, so my Uncle Jim, perhaps in his naval togs, must once have dandled me in his arms, but I don't remember him. Nor do I recall my mother's being plunged into sisterly mourning. But a framed photograph of Jim was one of the few personal remnants of her past which she allowed herself to keep. It disappeared when she married Sam. I could see why Sam would never have liked it. It was only after her death—the photo is mine now—that I discovered that she hadn't disposed of it but had simply hidden it from view.

He looks appallingly young and appallingly ignorant. Life has a thousand avenues, but he is fixed for ever—a perpetually grinning midshipman. He has my mother's sparkle, none of her cunning. And, of course—this was Sam's difficulty—I cannot look at that photo without seeing also the photo of Sam's brother, which Sam first showed me, slipping it confidentially out of his wallet and giving me the facts, in those very early days in Paris. A shrewd but ill-fated piece of emotional trading. Sam's brother (tropical whites; a lady-killer's smile), Sam's younger brother, Ed, who for these last forty years and more, just as Uncle Jim has been lying somewhere under the North Sea, has been lying under the South Pacific.

And what did my father—elevated now into some safer, more Olympian zone of warfare, touring the military purlieus of Berkshire, Hampshire and Surrey and sometimes being called to Whitehall, even to Washington—think of his new young bride? At his age, and after the first attempt, his notions of marriage must have been all to do (poor fool) with seniority, authority and self-esteem. He saw my mother as a pretty adornment to his own advancement. Or perhaps—after all those years of rigour under the Indian sun—he melted in the mild air of the Home Counties and in a wave of sweet self-delusion took this rather showy flower to be the perfect, adorable English rose.

And perhaps it was her voice, her gift, that swung it. That turned him from protector (perilous role) into worshipper (even more perilous one). His career; *her* career.

He might have fostered, guided that career—he was prepared to be humble and generous. And the two things were
not uncomplementary. A vision, a consummation: the
steel-haired diplomat and his diva wife; he sits in his box,
proudly and conspicuously clapping, while she, on the
stage, receives an avalanche of bouquets.

(Didn't *his* dream come true in *my* life?)

But scarcely was he married than she gave up her career.
And he was left clutching the rags of his dream, her abandoned stage robes, not knowing—so he would discover—
how to deal with her naked yet somehow less graspable
self.

I think I knew her, in some ways, better than he did. I
think I was closer to her than he ever was. I remember,
for instance, one afternoon in the autumn of what must
have been either '43 or '44. He is away on one of his
mysterious trips, and she, in defiance of the black-out reg-
ulations and with my collusion, is tending a bonfire. There
is the usual pile of dead leaves and garden debris, but on
top of this she is strewing—and I am helping her—so-
called "rubbish": papers, files, letters.

I only guessed later what she was doing. She had decided
that the time had come to dispose of all that "junk" of
Uncle Ratty's that had come to her via her brother and
which her brother had never had time to sort out for himself. All that research. All that *evidence*. All that burrowing
after noble origins. And in amongst the junk there might
so easily have been the disregarded notebooks of Matthew
Pearce of Burlford—who knows if some other, unknown
manuscript was not casually cremated that afternoon?
With my own ignorant hands I might have tossed Matthew
on to the pyre.

I don't remember her showing any special emotion, only
her evident pleasure in what she called a "jolly good bon-

fire, sweetie." She wore for this occasion—but this was typical of her—not some sloppy gardening outfit, but an *ensemble* much more chic than practical: sleek, well-cut trousers, which at that time must have been a matter of fashionable novelty; a figure-hugging, collared jersey, with a Paisley silk scarf; all of which would have looked well at the best golf club. While she wielded the rake and struggled with branches, this gave her the appearance of being skittishly feminine, sillily, fetchingly out of her element, so that any male passer-by (though we were alone and at the end of the garden) would have felt compelled to say, "Here, let me," taking the rake from her; and my mother would have stepped back in blinking, coquettish satisfaction....

The memory of the smooth pear-shape of her waist and bottom, which her trousers calculatedly set off; the memory of our faces glowing greasily and mischievously while the sparks danced and a blackbird tink-tinked indefatigably in the beech hedge; the memory of her, on a sudden whim and without explaining, going into the house and returning, through the thickening twilight, having raided my father's special reserves, with two glasses, one, filled only partially, for me; of her raising her glass to catch the full rubescence before the fire, then bidding me, with a wink, sip with her. My first taste of wine. "Chambertin, darling—divine." My mother: Sylvia Unwin, née Rawlinson. I don't believe my father ever communed with her more intimately than this.

I see her, in the gathering dark, rake the embers of Uncle Rupert's dreams. And I hear her, as she steps back, grasping the rake like a spear, and as the blackbird in the hedge at last admits defeat, begin to sing:

"Who is Sil-via . . . ?"

· · ·

She lay in that rufous, glowing light, and the wipe-clean clipboard lay untouched beside her. I realised she was too weak to use it. If she had wanted to use it, I would have needed to guide her hand. I will never know what she might have said. But surely while she still had her voice she would have said all she meant to say. Or written one last letter . . . I will never know how much she felt the agony of willing words but having no means to utter them. I will never know if, to her, the words and all the resources of her voice still seemed to be *there*, as they say amputees still sense their absent limbs. Fish are mute when they tumble into the net. Perhaps the near-to-death (but I should know this) have already retreated a long way into themselves. They cannot waste their energies on those strange irrelevancies the living, on all those wearying trans-actions that happen on the surface of things. They can do without words. Perhaps my mother's silence was golden.

I held her hand, which could only muster a faint re-turning grip. If I had not known this was my mother, I would scarcely have recognised her. All the cheerful plumpness she had gained in middle age had gone. She was a bag of bones. Her eyes, little trapped pools in their sunken sockets, seemed the only living things about her. They looked at me, over the wall of her speechlessness, and I could not tell what their infinitesimal glints and dilations meant. Apology? That I should have to witness her in this state? Or just apology? Defiance? Yet it seemed to me that whatever those eyes expressed, they were look-ing, intensely, *at me*, they saw me clearly; they were looking into me, assessing, questioning.

There was this sound of tennis balls. She lay with her thin arms above the covers, and her head in the peculiar, chin-jutting pose necessitated by all the scaffolding be-neath her jaw. I will never know if that air of queenly serenity was a trick of that enforced posture and the drugs circulating through her, but I like to think of it as her genuine state of being. The curtains stirred, allowing a fuller beam of sunlight momentarily to penetrate the room, and she smiled, faintly but distinctly, the way a child smiles at some simple distraction. So she was not that far within herself. But as I bent towards her—it seemed to me that in order to speak to her, I had to whisper almost directly into her ear, otherwise she would not have heard—her eyelids slowly closed. I knew this was not death—she lasted almost another twelve hours. I knew her eyes would open again, for Sam. But I knew she was saying, after her last smile to me, Go. Goodbye.

I kissed her brow. Whispered my own goodbye. I left the room like a tiptoeing parent at bedtime. I felt perfectly calm, as if I were doing something familiar and routine. Immunized? Perhaps. Along the corridor, I found Sam, all alone, in the waiting room. The look of terror on his face focused for a moment into a sort of searching expression that was an echo of hers, then dissolved into bewilderment. He might have been going to his own death. I squeezed his arm. But our little change of sentry duty was conducted, fittingly perhaps, without any exchange of words.

I went out immediately into the park. Into this Indian-summer balm, this land of the living. The air was almost completely still; only an occasional breeze stirred the trees, as it had stirred my mother's curtains. The sun was low and rich and everything under its touch—the midges whirling under the trees, the veins of leaves, the mica in the path—appeared specially illuminated. People's voices sounded slow and hushed.

It seemed important that I should track down the tennis game, and I followed the sound of the balls, which, strange to say, was harder to make out at ground level. There were only two courts beside each other, in their tall, wire cage, and only one of them was occupied. A young couple were playing. As I approached they stopped, and I thought for an anxious moment they had finished and were about to leave. But they were only changing ends. The girl's legs were slender and tanned. As they passed at the net, they paused to fondle and kiss, and it seemed again to hang in doubt whether they would continue their game or not. But then they walked to their respective ends—the whole court was bathed in the rays of the sinking sun—and then the reassuring, inconsequential sound of the balls began once more.

4

There are three things which have complicated my presence in this place and made me the subject of prying attention as well as recrimination among my fellow
collegiates—setting aside, that is, the principal fact that
my presence here is a joke. I am speaking now of the period
before my recent botched brush with death. It is too early
to say, except in practical terms, how this will have affected
my general status. The business of Sam's death, which
should, I suppose, be called complication number four,
has not helped. I sense outrage modified by pity. Not a
sweet combination. But then they do not know that I have
changed. . . .

There was first the fact that I had been Ruth's husband.
This, along with Sam's money, was, I soon realised, my
chief asset and counted for a good deal of initial unction
—no, let me say genuine cordiality. Even envy. However
much the academic world likes to maintain its persona of
high-minded aloofness, it is not insusceptible to a little
glamour—even the vicarious, refracted glamour that belongs to the husband of an actress cut off at the peak of
her success. The contemplative life secretly yearns for the
active life—or, in this case, the acting life. I know this,
having once been, myself, the dowdy moth, meant for some
inconspicuous cranny of scholarship, yet drawn to flutter
helplessly round the flame of a show girl (which is what
Ruth then could legitimately have been called). I was lucky.
My wings did not get burnt. They even acquired, in the

fullness of time, a sort of borrowed iridescence, which seemed to linger on (I suppose it is all gone now) after her death.

Glamour, I know, having lived with Ruth, is only a kind of dressing, a trick, a concoction, the promise of something else. (Beauty, love, happiness . . .) It is as desirable and as meaningless as money. Yet these grave and erudite dons, these seekers after knowledge, they would trade not a little of their learning and wisdom for just a touch of glamour.

(Look at Potter. He does these absurd radio programmes. His big moment came when at last he progressed to TV. He offers watered-down or souped-up scholarship for the masses. Potter's potted history. Talks any old bilge. Even I can tell this. We will see him soon hosting a quiz show. He is, by all accounts, a genuinely accomplished historian. Yet he feels obliged to prostitute himself, for the sake of a little dubious limelight, by turning himself into something he is not.)

I was thus regarded when I first came here, not least by Potter, as something of an intriguing novelty. Something that might add a little pep and lustre to the otherwise sober atmosphere of academic life. Fellows' wives—and Fellows too, with a touch of resentment—itched for the moment when they could ask me what was it like, what was it really like, to be married to *her?* What was she *really* like? No one was interested in my (admittedly unsensational) thoughts on Renaissance prosody.

I was under no illusions. Iridescence lingered on, at least in the eyes of beholders. But I was fully aware (what was true of my former self is even truer of the thing I am now) that I possess no intrinsic magnetism. What worldly adroitness I can muster, what chutzpah and charm, what spring in my step (I suffered in my younger days from flat feet), I owe to Ruth. I was not slow to detect, amidst all the actual or implicit interrogation, another, unspoken question (I was used to it): Could I really have been the husband of Ruth Vaughan? What—him?

But here the pathos factor came into play. I was not only the former husband of a well-known actress. I was the former husband of a well-known actress who had died in circumstances publicly reported and lamented and officially labelled (is there no other word?) "tragic." I was no ordinary widower. A school of thought which held that I should be treated gently—and therefore girded around with a sort of halo of knowing looks and evasions—was largely overruled by the school of thought which held that now was the very time (five months after the event) when I should be encouraged to "talk"—an excuse for fêting me liberally (if you can fête the bereaved) and milking me for the "inside story" I was supposedly bursting to tell.

And in all this, all this being the centre of dubious attention, all I wanted was to be the opposite thing, to be the dowdy, forgotten moth again. Yes, Sam was right—devious revenge or not—I accept that he was right. Perhaps I could never have coped. How much longer could I have gone on, holed up in that Kensington flat, in those roomfuls of memories, a redundant theatrical manager (my sole client had died on me), besieged by the commiserations of stage and screen, by agents, lawyers, morbid hangers-on and prurient journalists. I needed shelter, I needed sanctuary.

The contemplative life.

My period of spurious celebrity here lasted some three months. It carried me through to my mother's death, which did not have the effect of extending the prerogatives of grief. Rather, it was about that time—summer turning to autumn and a new academic year looming—that my special privileges fell away from me like some ineffective disguise, and I began to be scrutinized for my real credentials. It was then that the general view took hold that my academic qualifications, though not entirely absent, were way below the college standard, and that, Ellison Fellowship or no Ellison Fellowship, I was an impostor.

And it was then that the Pearce manuscripts, which my mother's death released into my hands, came—in more than one sense—to my rescue. I should explain that the terms of the Ellison Fellowship are generously vague. The incumbent, with all the resources of the College and the University at his disposal, is at liberty to pursue whatever line of scholarly research he wishes. The question of the duties he owes in return is left largely a matter of unwritten agreement. I had already undertaken—primarily to give myself something to do, but also to show willing and spare the College embarrassment—some supervision of students. After a gap of fifteen years, I found myself once more speaking to these strange, young—even younger now—people. (They too blurted out their little condolences.) I flattered myself that my teaching was not ineffective, though how much this depended on my students', like others', suspending their usual rigorousness of appraisal, I don't know. But now I was to understand that because of certain "feelings" in the Faculty (I will come to this) the continuation of my tutorial services was under review.

What was really under review was not my teaching but my whole contribution to scholarship. What exactly was the line of research for which College and Faculty were providing me with such superlative amenities? It looked very much to them—it looks the same to me too (Sam, you bastard!)—that my line of research, apart from a little desultory and random browsing, was doing nothing at all.

But then, with my mother's death, there was Matthew

Pearce. There were Matthew Pearce's notebooks and his last letter to his wife, Elizabeth, which had survived miraculously Uncle Ratty's depredations and my mother's successive "clear-outs" and incinerations, not to mention Matthew's consignment to the murky recesses (ah, but it seems I am heading that way too) of family failure and disgrace.

It is quite possible, entirely plausible, in fact, that she never knew she had them. There was more "junk" than you would credit, for a woman given to severing herself from the past, in those two old, rotting leather suitcases— one with its brass locks completely seized up. I took it upon myself to open them. Sam seemed unduly angered that I should have done so—I can understand this now—but he calmed down when the contents were made known. In fact, the occasion seemed to mark the end of the dazed, quarrelsome mood into which my mother's death had thrown him. "I'm sorry I bit your head off, pal." I didn't show him the photograph of Uncle Jim. But I showed him the notebooks, which he quickly flipped through, then returned to me with a shrug. And I showed him the cutting of my mother's singing début. "No, no, you keep it, kid. I'm sorry I yelled at you. You keep it all." There was the old, avuncular look in his eye.

But my mother had certainly known about Matthew Pearce. And so had I—from an early age—if only because of the clock: the little mantel clock with a rosewood case that was made in 1845 by Matthew's own father, as a present for his son and his bride, and which has served as a wedding gift over successive generations ever since. Ruth and I received it in 1959. Since our wedding was an impromptu, unannounced affair, we received it rather late in the day. Nonetheless, my mother felt it proper we should have it. It was one of few heirlooms she cherished and did her duty by. It used to tick and chime away, amongst relics—long since discarded—of the "India days" in our old home in Berkshire. I don't know what my father made of it. Then it kept watch over Ruth and myself, first on our various mantelpieces in London, then in the cottage we bought in Sussex in 1975 and made increasing use of, Ruth's schedule permitting, up until her death. Now it sits here—that is, on the sturdy mantelpiece of my august Fellow's chambers—one of a little nucleus of objects I brought with me from the flat. I sold the cottage over a year ago. The cottage, of course, was where Ruth died.

It has a gentle, modest tick-tock. A crystalline, elfin chime. Inlaid in the rosewood, above the face, are little scrolls, rosettes and a pair of cupids. On the hinged brass plate at the back, which covers the winding mechanism, is engraved *M. & E. 4th April 1845*, and above this, the motto, *Amor Vincit Omnia*. All of which my mother interpreted for me long ago, before our Paris days.

"It's Latin, darling. You'll learn Latin at school. 'Love conquers all.' If only it were true."

Then she told me the tale, such as she herself knew it, and with a tolerant sigh, of Matthew Pearce. A rare exception to her story-telling habits.

Now that I have the Notebooks, now that I know so much more about Matthew, the clock has taken on a new significance for me—not that it wasn't always an object of special value. If its discreet face had eyes and a mouth, it could tell me so much more (than even my scholarly surmises) about Matthew—and Elizabeth. It is a simple deduction that Matthew himself must once have opened the little hinged plate and turned the key. But only now does that fact seem extraordinary, mysterious, teasing—like the fact that Matthew wrote the sloping, regular hand (expressing such irregular thoughts) that fill the Notebooks.

_____

That when I open their pages, I open, I touch, the pages that he once touched. I occupy, as it were, his phantom skin.

The little brass winding-key, with its trefoil handle, is, so far as I know, the original key. After we acquired the clock (I told Ruth its history), it somehow became Ruth's self-appointed task to keep it wound. It was a point of some concern to her that she should not allow the clock to stop, at least—given her frequent trips away—while she was able to attend to it. I wind it now. Ever since that moment of panic, less than two days after her death, when I remembered that the clock had not been wound (but it had not stopped), it has been my resolution never to let the clock wind down. I cannot explain this. This was before Matthew entered my life. When I wind the clock, I hold the key which Ruth once held, and holding the key that Ruth once held, I hold the key once held by Matthew.

The people go; the patterns remain. Something like that . . .

It is a moot point why this little clock which presided not only over Matthew's marriage but over his scandalous divorce, and seems to have presided since over a good many marred marriages, including my mother's to my father, should have become such a token of nuptial good will. Elizabeth might so readily have disposed of it. She might—who knows?—have picked it up and sent John Pearce's loving handiwork smashing to pieces. Yet, when her second marriage had already fallen on hard times (this would have been after she received Matthew's letter) she gave it to her daughter as a blessing on hers.

But I think I know why. There is surely no other explanation. She kept the clock, and passed it on, for the same reason that she kept the letter and the Notebooks. For the same reason that the clock has kept its perversely benign status ("One day, sweetie, when you get married . . ."). For the same reason that we keep, in spite of all, in spite of ourselves, certain things it proves impossible not to keep.

Matthew was a clockmaker's son, from Launceston in Cornwall, who one day fell in love with the daughter of a vicar from a village in Devon and married her and had children, and it seemed they would all live happily ever after. Then one day Matthew told the vicar that he no longer believed in God. Result: scandal, divorce, Matthew's unseemly exit from the village, never to show his face there again . . .

Thus, my mother's version ("They took things seriously in those days, darling"), first told to me one day as she wound the clock, when I must have been seven or eight, and never significantly enlarged since.

The Notebooks; the letter to Elizabeth: my "line of research." There is no stipulation in the terms of the Ellison Fellowship that prevents the appointee from switching subjects. Complication—resentment—number two. I had no wish—whatever the College planned—to give up my scheduled tutoring of first- and second-year students in the Elizabethans and Jacobeans (always my strong period). But I happened to have drop into my lap what is the dream of every scholar, if granted to few, not even to those proudly inured cases (this place abounds with them) who have toiled for decades, heroically but aridly in their chosen fields, without ever stumbling across the spring of something Original or New. I was the owner of hitherto undiscovered *material*, of fresh *data*, of (I am quoting Potter now, but what the hell?) "an historical document of enormous value—a testimony to the effects on a private life of ideas that shook the world" (he had slipped—anticipatorily, perhaps—into his media style).

It was therefore my duty—let alone my new-found, galvanizing purpose—to give full priority to this matter. To see that it was properly presented (a book: editorial preface; introduction; notes) to the world of learning, if not to the public at large. My only mistake was to have spoken when I did to our resident whiz kid (history of Victorian ideas a speciality); to have *shown* him (goddammit!) the manuscripts. To have become, once more, *persona grata* at the Potter dinner table—an enviable privilege, I gather—but no longer for my cachet (though Katherine Potter is another matter) as a refugee from show-business and grief.

Potter's argument was, of course, that by the same token that I had a duty, in respect of the manuscripts, to the community of learning, so I had a duty to entrust my material to a specialist best equipped to serve that purpose: i.e., an historian, i.e., Potter, *him.*

You see, we old, doddering savants, we harmless, cloistered fools, are real cutthroats, when it comes to it. There is no fury and spite, no venomous chicanery, like that of the thwarted scholar. We are bandits, pirates, pillagers, when it comes to that all-important stuff: recognition. I can see now why men have duelled over questions of attribution, why they have come to blows in laboratories, why they have fought over who shall be first to name some particular species of plant or spider—why they have journeyed to the ends of the earth just to *find* some hitherto unknown species on which to bestow their names. No one owns knowledge (Potter's own argument): what does it matter if the unimagined Amazonian beetle is named after Miller or Müller or Martini?

So why should I be so possessive? Why not yield to Potter, to the community of learning, the pool of knowledge, or whatever? Why should I hug Matthew Pearce to me and not want to let him go? What is he to me? And why should it be my task to set him before the world?

———

And I have not even begun to write the "book"—the "edition"—which is my purported justification for being here. Perhaps now, in my changed state, I never shall. I don't know at what point the "book," the scrupulously scholarly exercise, ceased to matter, if it ever mattered. You see, it is the personal thing that matters. The personal thing. It is knowing who Matthew Pearce *was*. And why he should matter so much to me. And why things mattered so much to him, when (what difference did it make? What difference does it make?) he might have gone on living happily ever after.

5

Plymouth, 12th April 1869

My Dearest Elizabeth,

I beg you to forgive this liberty in writing and in reawak-
ening the pain of some nine years ago. Yet I take the further
liberty of presuming that perhaps in those nine years I have
not been wholly absent from your thoughts (as you, indeed,
have lodged permanently in mine) and that you may agree
with me, at least on our little private scale of things, that
the past is not easily to be dismissed.

Such a dismissal is what I must now seem to be attempting, since I find myself here in Plymouth with a trunk
containing the residue of my possessions, which I will
shortly accompany to the New World. New Life also, I would
say, but I do not know whether the one thing confers the
other—nor, if it does, whether I am fit subject for the
metamorphosis.

In deference to Old Life—our old life—I send you, since
they have no place, I think, in the trunk, the notebooks that
I began to keep after our poor Felix died, and kept, inter-
mittently, until the dissolution of our marriage. What you
will do with them—read them, ignore them, keep or destroy
them—will not be for me to know. But I could not offer you
this my last farewell (for that is what it is, my dear Liz)
without offering you also the testimony of the man you once
knew and (this is no presumption) loved. Perhaps it may
reconcile you to the pain I caused you, perhaps only revive
that pain. For you may charge me with the fact that had I
confided to you, at an earlier stage, the things I confided
only to these notebooks, then matters might never have
reached their fatal pitch between us, and I might never have

become, even before they did so, increasingly a stranger to you.

Yet I am not the first, I imagine, to have had a conscience about having a conscience, and to have struggled to keep doubts under guard while maintaining a sanguine face to the world, like a sick person wishing not to infect others.

What good, you will say, was my well-intentioned deception, if it served only to tear me, and us, apart? But at least I return to you now that part of me of which you had every right to be jealous—though never once, my long-suffering Liz, did you upbraid me with my private and late-night assignations at my desk.

I have added, excised, changed nothing. As to the temerity of my affronting you with what I might have spared you, I can only hope that as we grow older, we grow more forgiving, and plead that I still believe what I came to believe then— was this not the root of the matter?—that though ignorance may be bliss, happiness is not to be purchased by a refusal of knowledge. Where there is evidence, so we must look, so we must examine.

Keep them, burn them—they are evidence of *me*.

I sail in the *Juno* on tomorrow's evening tide. Plymouth Sound will be my last picture of England. I mean to take the train to Saltash and take one final look at the Bridge: that for particular memories, and my small part in its construction.

Do not ask what I shall do in the New World. In a new world there should be work enough for surveyors (if I still have credit as a surveyor). And I am not alone, it seems, in being drawn thither. The streets of Plymouth, as also, they say, of Falmouth and Fowey, are full of miners awaiting passages, some with their wives and children still about them, all putting a brave face on their exodus.

Times have changed. I do not mean to wound you. I have heard that Wheal Talbot is all but finished and no capital is left to explore for tin. You will think I write only out of vengefulness. True, I am human; I can summon few tender thoughts for the man who has taken my place with you. Yet I pray (ah, you will say, me—*pray*?) that fate—let me use that word—will not be unkind to you in these harsh times.

The same prayer for our little ones, though I know they are little ones no longer. They are grown up and old enough to have families of their own—is it so? I had hoped that they—but enough of that. Bid them farewell from me. May they be a comfort to you. I miss my Lucy.

The same prayer, if they will accept it, for the Rector and his dear Emily. They age well, I trust. Your father owes to me not a few of his white hairs. But white hairs become a clergyman, and he is a good shepherd, who is rid now of the black sheep of his flock. Salute my old adversary!

I should tell you—but perhaps you know—that my own father breathed his last in Launceston some four months ago. Since then only the necessity of putting his affairs in order has kept me from my present purpose. I was at his side at the end, as I have been these last years. We had become friends once more, after the cooling of our relations. In truth, I always loved my mother more than I loved him, and he had always known it, though only in his last days could we freely acknowledge this to each other, as he could acknowledge what his whole life, for all its lapses, has manifested: his undying faithfulness to her memory. There is no justice or logic in our favouring, in certain circumstances, the dead over the living (who surely have greater claim to our benevolence) and crediting the flame of remembrance more than the warmth of life. But perhaps in these last years I have done something to restore the balance.

We were not so different, perhaps, he and I. We came to the same place, he by the road of that early loss, I by the road of my own thoughts. Who is the more blameworthy? Yet, at the very end, he confounded me utterly. Bade me rummage in the depths of an old, locked cupboard, where I found the little old, leather bound clasp Bible—I supposed I would never see it again—from which my mother used regularly to read to me and which I had thought, in the wilfulness of his bereavement all those years ago, he had thrown away. Then he confessed, if not in so many words, that he was always jealous of the faith that *I* had kept but which he in his innermost heart had lost. Jealous, furthermore, of the good Rector, in whom he thought I had found a father—since a spiritual father—preferable to him. Yet surely it was my father who, if anyone, found me my father-in-law and steered you and me (happy, ill-fated steersmanship!) into wedlock. And if he supposed that I found thereby a sanctuary he could not provide, I did not refuse, in the end, the sad sanctuary of his own neglected hearth.

You are wondering, perhaps, how much his habit of the bottle hastened his death. I must tell you that for at least eighteen months before he died he touched not a drop, though I would not have begrudged him a dash of brandy in his milk, if it had eased the wretchedness of his illness. He died the devotee of temperance he was when my mother lived. All his confessions were soberly made. We said no prayers (how could we?), and what inward prayers he may have uttered I do not know. But my mother's Bible, which now I keep, was beside him. Death is a strange breeder both of truth and of superstition.

It is late. Rain is falling, and there is scarcely a footstep in the street. Part of me feels—a fine confession for a man who has just turned fifty—like some small boy running away to sea, with as yet no better conception of the perils of the ocean than the comfortable sound of rain beating on a window-pane. My dear, dear Liz. How many voyagers, how many ocean-goers have sat up late in this town, penning letters to their loved ones?

Superstition? Yes, I must say that. There has been no counter-reversal, no retracting of retraction. I hold to my groundless ground. And yet as I sit here, a traveller about to submit himself to the deeps, my mother's Bible is with me. It has a place in my trunk—I clutch it to me as a savage must clutch his talisman—while my notebooks do not.

Fifty years! What is fifty years? Life is short, we say. And we guess not (but I will not harp on my theme) how infinitesimally brief, how as nothing, as a "twinkling of the eye," is the span of human life within the great duration of the aeons. Yet life is long too. We feel it so. We feel ourselves become part of the ages. I remember, when I was a small boy, my poor mother telling me of her own visits to this town when she herself was a girl. How she had been in Plymouth when it was red with the coats of Sir John Moore's army bound for Spain, and how again she had gone with her father and mother to behold with her own eyes the fallen Emperor of the French, who was then a captive on the *Bellerophon*, anchored in the Sound, and daily drew out crowds in boats to observe him.

These things seemed to me to belong to some distant era, even to the realms of legend, and I confused in my mind Sir John Moore's army with the gathered bands of the Israelites at Hebron, which must have been at the time the subject of my Scripture readings with my mother. As for the Emperor of the French—"Boney," as he was called then—he seemed to me a figure entirely out of fable, out of *commedia dell'arte* or Punch and Judy. And this, perhaps, was how my mother conceived of him even as she beheld him, for she would insist—and I will never know if this were some nice embellishment on her part—that as she was rowed with my grandparents by the stern of the warship, the Emperor, in full view on the quarter-deck, raised his hat and smiled, expressly at *her*.

"How are the mighty fallen" was her gloss on this little digression. So we continued on our path through the Old Testament. How strange to think that three times as many years have now passed since she related these things as had elapsed then from the events which she recounted. And what an age it seems since I heard her voice and since I sat beside her at our parlour table with the Bible between us.

The time may come, my dear Liz—perhaps it has come for you already—when it will seem just as long ago, just such a thing of fable, that we ever married and shared life together. But come what may, dearest Liz, you may trust that, as I revere still in my memory my poor mother—who showed me the way to a world that can no longer be mine —so will you always be remembered by

Your loving

Matthew

6

I was born in December 1936, in the very week that a King of England gave up his crown in order to marry the woman he loved. Naturally, I knew nothing about this at the time and, of course, other events than the Abdication Crisis were then at large in the world. But I have always felt that the timing of my arrival imbued my life, for better or worse, with a sort of fairy-tale propensity. I have always had a soft spot (a naïve view, I know) for the throneless ex-king sitting it out on the Riviera. And I have often wondered whether my mother's pangs with me on that December day were eased by that concurrent event which must have been viewed by many, rather than as a crisis, as a welcome intrusion of Romance, allowing them fondly to forget for a moment Hitler, Mussolini and Franco. All for Love. Or, the World Well Lost. "Let . . . the wide arch of the ranged empire fall!" (As indeed it began to do under poor, put-upon George VI.) All for love, yes. *Amor vincit* . . .

And Paris, fairy-tale city, might have endorsed the point. Paris, with its enchanted streets and eternal air of licensed felicity, might have taken me to its heart. Was there any other city in the world in which to live but Paris? (I thought this even aged nine.) I might have become one of those countless aspirants who have flocked to the city by the Seine and become great artists, great dreamers or great liars. I might have become, trained in the free school of my mother and Sam, a great *boulevardier*, a great philanderer. I might have lived the life of Riley. But my father died before I had even passed the gates of puberty. And what I became was—bookish.

Though this did not happen immediately. If the truth be known, when we returned to England I didn't grieve for my dead father. I didn't want to grieve for him. I didn't want to think of him. I didn't want to think of my father as the man who had fired a gun at his head. I grieved for my adorable ballet-girls, who by this stage had received honorary names—delicious, seductive French names, Yvette, Simone, Michelle—who, even then, were alive and literally kicking, stretching their beautiful limbs in the ballet school, utterly ignorant of my distant worship and entirely without need of it.

And this was not a good time for grief. Or rather, it was a very good time for grief, which made one little parcel of it unexceptional and negligible. People had got used in recent times to the fact that every so often, so it seemed, nature required a culling, and thus to mixing a little callousness with their sorrow. Perhaps it was only after my father's demise that the war, which I had lived through but conceived of as some remote, rumbling, impenetrably grown-up affair, became real for me. It was about death: slaughter, bodies, casualty lists.

And if I did not grasp the general point, I had the specific reminder of Ed. Shot down, aged nineteen-and-a-half, over the blue Pacific. That photo of his grinning brother became Sam's trump card. How could I take out my feelings on Sam, how could I unleash on him all the venom due an arrant usurper (a murderer in all but name), when he neatly reminded me that we were companions in the same grim business of bereavement?

And what was an "accident" with a pistol in a Paris office to the Battle of the Coral Sea? ("Yep, a lot of brave boys went down. . . ."—his sentence would end in a mimetic gulp.) And what was my father's death to the deaths of the fathers of other boys (I met them, these high-grade orphans) who had died, as the saying went, "in action?" My father, soldier though he was, had died in circumstances which required from me either a considerable degree of risky inventiveness or a suspect, rumour-breeding silence.

And how could I deny—for all his exploitation of it—Sam's plight? You are twenty-one years old, happily exempted, for complex reasons of primogeniture and your father's involvement in a new and militarily useful industry ("Perspex, pal—you heard about perspex?") from armed service. But your younger brother, your little kid brother, Ed, joins up, learns to fly and is killed. It might have been you, you think: it should have been you. Whatever you do now will be over your brother's dead, sea-shrouded body. You have to live for Ed now; to take on all Ed's lost chances (and Ed was great with the girls; they just fell over him). To become a perpetual nineteen-year-old . . .

"Sure—it's tough. I know. It hits you hard," was the extent of his attempts to sound out the measure of my sorrow and show his willingness, if necessary, to console. I have to admit he handled with a degree of delicacy the problem of disguising his relief that I didn't appear to be hopelessly distraught, while preparing for the onset of a possibly vicious delayed reaction. And there was, in any case, that air of frank confidingness (so unlike my father), that bluff disavowal—I'm sorry if I have no conscience, if I have no shame, but it's not my fault—that thick-skinned, businessman's charm.

But I knew just how thick-skinned he really was. I had seen him with his hand trembling—I would see him, twice again in my life, with his face as drained of vigour as it was on that day. I knew his weakness. His tactical strength was his strategic disadvantage. Even I could see that, with all its fraught implications, with all its dangerous blend of the expedient and the needful, Sam saw in me a bizarre substitute for Ed. (And you gotta have substitutes.) That he side-stepped the dread question of his surrogate paternity—not to say his entire adult responsibilities—by this appeal to the chummily fraternal.

And he was right to prepare for a delayed reaction. He underestimated, that's all, the extent of the delay and the persistence of the reaction. It seems that I'm a slow burner, a long-term investor of emotions.

We returned, briefly, to Berkshire in April '46, to follow my father's coffin, then permanently in June to settle in his home. I had a strong sense now of its being "my father's house" rather than "home," though my mother rapidly began asserting her proprietorial rights. Furniture was replaced. Decorators appeared. There was plainly money on tap. The little gallery of framed photographs from above the sideboard, recording the "India days" (cane chairs; verandahs; turbans; polo sticks) disappeared one morning in the van of a man collecting for a jumble sale. I did not believe, any more than my mother, that the place should become a shrine to her husband's memory, but I felt the injustice. And I felt, as the physical remnants of my father were whittled away, the accretion, as it were, of his ghostly stock. It was *his* house. He may not have earned his plot in the ethereal fields of fame, but he had left this solid enough memorial. It was the husk of his life.

I should have protested. I should have said, at least, about those photographs: take them from the dining-room, if you will, but let me keep them in my bedroom. But the hypocrite and the coward in me stopped my tongue.

They got married the following March. There was a decent interval in which she practised being a widow and

Sam, to give him his credit, kept his relative distance, turning up only for plainly licentious weekends. It's true, he had much to occupy him. He was sowing (also) the seeds of his little empire—spreading the bright new gospel of polymers. I still have a vision of him offering his New World marvels to a depressed and war-wrecked England. The picture merges with all those smiling GIs, in their jaunty jeeps, handing out gum and being kissed and garlanded in the ruins of liberated villages. This was not Sam's experience, but he was built in the appropriate mould, and perhaps even imagined himself in the same blithely triumphal role.

Unlike many of his countrymen hustling their way round Europe in those days, Sam did not simply have a suitcase full of nylons, he had a father in Cleveland with a factory that *made* nylons and, young as he was, a sound working knowledge of industrial chemistry. Above all, he had an inborn flair for business. I think of Sam as a perpetual juvenile in all other respects, but in business he had powers beyond his years.

Of the origin of the flair, of Sam's parentage, of "old man Ellison," clearly one of America's leading plastics pioneers, I know very little; only that he and Sam had had a falling out, the roots of which seemed to have been the old man's egotism and Ed's death. There was Ellison senior, the self-made tycoon, and there was Ed at the bottom of the ocean. And in between the two was Sam, the dutiful, filial protégé, the safe, underwritten, overshadowed, guilt-ridden schmuck. Sam had to go his own way or become the eternal stooge. The necessary scenes of confrontation and rebellion should have prepared him, you might think, for my own act of rebellion in flatly refusing (I could see it coming a mile off) his own bountiful offer of a life in plastic. He might have been mercifully inclined, even nos-

talgically respectful. Not a bit of it. There was not even
what I took to be old Ellison's final compromise: a sizeable
pay-off and the injunction to get lost and get rich.

Like father, like son. I wonder. In going his own way,
you could say Sam only did in reverse what his own father
had done some decades before when he upped sticks and
crossed the promise-laden Atlantic. Sam pitched his hopes
in the opposite direction, in an old continent which history
had nonetheless turned into a new wilderness, where opportunities abounded for the bold and the resourceful and
where it was still possible, in such callings as plastics, to
be a pioneer. Thus he partook of that post-war spirit of
inverse colonialism which beguiled and affronted the ex-
hausted folk of the old world—yet which, in Sam's case,
was to be reversed yet again, to melt in that grotesque
dream of actual assimilation, actual assumption into the
true, old world.

But the release from paternal oppression also gave the
perpetual kid-at-heart within Sam its liberty. Thus it was
that, with a view to a little holiday, a little sight-seeing
before the serious business of life began (and with Ed's
robbed youth as well as his own to think of), Sam came
to Paris.

It seems to me now that, but for my father's extreme
action, my mother might have been for Sam only a ship
that passed in the night. He was too soft-centred a soul
simply to run away from the mess, and he found himself
caught. But this is only one interpretation, and it begs the
question of who was the predator and who (or what) was
the prey. There was the factor of my mother's (i.e., my
father's) money, which would indubitably have come in
handy for a young man pledged to an independent life, let
alone to setting up his own business. However big the cut
he received from old Ellison, Sam must have been running

through it fast enough in Paris. My father died; Sam saw his opportunity. It would, of course, be interesting to know whether he saw his opportunity *before* my father died.

Then there was the factor (I cannot overlook this—I heard the squeals from the bedroom) of sheer carnal compulsion. They hit it off. I have to say it. Sam brought to a yielding ripeness the full fruits of my mother's womanhood, poorly tended as perhaps they were by my father. Perhaps because of his obligation to function for two, Sam was on some sort of biological overdrive. But—I have to say this too—my mother could give as good as she took. And in all this she was not blind. Sam was the blind one, at least when his eyes (I only quote an expression he once used, with rare self-appraisal, of himself) were only in his balls. I think she took stock of her precarious seniority. She gave herself an interval of fleshly fulfillment, during which time she would set Sam up (the question still stands: how much was Ellison Plastics my mother's work?), and thus enjoy, in her mellower years, with a little diplomatic flexibility (the biological overdrive was an ongoing thing), both the rewards and the control.

An image of Sam, indelible in the memory, from one of those weekends during our first months back in England. A sultry summer's night; I get up to fetch a glass of water: Sam on the landing, stark naked, caught between bedroom and bathroom, and in a state of livid tumescence. He drops a hand in almost maidenly alarm. He says, "Oh, hi, Billy," with a kind of strangulated nonchalance, as if we have met on some street corner. Never thereafter is the encounter mentioned by either of us.

And he would have died, so it seems, "in action," in mid-erection, even in mid—

Sam, Sam. Led by his prick to his perdition. Switched off but still plugged in. Mr Plastic. Mr Plastic?

Only when the image of my ballet girls faded did grief for my father emerge to take its place. Or rather, not grief itself (what did I know *then* about grief?), but a nagging, self-pitying, self-accusing emotion born of the guilt at not feeling grief (how could I sigh over young sylphs in tutus when my own father was dead?) and out of a mood of redundancy, which it occurred to me my father must have felt too. There were Sam and my mother testing the springs of a new double bed, and there was I, an adjunct, an accessory, a supernumerary. This had been my father's position. I stood in his vacant place. And out of this ghostly identification I began to summon a father I had never really known: noble, virtuous, wronged.

I'd like to think I wasn't as slow as I was in opening my account of vengeance; that at least by that day the India photos were removed, I had taken my first vow of retribution; and that if I took such a vow, it was as authentic and spontaneous as the pang that prompted it. But I'm not so sure. I'm not so sure if our passions seek out models of behaviour or if models of behaviour are the springs of our passions. It was a while before the first blow was struck.

When I was eleven I went to a new school. I expected to excel in French. Instead, I excelled in English; I took comfort in books. I'd like to think that the love of literature which fell into my life around this time, and which one day would embolden me to snub Sam's patrimony of plastic, was a pure and genuine love, lighting my darkened and orphaned days. But I cannot be sure. I cannot be sure which came first: the love of literature, which ensured I would cherish the play; or the play, which guaranteed I would venerate literature. In any case, my English master, as you know, was Tubby Baxter: a thin and cadaverous man, naturally, thus having the air now and then of a haunted and death-obsessed Renaissance hero. And the play, which you might have guessed if I hadn't already told you, was *Hamlet*.

So what should I have done. Drawn my poniard and stabbed his unguarded back? "Now might I do it pat . . ."

What I actually did was this. . . .

Sam believed in gifts. He persistently showered them on me, not merely on birthdays and special occasions—gifts that were so transparently aimed at winning my filial allegiance that it was a simple matter to rebuff him with formal gratitude and immediate neglect of the article in question. These gifts tended to have a masculine and practical as well as an American bias. So I received a *Walt Disney Super Annual* as well as a chemistry set and the inevitable trains (but here he hit a genuine soft spot and nearly weakened my resolve: before there were ballet-dancers, you see, there were trains).

One day I was handed a gift that, even in this tiresome succession of bribes, I appreciated was special. It was a model-aircraft kit. That is, a *plastic*, scale-model aircraft kit of a type soon to flood the British market. This, however, was a kit of American origin, in a large, spectacular box. Inside the box—somewhat belying its lavish dimensions —were fuselage and wing parts and, attached to thin strips from which they could be snapped off, a host of intricately detailed smaller fixtures: propellor, wing flaps, undercarriage and so on—even, complete with moulded flying-jacket and helmet, a little, rigidly alert pilot.

I wish I could remember the name of the plane. I ought to. It was a rather stocky-looking fighter plane, once in service with the U.S. Navy. But what I remember is the box and the almost CinemaScope vividness of the scene emblazoned on its lid. We are high in the air, amidst a tight attacking formation of the nameless aircraft, one of which is caught in fine close-up—diving angle, guns ablaze—at centre-picture. Below us is the blue sheen of the Pacific, and on it the Japanese fleet taking frantic evasive action: flashing guns, smoke, curving wakes. In the distance, a skirmish between our planes and the defending fighters, one of which, gashed with flame, spirals towards the sea.

The compound symbolism of this offering was not lost on a boy capable of reading and digesting *Hamlet*.

"You see what you can do with plastic, pal? This is a *scale*-model. Everything's an exact replica of the real thing. . . ." He went on, as if he were talking not about plastic but about some kind of protoplasm.

And I did not have to ask, though I did ask, with an ingenuous and reverent hesitancy, and received from Sam a dry-voiced reply and a melting look, as if we were on the verge of a breakthrough: "Was this the plane that Ed . . . ?"

We spread the pieces on the table. He interpreted the little leaflet of instructions. His face, with its clean, naïve features that would age so well (how did this man ever succeed in business?) hung close to mine. It was obvious that he was having to restrain himself from assembling the model himself.

"Well, kid—all yours. Make a good job of it."

And make a good job of it I did. How I pleased him by not rejecting this bribe but giving it my devoted attention. What pains I took to assemble each piece in the correct order and not to smear the glue. And this diligence had its strangely revelatory side. Under my hands, something came to life: a piece of history, a fragment of former time viewed down the wrong end of a telescope. When I fitted the little pilot into his cockpit—duly painted in advance: pink for the face, brown for his leather jacket—I felt that I was like the hand of fate itself. I could see very clearly an inexorable truth. The man thought he was in control of the plane, but it was the plane that was in control of the man. This was how things stood. The man didn't belong to himself. The man was plucked up from his real place and set down in the plane no less ruthlessly than I took his miniature counterpart and glued him down by his backside. The man was a fleshy anomaly, entirely at the mercy of his winged carapace. He might as well have been made of plastic.

When the plane was assembled, fastidiously painted in authentic camouflage and affixed with its markings transfers, I hung it by a length of thread from the ceiling in my bedroom. This seemed both an appropriate aerial perch and to suggest the status of a treasured icon—I would look at it last thing at night and first thing in the morning.

But it didn't remain there for long.

The following morning, in fact, a warm Sunday morning, I took it down. Below me, on the paved terrace at the rear of the house, overlooked by my bedroom, Sam and my mother were lounging in deck-chairs, a late breakfast over. There was, I remember, a peculiar calm about this Sunday morning—the rustle of papers, the clink of coffee cups—a feeling of probation served, as if we had reached a pitch of domestic equilibrium not achieved before.

I held the lovingly constructed aircraft in one hand and with the other applied a lighted match to the propeller. Plastic, as Sam liked to drive home, does not oxidize or decompose and is resistant to electricity; but it is not uninflammable. It burns with a spluttering, tenacious flame and a thick, black smoke reminiscent of burning oil. Thus a plastic plane can be destroyed as well as built with a good deal of verisimilitude.

The propeller, then the engine cowling, ignited, filling my bedroom with evil fumes, of which Sam and my mother had so far no inkling. Holding the plane with the bold patience of a grenade thrower, I waited till the flames—the propeller already a bubbling goo—began to lick the cockpit and the little trapped pilot. Then, standing before the open window and throwing back my arm, I hurled it up and out, so that it soared first high over the heads of Sam and my mother, then plummeted downwards, with a remarkably realistic smoke-trailing effect, to crash just a few feet in front of them on the lawn, one wing dislodged, but still ablaze.

I went to the window—partly because it was my intention to be brazen, partly in order to gasp for air. I heard my mother's startled "Good God!"; Sam's "What the—?!" They both leapt from their seats. My mother tried to beat out the fire with a hastily folded *News of the World*, while Sam, telling her to get out the way, took the lid from the coffeepot and emptied its contents over the wreckage. Only then did they look up. My mother was a picture of exasperated accusation, as if I had simply spoilt a promising day, but Sam was already making for the house in an unprecedented rage. I sat calmly on my bed. He appeared in the doorway, and checked himself momentarily—either because my composure unnerved him or because of the fog of smoke filling the room. As he paused I had time to see—through the murk—that though his face was twisted with anger, it was also blanched with horror. It was the look of a man whose direct thoughts, whose worst fears, have been exposed.

"You little son of a bitch!" he yelled. "You little goddam son of a bitch!"

Through the open window my mother must have heard. And I wonder now how much Sam supposed he was uttering the truth.

7

But I have not told you yet about complication number three. I have not told you the third reason why my reception here has been such a mixed affair. I am referring now to my pretensions in the field (forget, for a moment, the Pearce manuscripts) which is properly my own. Namely, English Literature.

This is not a simple case, I should make clear, of inadequacy on the one hand and condescension on the other. I am not unequipped. I have read some books in my time, and I was for some ten years, as I may already have hinted, a lecturer in English at the University of London. Even when I abandoned that to become Ruth's manager—a move which earned me at first as many frowns in the theatrical world as my reappearance now in the world of scholarship has done—I did not lapse. I was—you may have noticed, if you ever looked closely at your theatre programmes—a "literary consultant" (whatever that means) to certain productions of Elizabethan and Jacobean plays, and not merely those in which Ruth appeared.

In short, the love which Tubby Baxter fired in me has never faded. There has always been, for me, this other world, this second world to fall back on—a more reliable world in so far as it does not hide that its premise is illusion. Even when I left it to enter—what? the real world? the theatre?—I acted with shrewd and miserly husbandry. I made sure there was a good stock of that other world still stored in the barn (the little library I set up in our Sussex cottage—while Ruth learnt her parts). Waiting for winter. I paid the real world the solemn respect of supposing it might not be real, and I paid happiness the compliment of supposing it might not last. "Call no man happy . . ." Isn't that what literature says?

I did all these things. And, you see, I was right, I was prepared. But none of it helps you. Not one little bit.

So when Sam came up with his little arrangement for me . . .

I appreciate that from the point of view of these hallowed precincts my claims must seem paltry. I am not proud. I do not seek eminence (does my mother hear me?). All my life I have been—quite literally so in recent times—a man behind the scenes. A one-time academic who never aimed at professorship, a poetry lover who never aspired to poetry. All this, I'm sure, given the Ellison Endowment, would have been tactfully overlooked, even cheerfully indulged. But what has put the learned noses out of joint is the so-deemed simplicity of my actual views on literature. My latter-day return to scholarship has not, it seems, displayed any gathered maturity. Apparently, word has got out that in those tutorials of mine (which now seem to be a thing of the past) I have been doing little more than urging my students to acknowledge that literature is beautiful—yes, the thing about a poem is that it's beautiful, beautiful!—and other such crude, sentimental and unschooled tosh.

Now, I admit that in my former days I could wrap this around a little more. I still can. I admit that if you stop at such a view you hardly leave the way open for those lengthy critical discussions and erudite commentaries which are the mainstay of the professional study of literature. I admit it is stating the obvious. But why shirk the obvious? Literature doesn't, after all. A great deal of literature—why not be frank?—only states the obvious. A great deal of literature is only (only!) the obvious transformed into the sublime.

So is it a trick? Is it the case that if we can take it apart and discover that all there is is the crashingly common-place, we are no better off than we were before? I don't think so. I think (perhaps I should say now "thought") there is something really *there*, something that comes out of the obvious. Something beyond the obvious.

Why should the simplest, tritest words (excuse this extemporary lecture) touch us with pure delight? "My true love hath my heart and I have his." Why do the most tired and worn (and bitterest) thoughts—the thoughts we all have thought—return to us, in another's words, like some redeeming balm?

> *Even such is time, which takes in trust*
> *Our youth, our joys, and all we have,*
> *And pays us but with age and dust;*
> *Who in the dark and silent grave*
> *When we have wandered all our ways*
> *Shuts up the story of our days.*

So? We all know this. We have heard this before, and we would rather not dwell, thank you, on the subject. But the words hold us with their poise, their gravity—their beauty. They catch us up and speak for us in their eloquence and equilibrium, and just for a little moment (are you listening, my fine Fellows, my prize pedants?), the obvious is luminous, darkness is matched with light and life is reconciled with death.

I rest my case.

(And, by the way, the words were penned—on the eve of his execution, they even say—by a putative ancestor of mine, Sir Walter Ralegh.)

Where is Tubby Baxter now? I should blame him, or

thank him, for setting the whole course of my life. For if I hadn't succumbed to this lifelong addiction, this lifelong refuge of literature, I would never have become, via my stepfather's maledictions ("You like books so much, pal— you better learn how to eat them!"), a starveling student, perched in the chilly eyrie of a bed-sit in Camden, living, indeed, only on poetical nourishment and the irregular and surreptitious cheques ("Flesh and blood, darling, flesh and blood") my mother sent me. And if I had never become a starveling student, I would never have been impelled, despite those maternal subsidies, to seek casual, nocturnal work to support my daytime studies. And so might never have entered, as part-time bar assistant and general dogs-body, a tinselly little temple of illusion, a den of late-night delights, called the Blue Moon Club in Soho.

And so (but aren't these things meant to be?) would never have met her.

I see him now, that former, unformed self of mine. That spectral, prehistorical being. Hunched in the aura of a reading lamp (but what has changed?) like a creature suspended in amber. Like a creature still in embryo. Neither in nor out of the world. He is free, he is proud. He has Hamletesque pretensions: "You would pluck out the heart of my mystery . . ." He is studious, he is callow. His head is in the clouds. But the days are coming when the poetry will come alive. When the books will turn inside out. When the sighs and raptures and entreaties of all those love-sick bards will no longer seem like wishful thinking. And all those dubious and apocryphal mistresses, all those impossible and enslaving Cynthias, Julias and Amaryllises, will no longer seem like moonlit phantoms, like paper dreams.

The Blue Moon Club in Soho. What a far cry from this place. Do not imagine anything too wicked. Nor, on the other hand, too demure. This is the year of our Lord 1957:

half-way between the age of rationing and the age of permissiveness; half-way between the syrupy ballad and the full frenzy of rock-and-roll.

The Blue Moon was a "night-club," not a dive, and definitely not a strip joint. There was no disrobing, even if there was scant attire. Its atmosphere was charged with a piquant ambiguity in which it was hard to distinguish failed innocence from failed sophistication. The girls (there were three of them—as many as the tiny stage could hold—along with three musicians and a "resident" singer, a buxom, brassy trouper called "Miss Rita") were only "passing through" this slightly risqué venue en route (you could gauge their degrees of conviction) for "real" work in the "real" theatre. Hence their fondness for an impoverished student who, like them, was only dabbling in this dubious night-work to serve his aspiration to higher things. He was no more interested, therefore, in their frivolous titillations than they were in teasing his callowness. So when, in the narrow, rear-of-house passage, they scampered past him in single file (Mandy, Diana, Barbara— where are they now?), forcing him to press his back against the wall and smile weakly while he was successively brushed by their frills, plumes, flounces and tassels; or when one of them slipped in or out of their cramped communal dressing-room and he caught a glimpse of fevered undress—this was only accidental. Their winks, tut-tuts and little blown kisses were just their excuse-mes.

He is callow, he is studious. Brought up on ballerinas worshipped from afar and the high jinks of Sam and his mother just across the landing, he has acquired a certain tentativeness in a certain area (in which Hamlet himself did not exactly have plain sailing). He is gauche, he is guarded (believe me, he is no Errol Flynn), but he is Paris-trained. And here he stands again, on his army-exempting flat feet, with his brain in a spin, gawping at dancing-girls.

At a certain point in the "show," around midnight, when Miss Rita took her solo spot, it was my task—a strangely domestic ritual—to slip out to the kitchen behind the bar and make the girls mugs of hot, sweet tea (they drank nothing stronger while they performed). I would knock on the dressing-room door, while from the stage would come Miss Rita's husky imprecations—"Got a crush on you, swee-eetie pie . . ." A polite pause. *"Entrez."* And I would enter, bearing the tray on the outspread fingers of one hand, consciously imitating the gestures of a waiter I had once seen in a Left Bank café. An aroma of perfume, talc and cigarettes never quite disguised the smell of sweat. Three pairs of eyes would greet me. And then one night, in June 1957 (it was Barbara, I think, who left with unexplained suddenness), a new pair of (melting-piercing, greenish-brown) eyes.

You could say I saw her in her first performing role. Girl Number Three at the Blue Moon Club. When she had yet to make her name. Though her name was then just as it would be later, and she was surely no less herself. Ruth: a first-year drama student (en route, yes, for the real theatre), who had jumped into the deep end of this haunt of pleasure in order, like me, to make a little needed money, but also to cure—her stage fright.

In a diamanté-plastered leotard, white gloves, tiara and plume. In a little feminine mockery of black tie and tails, with fish-net tights. Wiggle, kick, smile, turn. She couldn't dance as well as Mandy and Diana. But she had something that made you not realise this. Something which Mandy and Diana didn't have.

A look of delicately courted danger, a look which, even as she cradled her mug of sweet tea, made you feel as if you were out on an adventure . . .

"Ruth, this is Bill, our tea boy. Watch him, he's a tiger."
Giggles.

One night Miss Rita couldn't perform—stricken with flu—and Mr Silvester, proprietor of the Blue Moon Club, a self-possessed East-Ender who had a way of suggesting he had steered himself capably through all manner of roughness to reach this haven of (as he liked to call it) "class," was thrown into untypical panic.

She volunteered. She had to do it. Of such stuff are show-business fables made. She even uttered a plucky "Don't worry, Mr Silvester." And she proved, not exactly that she could sing, but that she could disguise impeccably the fact that she couldn't sing, could act impeccably the part of a singer; and that she had, moreover, that indefinable, spell-casting quality called (but why don't we all have it, since we are all present?) "presence."

I think I saw—and perhaps only I saw—just for a moment, the terror in her eyes, the hidden absence out of which the presence emerged. Then it was gone, she had overcome it, a little internal victory, and I was caught in the spell. And I knew then what I would always be and always want to be and need to be for the rest of my life: a perpetual stagehand waiting for the leading lady's kiss; a lurker amidst lights and scenery; a shambling devotee of poets and performers; a humble thrall to this business of show-business.

Somewhere in this vision was already a scene in which, in some hotel suite stuffed with flowers and invitations, where Ruth held court to journalists and photographers, I would open the door from the bedroom, a preposterous figure in a dressing-gown, blink, pause, then withdraw again with a mumbled apology. But in that brief instant she would have turned to me with a smile and a look quite different from that reserved for her sycophantic retinue.

And the retinue would have noticed and would think (much in the manner of some new acquaintances in this place): Can that really be—? *Him?*

A spotlight's moonbeam. A shimmering creature in a clinging dress, hurriedly spirited up from somewhere, of midnight blue, hung with silver sequins and slit to mid-thigh. Smoke-furls. The piano's tiptoe; the drum's whisper. Her lashes flutter over the microphone, her lips part, noise-lessly for a moment, as if inviting the audience to take delicious pity on her girlish trepidation.

Then: "I'm wild again, beguiled again . . ."

Pause: for the heavy-jowled patrons at the front tables to pull on their cigarettes, tap their cigars; for the old soak at the bar to bring his glass safely to his lips:

". . . a simpering, whimpering child again . . ."

Who would not have been smitten? Who would not have been bewitched? And yet it was strange how this little world of smoochy melody and sugared lubricity seemed to make way specially, deferentially, for us, its hesitant protagonists. How Mandy and Diana, professional sirens, became as gooey and conniving as bridesmaids. As if everyone could see it even before we did. As if it weren't supposed to happen, not the real thing, not in this dim-lit domain given over to the hint, the dream, the starry promise, but not the substance of love. But since it was happening—how sweet, how touching, how truly remarkable; and when were they going to get on with it?

When indeed?

Call it, also, stage fright. This stomach-fluttering period of waiting in the wings of love, this nervousness of lovers rehearsing the lines they will inevitably, redeemingly fluff. How strange to think, now, that there was a time when I did not know every inch of her body, every nook and niche and curve, when I had to imagine it—flaunted as it was, within proper limits, by her Blue Moon costumes. When there was as much a sweet shock of nakedness, of disclosure, to realise that this woman who could shine in the spotlight was the same woman who, backstage, would wrap round herself a simple fawn raincoat, run her fingers through her damp hair, light a cigarette or yawn with a sort of surprised intentness, one hand patting her lips the way boys make Red Indian noises. It was *her*, it was *her*, you see, never those roles she dressed in.

How strange to think there was a time when all those first times were yet to come. The first time we kissed (a mistimed, fumbling, near-bruising affair like a collision of birds in mid-air); the first time she shed her clothes for me; the first time my bare palms pressed her bare breasts; the first time . . . Then suddenly all these first times were passed through, like a dizzy mist; there was this woman who had stepped out of possibility into actuality, as if I had validated her existence. To put your arms round another. To say, be mine, be here, always be here. And then one day she was gone; where she had been there was air.

To think there was a time when I went back to my single, solitary, auto-erotic bed, on those summer nights which were already racing towards dawn, and hoped and feared and doubted and imagined, watched over by custodial and commiserative poets. And Mrs Nesbitt, my landlady, that old crow who hopped around below my eyrie, already had me down as a confirmed libertine. This "job" that brought me home, four nights a week, at three in the morning. At which hour, I suspect, she lay pruriently in wait, but never got her chance, hoping for a damning trail of scent, whispers and stifled giggles to ascend the stairs.

To think there was such a time when we hadn't yet stepped into each other's lives. When we never even knew each other. "I wonder, by my troth, what thou and I did, till we lov'd . . . ?" These things are meant to be. Life has a thousand avenues, but these things (surely?) are meant to be. To think she too must have wondered: will this happen? Shall I, shan't I? Will he, won't he? It is a kind of stage fright. This rendering of yourself to another. This saying: here I am. And even at the height of her success (you won't believe this) I would see her suddenly stricken with stage fright, enough to make her physically sick. That face (I try to *remember* it): so charged, so elusive (a thousand pictures failed to capture it). I never saw a face so brimming and in motion. So crystalline yet so liquid. So tender, so potent. A face that needed to be stilled. A cigarette helped. Better still, a kiss. Best of all, a part to play. A part to play. So fragile. So brave.

In the days before she was famous. Which was the greater fairy-tale?

I owe it all to a summer storm. The oldest ruse in the book of Romance. Dido and Aeneas. Ginger and Fred. Mr Silvester was a considerate, a courteous man. All that rough living that was now behind him had given him an exaggerated regard for the niceties of life. His club (or "establishment," as he liked to call it) was a good, clean club; his girls were decent girls. One of the decencies he showed them in return was to pay for taxis to take them home in the early hours. My own means of transport was a rusting bike. While the Blue Moon Club warmed up, the cabaret commenced and all Soho went through its nightly paces, it waited, in sad but faithful exclusion, by the rear entrance, to take me home. But that night that the heavens opened (they opened! They poured down blessings!), it remained there, as on many a subsequent night, to rust even more.

Chucking it down at half-past two in the morning. I would get drenched (said Mandy and Diana). I would catch my death (said Miss Rita). Mr Silvester was shrewdly silent. And at last she said it. At last we stepped into each other's limelight. And I dare swear that after we left, Miss Rita and the girls and even Mr Silvester and assorted unimpressible staff gave a little round of relieved applause. A midsummer night. No sylvan sorcery, no moonlit magic. But that night a wand was waved. I forgot I was Hamlet. I was a puckish soul. The world was no longer weary, stale, flat, and unprofitable, and for months I would not plot a single act of further reprisal against my wicked stepfather.

These things are meant to be. Jack shall have Jill; nought shall go ill. I might have lived thenceforward happily ever after. (But what does "ever" mean?) Her best line, her most unforgettable line, delivered with such casualness but with such depths of promise:

"Share my taxi?"

8

The little ironwork gate into this garden, which can only be opened by those honoured with a key, has a distinctive and now easily recognisable repertoire of sounds. There is first the exploratory scraping and clicking of the key in the lock—not a sound that carries far but one easily picked up by the ear if you are used to opening the gate yourself (the mechanism is temperamental and demands coaxing). Then there is the mixture of rattles and squeals with which the gate swings open; then, after a pause, the vibrant, percussive jingle with which it returns on its sprung hinge.

A tinkling bell, specially made for the purpose, would be no more effective in announcing someone's coming. Thus I lift my head, I am prepared: though her arrival is not unexpected—she has visited me now, here under the bean tree, for several days in succession. Nonetheless, as the gate gives out its warning, I take these pages (I am writing this later—days later) from the tray on my knee and slip them into my briefcase. Then I take my notes on the Pearce manuscripts from the briefcase and pretend to be working on them.

She walks towards me across the lawn with that by now familiar gait and that soft and bulging straw basket in her hand. One of the disquieting thoughts that beset me in this curious post-mortal condition of mine is that everything might be beginning again. This *is* my second life, my reincarnation. Perhaps there is life and life again, always and for ever. Perhaps the world has been reinvented for me in its full potential. This is the Garden of Eden. And here comes Eve.

But no, she is not Eve. And nothing is going to happen, not this time around, even if Potter is far away at a conference in Chicago. She is more like one of those pitying and piteous women of medieval romance—yes, that is more her style. And this garden, with its locked gate which only the favoured may open, is like one of those semi-allegorical gardens into which the Lady of the Castle steals (unknown to her absent lord) to solace some wounded knight-errant (ha!). Which, with a good deal of twisting and stretching of the imagination, is not unlike our situation.

A brief history of the Potters, Michael and Katherine. Part fact and part surmise, just like my reconstruction of the life of Matthew Pearce. Just, if it comes to it, like my reassembly, here in this afterworld, of my own life. A brief history of the Potters—pieced together from hearsay and conjecture and from what Katherine herself, in circumstances rather different from these decorous meetings under the bean tree, has told me . . .

Picture a scene in the office of Michael Potter, university lecturer at the University of X, it doesn't matter where. Year of our Lord, 1970. Potter is twenty-seven. Katherine is nineteen. And it is Katherine who has sought this not-so-common cross-disciplinary meeting between a lecturer in History and a second-year student in English. She would like some help with the background to her long essay: Arthurianism in Tennyson and his contemporaries. Potter has flipped through his diary (at the same time, let us suppose, discreetly appraising the young Katherine out of one corner of his eye) and said, "Okay. Say three o'clock,

Thursday?" And he is the right man to have come to. This is his special field: Victorian idealism and Victorian doubt. One day he will write a book on the subject.

She duly knocks at three. She has not quite broken free of the brittle mould of a clever schoolgirl. One part of her is actually drawn to that moody, broody, neo-chivalric stuff that forms the topic of her essay—all that loss of faith, all that elegiac Romance; another believes that this is what you do, this is what is supposed to happen at modern universities: you throw yourself at clever young lecturers.

What would she have worn for this fateful tête-à-tête? The ubiquitous miniskirt of those days? No, one of those long, ankle-length, slim-waisted, high-necked dresses in some dark, velvety material, which were also, conversely, favoured then and actually evoked the graciously draped women of past ages. Potter would have noticed it (winter light fading beyond his office windows, his desktop and bookshelves in a state of beguiling disorder): the nostalgia for the nostalgia of nostalgia.

Darkness descends. The talk goes on longer than envisaged. No problem, no problem, says our doughty lecturer. He pours more coffee into the trusty coffee mugs. Then at length, the last cup of coffee having gone cold, Potter says, "A drink . . . ? A bite to eat . . . ?"

She seduced him? He seduced her? The latter surely, knowing what we know, now, of Potter. But this Potter of yore was not the Potter of now—this I have on the best authority. The Potter of those days was a serious, forceful, unstudiedly charming young lecturer, with something of a reputation, it's true, as a campus heartthrob, but only just learning to take advantage of it. They seduced each other? They fell in love? Like Paolo and Francesca over the story of Lancelot? Why not?

Two years later they are married. And three years after

that, rather later than anticipated, Potter publishes the book that was to have made his name. But this, alas, is not before—in fact, it is almost twelve months after—a certain C—— at the University of Y has published, to considerable attention and praise, a work on much the same subject and incorporating a good deal of the same material.

The trials of the academic life! How the true, chaste scholar is tested. Those years of study and research! Potter the star student, Potter the professor-to-be. It doesn't matter if people tell him, as many do, that his book is actually better than C——'s, more thorough, more cogent, more perceptive (it's true: it's an invaluable aid to my researches—you see the trickiness of my situation). C—— stole the limelight, C—— got the credits. And if he, Potter, hadn't been seduced by her, by Katherine, by marriage, domesticity, kids, he might have finished it earlier, might have got there first.

So it was she who seduced him? It's funny how the memory blurs. And as for the kids—there were no kids. Only in the mind. Only the two miscarriages—memory doesn't mix matters here. Then nothing.

And maybe it's around this time—the time of the second miscarriage or the time of the publication of his abortive book—that Potter begins to wonder whether, in any case, this scholar's life is really for him. This contemplative life. This life of the mind. When you are sitting at home by the fire . . .

It is a well-known fact that the Potter marriage is a façade, of which the relentless people-collecting and opportunity-seeking and throwing of dinner parties are compensatory symptoms. The marriage may have died, but the wake goes on—and how many perfectly thriving couples could generate such buzz and *esprit*? It is generally known and accepted that Potter's academic and extra-academic adventurism has been at the expense of domestic harmony. In a word, that Potter screws around.

It is also generally known that Katherine Potter knows that Potter screws around, and somehow accepts or submits to the fact, is long-suffering and diplomatic about it, and has not taken up other options open to her. Such as screwing around herself. Though she is eight years younger than Potter and still undeniably attractive. Undeniably attractive. But I can be pretty sure—in fact, I can be certain—that Katherine Potter has never once in her life committed an act of adultery. Not once.

Time goes by. A new Potter emerges out of the fragile, if still intact, fabric of his marriage: radio and TV pundit, would-be celebrity, but also (the scholarly career has not been entirely forgotten) Fellow of this worthy College.

Then there appears on the scene a figure of dubious credentials if intriguing provenance: the Ellison Fellow. He is briefly courted by the Potters (among others), then dropped—the man has only a borrowed lustre. But then, following the death of his mother, he acquires a certain set of notebooks, hereafter referred to as the Pearce Notebooks. And, after a period of dwelling extensively on their contents, makes the mistake of showing them to Potter. And Potter makes the mistake of not making a copy.

Once again, but for different reasons, the Ellison Fellow is pursued. After some initial exchanges of surprising animosity (it seems that Potter feels that the Notebooks are best left with him, but the Ellison Fellow demands them back, makes three copies of his own and keeps them under lock and key), Potter is anxious to smooth relations. The invitations and blandishments begin again. Furthermore, by the personal example of his renewed friendliness, Potter is at pains to uphold the Ellison Fellow's status, by now somewhat open to question, as a genuine and good Fellow.

He is doing "serious work" after all, something really rather special. In short, having missed his chance simply to grab the Notebooks, Potter sets about trying to wheedle them into his possession.

Now, throughout this period, let it be noted, even during the interval of his relative ostracism, Katherine Potter has maintained an unbroken interest in the Ellison Fellow. It seems (you will find this hard to believe, even harder if you were to take one look at me now) that for her he has the stubborn attributes of a Romantic Figure. Which perhaps only means that Katherine Potter (despite everything) is a Romantic Soul. It is true, as previously observed, that he arrives in his new quarters with a certain aura of glamorous pathos, or rather, pathetic glamour, with a certain poetically construable personal baggage, positively Tennysonian in its freight of dolour. But this was at the beginning. And time— And surely, in the end, as we all know, poetry is one thing and life is another. These big, sonorous, laden words, how inflated and archaic they sound, as if they *could* only belong to literature: heartache; sorrow; grief.

And as for the Ellison Fellow's feelings towards Katherine Potter—to be honest, they involve a good deal of confusion. He reacts before Katherine Potter, in fact, as he has reacted before all new, strange (attractive) women who happen, since a certain event, to have crossed his path. He does not know how to deal with them. He is filled with dismay, a giddy sense of arbitrariness, an apprehension that the universe holds nothing sacred; all of which is only to be stilled by the imperative of loyal resistance.

He is not immune to the prickle of passing lust. But he deals defensively with it. He reacts either with disdainful dismissal (Not your type, definitely not your type) or with a rampant if covert seizure of lecherousness (Christ, what tits! What legs! What an arse!), which serves the same forestalling function by reducing its object to meat and its subject (he is past fifty, after all) to a pother of shame.

But none of this—so much as is apparent—deters Katherine Potter's interest. Rather, it stimulates it. If someone is on their guard, then you know there is something to be guarded. Somewhere, if it is only within the hidden vaults of memory, there is treasure. You see, in this hotbed of sophistry and pedantry, Katherine Potter applies simple instinct and logic. She sees that if the Ellison Fellow is unhappy, it is because he was, once—happy.

And one night, when, thanks to the Pearce Notebooks, the invitations to the Potter home have been renewed, Katherine Potter touches the Ellison Fellow's wrist with the fingertips of one hand and even runs the fingertips, just a little bit, brushing the hairs, up his forearm—a gesture that strikes him, among other things, as simultaneously impetuous and calculated, and certainly audacious, since there are several other people in the room at the time (though only one sees).

But this is not before the Ellison Fellow has been subjected to a concerted campaign of persuasion, across the dinner table, to release his close-kept manuscripts, there being among the assembled guests at least two other members of the History Faculty, previously briefed, no doubt, and there to voice the wider view of the Faculty that, with all due respect, he might not be the best man for the job, etc., etc. To which he responds, let it be said, with unbudging tenacity. And not before, unobserved himself, he has observed, in the kitchen (this will give some idea of the fluid nature of Potter's soirées and his delight in mixing old and young), Potter with his hand firmly on the left buttock of one of his guests, a research graduate called Gabriella (black eyes, black hair; flashing, Italian glances), who is definitely not, as it happens, the Ellison Fellow's type.

And whereas Potter did not know that he was observed with his hand on Gabriella's buttock (let us be plain, his hand was thrust beneath the waistband of her undeniably fetching, tight black evening trousers, so we are not talking about the seat of her pants), it is clear to the Ellison Fellow that Potter sees Katherine, his wife, put her hand on his, the Ellison Fellow's, wrist and, what's more, that Katherine knows it, and doesn't take her hand away. Which makes the Ellison Fellow, who still likes to put into his thoughts the words, if not of Hamlet, then (more appropriately perhaps) of Polonius, think springes to catch woodcocks. But since she does not take her hand away, he is forced to look into her eyes. They are blue-grey eyes. His eyes are grey. Gabriella's eyes are black. His dead wife's were seaweed-brown. How strange that we each have these different eyes, like jewels set in our bodies, and that when we look into someone's eyes we think we can see who they are. These are not the eyes of a natural temptress. They seem to be pleading for his co-operation and at the same time to be saying, "I know, I married the wrong man." And he cannot tell if she is acting.

She walks towards me across the lawn; waves; I wave in return. She is wearing a sleeveless, mutedly floral summer frock of some thin fabric, which, if it were not for the dark yew hedge behind her, would allow the sunlight to show up, in hazy outline, her still slender-but-firm body—which, let me make this plain, I have never seen otherwise exposed.

Though the point came near.

She walks with a fluid stride, which would be truly

gazelle-like if there were not a touch of sheepishness about it, a self-induced and long-practised hesitancy, an air of brave cheerfulness undermined by contrition. She carries this large straw bag, out of which there peeps the glossy cap of a thermos flask and a rumpled blue-and-white-check cloth; and I know, without seeing, that also in the bag, along with the decanted, chilled white wine in the thermos, are a few choice morsels purchased on her way: the rudiments of a little *déjeuner sur l'herbe*. Though there will be nothing scandalous, not now, in this picture.

The straw bag is strangely affecting. It reminds me of those ubiquitous, oddly rustic "shopping bags" that were once, in those far-off days before the advent of polythene, a standard accoutrement of every woman, including even my mother, but which now seem folksy and quaint. It somehow looks right in the hand of Katherine Potter, in whose simple, flaxen tresses, vulnerable shoulders and Arcadian attire you might detect the traces of a pastoral wistfulness: a former Sixties flower-child (fallen since on thorns), a one-time student of Eng. Lit., wallowing, Ophelia-like, in simpering, whimpering poetry.

Not my type. Not my type at all.

She waves. The nurse; the convalescent. The wounded paladin; the pitying lady. These titbits stolen from the lord's table. I think she thinks she is restoring me to life. That that is her duty now. I think she thinks it was because of her—

A little fact I omitted to mention above: When she touched my wrist that evening at Potter's, it was as though I had forgotten that I still had a wrist, as though I had forgotten that my wrist, with its little forest of dark, pliant hairs, still belonged to me. Later, alone, I looked at my wrist and said to myself, absurdly: This is my wrist.

And when I watch her walk across the lawn, she seems

to me (but don't trust the words of someone newly snatched from the grave) like life itself. Like life itself.

She crosses the lawn and halts in front of me. "Hello," she says. "Hello," I say. She puts down the basket. A light breeze wafts across the garden and just for a moment it wreathes her hair about her face and flutters her thin dress against her body with almost sentient, Botticellian tenderness. The bare shoulders are infallible. Their appeal goes to some helpless spot at the centre of the chest. She starts to unload the basket. There are real napkins, real wine glasses, nothing skimped. I take the notes I have only just placed on my tray—it reconverts, you see, to its proper use—and shuffle them into my briefcase.

"I haven't come at a wrong moment?" she says. She always says this, or something like it—"I'm not disturbing you?" "Would you rather be by yourself?" And it's then that she wears her most contrite looks.

"How's it going?" she says.

"Fine," I say.

I don't know which would hurt her more. To tell her (but I think she knows this, I think she really does) that it wasn't because of her, no, not exactly—and so deprive her of her stricken but gratifying role. Or to tell her that it *was* because of her, yes, as a matter of fact—and so turn that role into a lasting, remorseful truth.

I don't know which is true myself.

How can one person take the place of another?

She pours wine from the thermos, and condensation mists the bowl of the glass. She hands me the glass, then she says, meaning it lightly but somehow sounding reproachful, "What was that you had to hide in your briefcase?" And it's only at this moment that I know for certain that I'm going to go through with the decision I've made.

"I'll tell you—in a while," I say.

First, we eat, we drink. We are surrounded by warmth and flowers. Under the Indian bean tree, who loves to lie with me . . . In far-away Chicago Potter will be just waking up. I'm prepared to bet that he is alone in his bed. I'm prepared to bet that, for once, he will not avail himself of the customary opportunities of a conference abroad. He will be the chaste scholar. And he will think a lot of Katherine, and of me.

I drain my glass, then reach over to my briefcase and take out—no, not these scribbled pages, but a complete, freshly made copy of the Pearce manuscripts. What does it matter? Who am I to raise Matthew Pearce from the dead?

"For you," I say. "For both of you. I want you to have it now."

9

The thing was that he saw an ichthyosaurus. The thing was that he had come face-to-face with an ichthyosaur, on the cliffs of Dorset in the summer of 1844 (age: twenty-five).

I see him lurching, slipping, fleeing down that wet path towards the beach. Everything is chance. It might so easily have been otherwise. He might have gone to the aid of the young woman who even then, as he scrambled blindly by, sat on the damp ground, encircled by a little attentive group, nursing a twisted ankle. Only a minute before, under the flapping tarpaulin, he would have heard her sudden cry. And if he had gone with the others to assist, if he had not lingered alone for those few mesmerical moments, his whole life might have been different. He might have married the young woman. What an opportunity missed! There she was, pale, shaken, in need of rescue and obliged to show, for all the fussing of her chaperone, an unaccustomed amount of lower leg. He might have fallen in love with this pretty invalid and lived happily ever after. Instead of which, he chose to stare into the eye of a monster.

And it was meant to be a holiday. A week's recreation which, given Matthew's general cast of mind, would require an element of study—he would try his hand at this fossil business—but which might not exclude (Lyme Regis was well known not only for its fossils but for its summer crop of eligible daughters) a little amorous exploration.

The facts about Matthew Pearce as they stood in the

year 1844. The facts infused with a good deal of theory, not to say imagination. The Notebooks do not begin till 1854, though they begin with a backward reference to that summer day in 1844, which, scrupulous as Matthew's memory was, might have been subject to a degree of narrative licence. The facts, mixed with a good deal of not necessarily false invention. *Pace* Potter, I am not in the business of strict historiography. It is a prodigious, a presumptuous task: to take the skeletal remains of a single life and attempt to breathe into them their former actuality. Yet I owe Matthew nothing less. As Ruth would have said, the script is only a beginning: there is the *whole life*. Let Matthew be my creation. He would have appreciated the commitment—not to say the irony. And if I conjure out of the Notebooks a complete yet hybrid being, part truth, part fiction, is that so false? I only concur, surely, with the mind of the man himself, who must have asked, many a time: So what is real and what is not? And who am I? Am I this, or am I that?

He was born in Launceston, Cornwall, in March 1819, son of John Pearce, clockmaker, and Susan Pearce. And he began the Notebooks thirty-five years later, on the day of the death of his third-born, Felix. So much for plain, hard fact.

But I prefer, to get the measure of him, to picture him early one morning, in his twenty-second year, in an inn-yard in Oxford, about to leave that city, a fully educated young man, to take his modest and unsung place (he has no fond ideas) in the world. His journey home—for in the first place the world would have meant his father—would have been by stage-coach, a matter of some two-and-a-half days on the road. Thus at this point in his life Matthew would have belonged to the Old World. But only just. Within another five years he would have been able to have made the journey, at least as far as Exeter, by train. Within another ten years Matthew himself would have helped, in his small way, to guide the Great Western Railway—then nudging along the Thames valley—as far as Plymouth.

But there is no reason to suppose that on this summer's morning he feels himself to belong to a vanishing age. Or that he looks upon the coach and team that will transport him westwards with the sort of wistful feeling that one day, indeed, people will apply to steam engines.

I see him (I have no proof of this; I have no idea what he looked like at all) as one of those robustly sober-looking young men in whom youth puts in only a tenuous appearance. He has the solid build and steady movements of a precocious maturity. He is unostentatiously dressed, for an Oxford man, and as he stands in the bustle of the inn-yard at this unseemly hour of the morning, he shows no sign either of aloofness or of discomfort. There is even a hint that he feels at home amidst such workaday surroundings and that he is not entirely sorry to be leaving this cloistered and rarefied city.

The arm that swings his portmanteau is strong and sure. The eyes of women, more easily turned by any number of sprightly young bucks, might, having first passed over Matthew, return to him with a sense of revised judgement. The face cracks readily enough into a generous smile or to offer some casual pleasantry—he has an appealing way of hovering between thoughtfulness and affability. The gaze is open and frank and meets yours forthrightly. You would say it was an observant gaze.

The very last quality he emanates—he climbs up, naturally, to take his seat on top behind the coachman—is lack of balance. Stability, rather, an intuitive sense that all things must have their basis, might be called his tacit watchword. He will become a surveyor. That is an unambitious, even lowly profession for a man with an Oxford education. But Matthew is shrewd enough not to leap ahead of his talents—three years at Oxford have taught him that he is neither an idler nor a genius—and both Matthew and Matthew's father (though perhaps Matthew's father rather more) are shrewd enough to foresee that there will be much call in the years ahead for versatile surveyors, and that a surveyor with the asset of an Oxford education might go far, even given the limited spheres in which surveyors operate.

And look at it another way. It is true that in the coming years, great engineers and designers would win for themselves immortal fame—it would be Matthew's lot to know at least one of them (and feel a touch of pity mixed with his admiration)—but no surveyors. Yet what, in essence, was the surveyor's task? It was to establish the true ground of things; to provide a *basis*, a sure foundation on which the works of others might be raised. Was it not, literally, fundamental? It was as essential as it was unspectacular. It had nothing to do with risk and hazard; everything to do with stability and trust.

And trust, merging imperceptibly with the deeper stuff of faith, might have been the other, silent watchword of this dependable-looking young man. In his portmanteau is his mother's Bible. Matthew would have referred to it often in private and been able to quote large parts of it by heart. And now, in 1840, after three years' exposure to scholarly scepticism and the rigours of science, he would not have relinquished the belief that every word it contained was the literal and immutable truth. The world, too, must have its basis, and the nature of this basis had been indelibly intimated to him long ago on his mother's knee. The central fact of life was there. It was a wondrous thing, this central fact, a wonderful clarifier, encourager and liberator. It meant that the profounder questions of existence were settled and one was free to go out on to the surface of the world and do good, practical work. And the surface of the world only brought you back to the central fact: nature's handiwork, and man's too, since it exploited the unchanging laws that were part of nature's design, was evidence of God's.

The coachman cracks his whip. They leave the city. The sun fills the green bowl of the world.

A further reason Matthew might have given for choosing a career unlikely to be meteoric or all-consuming was simply that it allowed time for other things. If Oxford had shown him he was no scholar, he recognised in himself a naturally inquisitive mind. He liked to be out and about, to get the touch and tang of things (he looked forward to this stage-coach journey which others would have regarded as a three-day purgatory), to look, take note, assess, compare—all admirable habits for a surveyor. In this sense, Oxford had constrained him (the truth was, perhaps, that he had shielded his mind from some of Oxford's more unsettling influences). He thought of his interests as being ranging and extra-curricular: natural history, geology, the ever-absorbing study of his fellow men.

Geology, of course, bore directly on his chosen profession. But Matthew had not yet begun to sound (it would come, before that holiday in Lyme) those intimate links between geology and palaeontology which were not essential to a surveyor's broad understanding of rock and soil, that mysterious paradox by which this study of dead stones offered the clue to Life itself.

Geology drew him, in the first place, precisely because it was the science of solidity, the very key to that thing on which all human endeavours began and must surely come to rest. Ask Matthew, aged twenty-one, what he most loved about the world, and he might well have said: land. He couldn't have said where the passion came from—from the rolling prospects from his native Launceston—but it is there. Matthew loved land as a surveyor and a believer in God should. "And the little hills rejoice on every side . . ." His palm sometimes tingled—he wouldn't have known how to explain it—to reach out and stroke the contours of a particular landscape, as one might stroke the flanks of a horse or the head of a child.

And he will have plenty of cause to feel such an itch, plenty of opportunity for geological reflection, as his coach carries him across the broad belly and down the crooked limb of England, over limestone and sandstone and peat and clay, through an old, old world.

Yes, he is glad to be free of this dreamy city with its fogs of ideas (I know the feeling). Out among real things. He has a handicap, a blemish, which he has endured and tried vainly to eradicate for three years: his accent. It is a Cornish accent, an east Cornish accent, but to most Oxford folk it is a yokel's burr. From time to time it has miserably betrayed him by substituting a "bain't" for an "isn't." But now, as he travels ever south-westwards, he relishes the release of allowing it progressively to return. He even prankishly indulges it (let's suppose) before some enforced travelling companion, some dapper fellow-*baccalaureus* (let's imagine) going as far as Bath, for whom "land" only has a meaning when it is translated into "income."

Matthew's father married Matthew's mother in 1817. It seems to have been a union which demanded compromises, since the former was of the Methodist persuasion, while the latter was of staunchly Anglican stock. But John

Pearce, like many of his kind, perhaps, when improved prospects presented themselves, was prepared to remodel his faith so far as to exchange chapel for church. His marriage, in short—since Susan's father, once certain conditions were met, was not ill-disposed—was the means of his setting himself up in trade.

From his father Matthew would have inherited the conscientiousness, the self-reliance and that same will to self-improvement which stemmed from his submerged Methodist heritage. But from his mother he would have inherited his simple, sanguine faith. Susan Pearce was perhaps not exceptionally God-fearing: she merely accepted absolutely the traditions in which she had been raised and took parenthood responsibly enough to become in Matthew's earliest years his moral instructor. The instruction apparently consisted almost entirely of direct readings from the Bible, with her comments and interpretations, though she seems to have been not averse to the occasional digression and to telling tales, as Matthew would later describe them, "of the old days."

None of this, perhaps, would have had such far-reaching effects on Matthew, were it not for the peculiar vividness of his mother's personality and for the fact that she died suddenly when he was only eleven and she was thirty-two, so that her memory became a shrine for all his religious feeling. At an early age there was cruelly brought home to him religion's intricate connection with mortality. The Bible would remain for him the sole consolation for his mother's inexplicable departure, the only true reply to death. Though, for all his early training, he does not seem to have been able to sustain the same trauma from the opposite end: the death in 1854 of his son Felix, aged two. Rather, this heralded the collapse of Matthew's spiritual certainty. However, by this time Matthew would have retained not only the undimmed memory of his mother but the memory of his encounter with an ichthyosaur.

His mother's death would also have made clear to Matthew, if he did not guess it already, that his father had married not just as a means to material advancement. Until in later life he succumbed increasingly to drink, John Pearce does not seem to have been given to extravagant displays of emotion. But his son must have perceived what was seldom voiced: John did not remarry; grief became an abiding fact of his life. And it must have dawned on Matthew sooner or later that the loss of his mother was the beginning of his father's own gradual abandonment of his faith.

One result of his bereavement might have been John Pearce's return to the chapel. He turned, rather, to the world. He was the former industrious apprentice who had assiduously bettered himself so as to run his own modest workshop and his own modest household: it now meant everything to him that the amelioration should be continued in his son.

Only some intuition of the inner motive at work could have kept young Matthew from rebelling against the cajoling, insistent overseer his father must have become. It was all a form of tribute—a mutually binding tribute to his dead mother. On that basis Matthew would have learnt to serve rather than resent his father. He would have understood the responsibility placed upon him and grown up with a sense of obligation and duty as springing from some tenderer source than mere obedience. His appetite for knowledge would have been released and, behind all the paternal coercion, blessed. And all this would have reached its apogee on that day when, against all the laws of social expectation (though his father was now operating a thriving business and his clocks were sought after by the local gentry), a place was secured for him at Oxford. His father's features, so long the stern features of a determined taskmaster, must have at last allowed themselves a broad, proud grin.

And now, as Oxford recedes behind him, Matthew imagines the scene of his homecoming. His father will be waiting in the market square. He will not be cowed by his son's attainments, nor parade them too vainly before his neighbours; but nor will his son be cowed any more by his once overbearing father. They will greet each other amicably, as equals. In the White Hart they will clink glasses (one Methodist pledge John has long abjured), and Matthew will be aware of a sense of mission fulfilled.

What he will not be aware of, not until, years later, he confides the realisation to his notebook, is that while it is he who has enjoyed the benefits of education, it is really his father who is the more free-thinking, the more forward-looking and certainly the more calculating. It is John who, adroitly exploiting the connections of his clockmaker's clientele, has secured for Matthew (he will start next month) a position with the Exeter firm of Westbrook and Cross, newly appointed consultants to the Bristol and Exeter Railway. And it will be John who, some four years later, will write to his son, pointing out that one Robert Makepeace, a crusty soul who runs a surveyor's business in Tavistock and has so far found no junior partner to his permanent liking, is ailing and contemplating retirement. Tavistock is not Exeter, and a partnership in the Exeter firm is almost guaranteed, but now that the Bristol and Exeter was complete, the railway would forge its way westwards across the county to Plymouth: Matthew, with all his experience, would be well placed. And, as Matthew surely knew, Tavistock was no longer a sleepy market town:

the talk now was all of copper mining. Here was an opportunity for Matthew not only to acquire a business of his own but to extend his experience into new fields. . . .

The coach rocks and trundles on through the long, midsummer day, through the drowsy heart of England. As evening sculpts the hills of Somerset, it rattles into the honey-stoned, eighteenth-century city of Bath. Matthew's graduate companion, who has tried him all day with his stabs of wit, proposes a night's dissipation—"one last bachelorly bout before we wed the stern bride of the future." Matthew resists the wilder suggestions in the proposition but submits to supper and a good deal of claret before his companion finally takes his leave—whether to some house of the night or to the clutches of a guardian aunt, Matthew cannot be sure.

He goes to bed drunk. Upsets a candle. It would be like him, the next morning, to be a little ashamed of his behaviour. Nearly twenty years later, recalling, with some wistfulness, the days when his father's abstinence was total, he will remember his saying, as they passed some grinning, lolling drunkards in a Launceston street: "They have swallowed the devil and now he makes them feel pleased." But now, standing at his inn-chamber window, open to a starry sky, feeling the lift of the world beneath him like the pitch of a ship, he cannot resist a certain festive mockery of his own inner seriousness. We are not who we think we are, only figures in some eternal, amoral masque. . . .

There is a strong conservative streak in Matthew's nature—an instinct, for all his inquisitiveness, for not looking too far about him, or looking only at what he wishes to see; and a tendency, for all his self-reliance and capability, to take a good deal for granted. During his spell at Oxford, the Tractarian question has been raging; but there is no evidence that, young man of religious conviction, he interested himself in the turmoil of an old Church facing new times. Nor, while he was at Oxford, does he seem to have pursued, though the opportunity was there, those areas of scientific debate which in later life he would grapple with for himself, as if they were new.

He sees himself as setting out to take his place in an advancing (if essentially unalterable) world: it is really his father who will have put him there. He thinks he has decided, himself, on his future profession: it is really his father, with his own instinct for not setting his sights too high, who has chosen it for him. And though John Pearce is no gambler (one Methodist vow he has not abjured) and would frown at his son's forsaking the noble duty of Work so far as, for example, to dabble in railway or mining shares, Matthew would be astonished that his father's dreams for him, if only when under the influence of brandy, extend beyond his becoming merely an accomplished, successful surveyor for the rest of his life.

It might also be claimed that there is in Matthew's nature a strong capacity for happiness. Contentment, at least. A man who likes to think—and who does not like to think. Who has time for ideas but is peculiarly at home in the world of things. Who has no sense of his own importance but no vague notions, either, of his own abilities. Who has no airs and graces but a natural social ease—he is at home with people too. Who has the knack of knowing and not knowing.

Look at him now as, his journey resumed, the coach bears him onwards. Look into this bluff, obliging, earnest, amiable, in no way special face, which combines, right now, the stolidity of a man twice his age and the innocent glee of a child released from school. He has—he doesn't know it yet—depths.

10th June 1854:

We are all aware, though none of us announces the fact, that today would have been the second birthday of little Felix. One and a half months dead—as if such posthumous calendars were significant. We go to the graveside, though I truly believe poor Felix, if he could speak, would bid us not to mark the inaugural day of a life so wastefully short.

A blooming, midsummer's day. Swallows swooping around the church tower. A day designed to banish dark thoughts. Yet the thought does not escape me that it is almost ten years ago to the day that I made my excursion to Lyme. How I knew nothing then of my darling Liz, of my John, Christopher, Lucy and poor Felix. And yet how neither the passage of ten years nor all the heaped contentments they have brought me can expunge from my memory that former incident. How different my present powers of patience, of humble submission to Providence, had I not taken that journey. God knows how much since then I have pretended. God knows!—but there, in a phrase, is the essence of my pretence.

How earnestly have I endeavoured to persuade myself that I was the victim of some circumstantial or atmospheric "effect." Was not the tableau perfect? The darkening sky, the lightning flashes at sea, the flapping and straining of the tarpaulin pitched above the exposed skull. I recall every detail. The sudden cry of the young woman who had slipped on the wet surface further down the path, so that everyone rushed from the enclosure to attend the accident, leaving me alone with the creature.

Why did I not rush too? To assist the damsel in distress. A little common gallantry might have saved me.

Yet I know—ten years cannot undo the knowledge—that what followed was not a moment of unreasoned panic and confusion but a moment of acute *perspicacity*. Truly, I was to rush too, a little while after the others, from under the tarpaulin; to rush quite past the little group helping the young lady, who must have regarded me with astonishment. I recall a cluster of umbrellas bouncing in the wind; the pale face of the victim (victim!)

supported by one of her party while she tried the strength of her ankle; mud on her garments. But of what little note to me was this touching scene of mere human misfortune. . . .

He saw an ichthyosaur. It is difficult to know how people will react when they see an ichthyosaur. I can understand it with Felix—though I have never had children. Yes, I can understand it with Felix (though, even then, such a man as Matthew, cognisant of the infant mortality rate of the times—they bred hard, these Victorians, and with reason —might have thought: not so terrible, one in four). But with an ichthyosaur? An ichthyosaur.

Quite probably, he had seen one before. (I too have seen ichthyosaurs, in museums, in books. I have made a point of it, in fairness to Matthew. I look at them and don't feel that much at all.) If he had been to London, which he probably had, he would have seen in the British Museum the famous ichthyosaur, thirty feet long, discovered (first of its kind to be so unearthed) by Mary Anning of Lyme Regis—beside which awesome exhibit this half-buried specimen, perhaps some fifteen feet, was a mere baby.

Yet museums are safe, orderly, artificial places, and here, still trapped in the rock from which workers employed by the same Mary Anning were labouring to release it, within sight of the plump hills of Dorset and the ruffled waters of Lyme Bay, was the thing itself. Here, in the very spot where— Here. Now. Then. He stood face to face with the skull of a beast that must have lived, so certain theories would have held, unimaginably longer ago than even the most generous computations from the Scripture allowed for the beginning of the world (yet which must have been created, so something inside him would have insisted, by God); so long ago that the fact of its existence had been almost irretrievably swallowed up in the fact of its extinction and only now, in the pathetically locatable nineteenth century, had it come to be known that it had existed at all; and thought— And thought what?

". . . The moment of my unbelief. The beginning of my make-belief. . . ."

You have to picture the scene. You have to imagine these scenes in which for most people nothing changes, nothing is essentially different—all this drama and fuss, a passing storm, a twisted ankle—but for some people the world falls apart. I think that's perhaps what Ruth did—all this drama! To picture how the world might be—how it might fall apart or hold, incredibly, together—in the eyes of other people.

Such a simple, unconscionable thing: to be another person.

A flapping tarpaulin. Sticky gobs of rain, a bruised, galvanic sky. The long, toothed jaw; the massive eye that stares through millions of years. He is the creature; the creature is him. He feels something open up inside him, so that he is vaster and emptier than he ever imagined, and feels himself starting to fall, and fall, through himself. He lurches on to the path, as if outward movement will stop this inward falling. He passes a startled young woman, who has fallen also, but less than her own length and on to solid ground. He blunders down another path, not the path he came up by but a path which takes him to the beach—as if to stop himself falling he must get to sea level. The storm swipes in off the sea. His hat blows off; he is soaked. Everything is lost and confused—sea, rocks, cliffs, sand—in swamping greyness.

17th June 1854:

An impossibility, a contradiction: to *pray* for belief. He knows everything. He "unto whom all hearts be open." He punishes me with Felix's death, for perpetrating this impossibility. Or: for my false belief, the belief in my own pretence.

Or: Felix's death: merely a proof.

18th June 1854:

No, I will not believe it. I will acknowledge the insoluble mathematics of nature, the wanton waste and the resourcefulness of her economy; that compared with the brief life of countless creatures, my Felix may be said to have lived an age; that everywhere, if seeds and eggs be counted, examples abound of gross destruction so that few may survive; that humankind, albeit leniently accommodated, is not excused from this scheme. But I cannot believe that in this prodigious arbitrariness there is any *purpose* that grants life to a child only to withdraw it after two years; that it is not the case, rather, that he might as well not have existed; that he holds, in truth, in the great course of things, no place, value or identity compatible with the vain fabric of loving recognition that I, that we all, have built around him. . . .

He walks and walks, to stop the falling, all the way back to Lyme. If Lyme is still there. It is—emerging from the curtains of rain. But how pathetic and pitiable it looks; the little huddle of habitation, the quaint tumble of roofs, the cluster of rocking boats cradled in the curving arm of the Cobb.

And it was meant to be a holiday. And now it has become an experience from which he must recover, slowly convalesce. Though no one can help or nurse him but himself. No one will even know how he is not himself, how far he has fallen through himself, except himself. And the only remedy he has is to pretend. To pretend so hard that one day, perhaps, he will forget he is pretending. He will do his best, and even achieve, quite soon, some outward approximation of recovery, so that, back in Launceston that same summer, even his own father will not guess the true extent of the damage. The lad is strangely out of sorts, to be sure. So much for the benefits of sea air. Some talk of an untimely ailment, a fever, a soaking in a summer storm. As like as not, some woman is at the bottom of it. At any rate, his son is oddly reluctant to discuss the whole Tavistock question. Well, well, let the cloud pass, give everything its time.

Matthew says nothing. And John Pearce treads carefully. But remarkable recoveries—or rescues—happen. And Matthew has a capacity for happiness. And John Pearce is doubly glad that Rector Hunt should call that afternoon about his clock, and that he should bring his daughter with him.

Or that is how I like to see it. That is how I wish it to have happened. I give to Matthew's life that very quality of benign design that he had already glimpsed might be lacking from the universe. I choose to believe that Matthew first met Elizabeth in his father's office in Launceston that same July. And I choose to believe that at the very first meeting Matthew would have had the overwhelming perception that here, when his thoughts had already shown him how terribly you could go adrift, was the true, sure ground of his life. That he would have felt himself falling, sinking, collapsing again, not with that fearful sense of falling into a void, but with a sense of miraculous, restoring gravitation.

The scene: John Pearce's workshop in Bell Street, Launceston. July sunshine—let's suppose there was sunshine—slanting through the workshop windows on to the scratched and worn surfaces of the workbenches and on to the little brass pieces—cogs, springs, levers—laid out like some miniature treasury on rectangles of black felt. Matthew would have been impressed by the improvements to the workshop. His father now employed two journeymen and one apprentice, but he still sat, himself, at his work-bench, eye-glass crammed into one eye, conforming to the image Matthew still retained of him from childhood: a vaguely magician-like figure, hunched over his little clock-work world, unwittingly miming the classic analogy for the existence of a Creator, and seeming to be engaged not only in the making of clocks but in the manufacture of this vital stuff called Time, this stuff which Matthew still thought of as being essentially human in meaning, the companion and guardian of human affairs.

A clock ticks on the mantelpiece. . . .

A desultory conversation in progress: Launceston gossip. John notes yet again the want of his son's usual buoyancy and curiosity. Then the little bell in the office tinkles and John says, "Ah," and drops his eyeglass neatly into his right hand, removes his apron, rolls down his sleeves and reaches for his jacket. "That will be Rector Hunt."

Or perhaps there was nothing so apparently casual about this encounter. Perhaps John had said to Matthew: "The Reverend Hunt, from Burlford, will be calling by about his clock. He would be pleased to meet you." Which is why Matthew was there. Or perhaps John, on a previous oc-casion, had said to the Rector, a man who, living in a household of women, felt a want of educated male con-versation and a vague sense of being out of touch with the world, "Matthew will be home in July, so please call by—and you can see how the clock comes along." But whether John had anticipated the Rector's being accompanied by his elder daughter is another matter. And whether Rector Hunt had said to Elizabeth, "I shall be paying a call on Pearce the clockmaker—I believe his son, a Brasenose man, may be there. Perhaps you'd care to join me?" is another matter still. But why should Elizabeth have de-cided to attend her father about so humdrum a matter as a clock, when she might have passed her time in Launceston much more pleasurably, at the dressmaker's or milliner's, say?

Matthew would have gone with his father into the office, ready to offer his hand to Rector Hunt, but his eyes would have been compelled to meet first—and have been met quickly, meekly—by the eyes (I see them as glossy brown) of his daughter. A just-detectable hiatus would have occurred in which a just-detectable mutual blush would have touched the faces of the two young people. Then, after exchanged pleasantries and at a polite inquiry from the Rector and some prompting from his father, Matthew would have found himself rehearsing what he would have already rehearsed to his father, namely his account of the opening of the Bristol and Exeter Railway and of the jubilant arrival, just two months ago now, at the Exeter terminus of the first train from Paddington. And Rector Hunt and his daughter (if with different motives) would have listened with genuine awe to his tale. Railways existed, had existed for some thirty years in Cornwall—little, narrow-gauge haulage lines serving the north coast ports. But the Rector and his daughter would never have seen a steam engine. And these hurtling contraptions, which could take a man from his breakfast in London and set him down for dinner in Devon, they would have regarded with amazement and not a little dread.

Matthew does not overdo his scene-painting, but his voice betrays a curious urgency, and he finds himself gratified, peculiarly enlightened, by the looks of astonishment and vague fear on his listeners' faces. As the train of his description is greeted by the cheering crowds at Exeter, a train of thought passes through his mind that fills him— he cannot say how much it has to do with Miss Hunt's look of appealing vulnerability—with a sudden gush of liberating relief. The fear of the new, he thinks, is as primitive, as superstitious, as the fear of the old. We fear what we do not know. To the vole, the hawk is a monster of tearing beak and talons; only a man sees its aerial grace and skill. How many things that are dreadful to man might not be, in the eyes of their Maker, comely and fitting?

He moves with sudden confidence (John is amused to note how his son's spirits are reviving) and with the aim of reassuring his audience, to give a practical and lucid account of that masterpiece of engineering, the steam locomotive, with a brief commentary on the dependability of Mr Brunel's Broad Gauge. Elizabeth thinks: he has a way, to be sure, of making the extraordinary seem perfectly acceptable—and such a dependable, broad-gauge kind of smile. But the Rector, who cannot get beyond seeing a steam engine as a sort of tamed dragon and forgets that he has initiated the whole subject, says, "Yes—yes, indeed. But tell me, is that Philpott fellow still peddling Divinity at Brasenose?"

"But Papa," protests Elizabeth, "you interrupt Mr Pearce."

Matthew notices the swiftness of this intercession on his behalf and the briefest flash of a look from her (acknowledged by a reflexive tightening of the corner of his mouth) which seems to say, "See, I do this for you."

"I'm sure"—she redeems any brusqueness with a smile—"he has so much more to tell us."

And Matthew is only too conscious at this moment that he does, indeed, have other things to tell—he has seen stranger and more awesome things, indubitably, than railway locomotives. The possibility comes rushing to him that *she* might be the very one—the only one—that he might tell them to. But responding to the awkwardness of the situation (she notes: he is not clumsy, he has natural tact), he saves the Rector's embarrassment—"No, indeed, I go on at too much length"—and, turning the conversation with a deferential inquiry about Rector Hunt's own Oxford days (aware with the corner of his eyes how the corner of hers is twinkling; aware of how her father, almost unconsciously, takes her hand and strokes her wrist), allows a cheerful exchange of reminiscence about Oxford, or rather about two different Oxfords, which each pretends, for the sake of good feeling, are the same.

"No, no, Dean Philpott must have retired before my going up."

"Ah, quite so. There would have been, I suppose, that man Newman. . . ."

And Elizabeth listens. And the Rector, on the verge of a theological disquisition, brings himself up suddenly with the remark (his turn for apology) that he has quite forgot the time and must be on his way. Whereupon Elizabeth says, and everyone laughs: "Indeed, Papa, you have quite forgot the time, for you have quite forgot the clock!"

The way things begin. The auguries of happy-ever-afters. A clockmaker's shop, where time ticks impartially away. Perhaps Matthew was aware that this first encounter with his wife-to-be had been engineered by his father and was the work of a witting or unwitting match-making by the two elder parties. But what did this matter, when he could be unswervingly sure that if he had met Elizabeth in some other circumstance, wholly free of behind-the-scenes manoeuvring and wholly subject to chance, he would have experienced the same thrilling emotion of a foregone conclusion?

Call it—heaven-sent.

A sober scrutiny might have judged that a man who had

lost his mother when he was small, and remembered her most clearly as the woman who had read to him from the Bible, might well be drawn to a clergyman's daughter; and that in that bumbling, kindly figure of Rector Hunt (the way his hand had touched hers) he saw something his own father could not offer. But this would have been to ignore the young man of only twenty-five, who, for all his, by now, increasing and debilitating proneness to thought, still possessed, in spite of himself, a healthy animal nature. He falls in love, heavily, thickly, thankfully (is there any other way?). He is still—thank God—open to experience. He sees himself, indeed, as "saved"—returned to the sweet, palpable goodness of the world.

He goes back into the workshop with his father and is strangely, tenderly struck by his familiar presence. The way his leather apron and his eye-glass seem to wait for him; the way the brass components on the bench have an almost sentient, obedient distinctness. Things fit, things have a purpose.

That evening, his steps light and every breath fresh and clear, Matthew strolls down from his father's house to the knoll at the edge of town on which stand the ruins of the castle. Once, his mother used to take him on this same walk, and used to tell him, like some made-up tale to warn impudent young boys, how men, wicked men, had once been hanged in public right here on the castle green. The air is soft and aglow. A breeze caresses the peaceful curves of the landscape, and Matthew is prompted by that old urge, that old itch in the palm—as if he were capable, now, of such a giant reach. Perhaps he need never tell her— better never to tell her—about his "thoughts." Let them be banished like demons.

"The little hills rejoice . . ." The land of the living.

He watches a buzzard hang over the hillside, then drop

from its shelf of air. He looks eastwards across the valley, where the Tamar severs Cornwall from Devon, and is struck by the pleasing notion that, like the best lovers of old, he and Elizabeth dwell on different sides of a divide.

Meanwhile, Elizabeth, riding home to Burlford in the carriage with her father, displays a tendency to pensive, absorbed silence. Several times the Rector ventures to strike a conversation, but then, with perhaps a smile to himself, thinks better of it.

I invent all this. I don't know that this is how it happened. It can't have been like this simply because I imagine it so.

That night, in the White Hart, there would have been a bloom about his son's features—more than could be ascribed to an evening's stroll—which John Pearce would have been too shrewd not to see the cause of. Just as he was too shrewd to dwell, for the time being, on the Rector's visit earlier that day. But, calling for another brandy and water, and knowing full well that Burlford was only three miles from Tavistock, he would have chosen his moment and said, "Now, about old Makepeace. What do you say?"

10

Romantic love. A made-up thing. A concoction of the poets. Jack shall have Jill. *Amor vincit omnia.*

Her last role was Cleopatra. Love triumphant and transcendent. Love beyond the grave: "I am again for Cydnus to meet Mark Antony." This was at Stratford, two summers ago. Then the symptoms made their appearance, and it had to be announced that because of sudden illness she could no longer perform. Early the next year she was dead. . . .

But you could say I was always a stage-widower. A stage-cuckold. The old joke about the actress's husband: he could never get his hands on his wife's parts. I would watch my wife go away. I would watch her disappear and turn into —these other people. With my own eyes I witnessed the inconstancy. How many times did I watch Ruth fall into another man's embrace? Play seductress and seducee? Run squealing, half naked, round strange bedrooms? How many times did I watch her—die? And it is true that, sitting in the darkness (proud, jealous, enthralled), I would have to concede that at such moments she didn't belong to me, she belonged to her audiences. She was everybody's. But the thing is, she would always come back to me. Me. I don't know why, but she did. Always. A dullness for her brightness? A nobody for her somebody? When you are out on an adventure . . .

I see her at the end of the garden of our cottage in Sussex, which backed on to a field that dipped down to a wood, with the Downs rising beyond. Against that backdrop, she would pace to and fro by the low, bramble-smothered fence, a book or script in one hand, gesticulating to the air, communing with invisible interlocutors, utterly bound up in herself, so that she would be unaware even of me, a privileged audience of one, watching from the window. Turning and turning again, wearing a path in the grass, now and then clawing a hand through her hair or hugging herself with both arms or offering up some half-conscious commentary on her progress—a "Now then, let's see" or a "Fuck it! Who wrote this thing?!"—and all the time lighting cigarette after cigarette from the pack jammed in her cleavage, chucking the butts away at random (once starting a small fire in the brambles). It was at such times, rather than in the darkness of theatres, that the truth of something would come to me: that people are fuel. They are consumed. Some, for some reason, more quickly, more brightly, more readily than others. But they are burnt, used. Fuel, fire, ash.

I think she knew. I think she knew all along, even before the outward symptoms appeared. But didn't want to spoil—not before she had to—that Cleopatra summer. What you don't know can't hurt you. One Sunday, that September, we drove out, with G—— (an actor), to a pub we knew, somewhere in the depths of Warwickshire. A day of sweet, cidery sunshine. G—— was in a strangely deferential, vaguely timid mood. If I told you who G—— was, you would guess that this was not his usual style. We sat outside. She wore dark glasses and nobody recognised her. I went to get the drinks, and when I emerged, G—— was kissing Ruth on the crown of the head. His own dark glasses—these *incogniti*—pushed up on to his brow, a hand on Ruth's shoulder, his lips in her hair.

It wasn't what you think. No, it wasn't what you think.

It was only the thought of the *possibility*. It *could* have been them, you see; it could have been Ruth and G—— all along, not Ruth and me. Them, not us. I stood there in the doorway with the drinks, like someone standing outside their life, like someone suddenly without a life. You see, it was a solemn, intense, decorous kiss. Like a kiss of farewell, like the kiss of a priest. Like the kiss you give to the small, hard head of a child, conscious of its vulnerability, the brittleness of the skull. And I knew then, by the chill inside me, despite that soft sunshine, by the feeling that my body was like an empty sack, that she was going to die.

And her first role was Girl Number Three.

It was after her father's death, some fifteen years ago, that I gave up my career (my blooming career as a third-rate academic) to become her "manager." All sorts of questionable motives might be ascribed to this—and perhaps were at the time. That I wished to be more at my wife's side—in order, that is, to keep an eye on her. That I wanted to live off her earnings. In any case, it was a bogus job. Other people—agents, theatre and film people— "managed" Ruth. I was no more than a privileged secretary-cum-minder. Since my talents were limited, I sometimes hindered rather than helped proceedings. But I would still maintain that I did it out of a desire to protect her.

He died of a brain tumour. Or so they say. If you ask me, the doctors (naturally, I thought of my great-uncle George) were as baffled as we were. In the last stages he simply lost all power of identity. A mild-natured, obliging man, he slipped towards death with a stony, empty expression on his face, speechless and unhearing, not recognising his own wife or his own daughter and having no idea, so far as you could tell, who he was himself. It was as though the Bob Vaughan we knew dissolved away before some other grim, usurping, unappeasable being. Then he died.

Her mother is still alive. She married again several years ago. But I have lost touch since Ruth's funeral and the bouts of strained communicativeness that follow a death. Now, of course, in my present woeful circumstances, I am beyond the pale. The fact is, we never got on; and neither were Ruth and her mother always the sweetest of friends. Without ever knowing it for certain, I have always imagined Joan Vaughan as the one who was against Ruth's preposterous choice of career from the outset, waiting ever afterwards, notwithstanding all the evidence of success, to say, "I told you so." While Bob was the classic, doting father of an only daughter, happy for his child to do whatever she wished. I picture Ruth as a young girl quarrelling with her mother, and Bob trying, rather ineffectually, to keep the peace.

I should pity Joan, who has lost a husband and a daughter, both before their time. But I don't. She still harbours, I think, an image of Ruth as someone who might have done something solid and sensible with her life (whatever that may have been) and therefore have still been alive now; instead of this foolishness—see, it didn't last long —this play-acting. Don't try to be something you're not. . . .

I should want to see Joan now, because only in the mother's features might I still catch a glimpse, a living vestige, of the daughter. But that's now how it works.

After her father's death, Ruth's acting took on this new dimension, this new depth and range. Everyone noticed it. But there was also—perhaps only I saw it—this new need of protection. This desire on my part to put my arms irremovably around her, as if I were holding her together, to beg for her a special immunity. Be there, always. I don't know what makes some people exceptional—so that we say the world would be poorer without them. I don't know why the distribution of love is so unfair. And it's strange that I say I wished to hold her together, since it was she, after all, who held things together for me, who held my world together. I mean the world that had fallen apart (it did, you see) with my own father's death.

You see, I protected her so she would protect me.

From Girl Number Three to the Queen of Egypt, from the Blue Moon Club to a palace by the Nile. A reviewer of those last performances wrote (without benefit of hindsight) that she evoked the "defiant incandescence of soon to be extinguished glory." The formal obituaries referred to them as her "crowning achievement" and the "culmination of her career." As if she had *meant* it that way. While the news columns dwelt on the "real-life drama" —"found dead," "overdose of drugs"—and bandied about, without a trace of irony, it seemed, the phrase "tragic death."

And no one, out of tact or impercipience, alluded to the simple fact that Cleopatra is a woman who, with serene and regal deliberateness, commits suicide.

"Finish, good lady, the bright day is done, and we are for the dark."

I had to play this scene. I understood how hard it is to act. The lines were so awful, so unconvincing. I found myself uttering the hackneyed words "How long does she have?" To which, however, there was a perfectly actual, factual reply. I didn't want to tell her. If you don't say it, perhaps it won't be true. If you don't think about it, it will go away. But she simply faced me with the same question: "How long do I have?" She didn't blink. I found I couldn't lie. "Two or three months." She came back with a little flurry of brightness—she was an actress, you see: "That much?" Then she gave a look, just like a little girl who's been punished for getting beyond herself, for having big ideas about herself. I told you so, I told you so.

And there was, after all, this simple, banal explanation. She smoked. She had lung cancer. The common vice and common nemesis of nicotine. The gifted and famous are not *exempt*, you know. I should have told her to stop (I did), to cut it down. I should have said (but I didn't *know*), if you don't stop, you will *die*. But, but. The side effect of a certain way of life. Fuel, fire, ash. It might have been drugs, alcohol, screwing around and regular psychoanalysis. It was none of these. None. Just cigarettes. So many packs to learn a part. And the only time, she used to joke, she could do without, was when playing a non-smoking part (e.g., Cleopatra).

And besides, our bodies are ours—aren't they? To do with as we like. And our lives. Our lives.

And right here in the Fellows' Garden I furtively chuck my butts into the nearest flower bed.

I should blame it all, perhaps, on that conjectural ancestor of mine, the resourceful Sir Walter, who, among his countless other claims to fame, I believe, popularized the noxious New World weed. But just take him for an example. Smoked all his life like a chimney: died by the axe. There is no accounting. We have to die of something: a lung cancer, a throat cancer, a brain tumour, a bullet in the head.

But not of love, never of love. Leave that for the sonneteers. "Men have died from time to time, and worms have eaten them, but not for love."

From the Queen of Egypt to a worried woman in a waiting room. From Cleopatra to a hospital case. From a thousand parts—tragic queen, frothy French farce flirt—

to the only, unfeigned dénouement of her stricken body branded with the scars of an unsuccessful operation. So why all this acting stuff? Why all this poetry stuff? Why all this imagining it otherwise?

We gravitated towards the cottage, neglecting the London flat. We moved in things that were dear to us, such as the clock made in 1845 by John Pearce of Launceston. For me—I won't deny it—this retreat from the publicity that was part of her life—this having Ruth to myself—was a kind of terrible boon. I think we did what most people would have done in the circumstances. We drew a circle around ourselves. We tried to carry on as if nothing were different. You could call this acting too, and one day, we knew, it would have to stop. But I ask myself: in those final weeks, were we happy? It's not an absurd question. The human frame, it seems, has this stubborn capacity for existing in spite of the facts. We went for gentle walks in the brittle winter days. Put logs on the fire. We summoned memories while trying to pretend we were not summoning memories. Made plans—as if plans were feasible. Spent Christmas with Joan and her second husband, Roy—an exercise so mawkish, so awkward, so like a piece of treacly black comedy, that you were tricked into thinking none of it could be real.

I fielded (still technically her manager) the commiserative calls, dealt with the kind-but-cruel welter of mail. I developed unsuspected skills as a nurse, chef, maid-of-all-work. We tried to submit to the illusion that all this was some kind of benign interlude, a period of rest, of convalescence. Not a— Then a look of quiet urgency, of concentration, would come into her eyes, which would seem to make my presence futile. As if somewhere, deep inside herself, she were searching for someone. I would think: I must distract her. *Distract* her? I didn't allow myself to think that all this withdrawal, this retrenchment in a country cottage, this privacy, this trying to be simply, at last, herself, was itself a kind of rehearsal (so rich with stage fright), a learning of the final part.

"Give me my robe, put on my crown . . ."

I think she wanted recognition. She achieved it. Some of us want recognition, some of us don't. Potter wants it. I can live without it (perhaps I should rephrase that). And some of us who want it never achieve it. It's a funny thing, recognition. You achieve it and then you have problems about being recognised. You go around in dark glasses. And though you are recognised, everyone wants to know about this other person, this elusive, hard-to-spot character called "the real you." The "real Ruth Vaughan," as the journalists would have it. No one would recognise me, but nobody would want to ask me about the real me.

(Though I wonder who he is—really I do).

She used to say—a strange thing for an actress—that she never knew what she looked like, she couldn't have described her own face if she were asked. My experience is different. When I look in the mirror (especially these days), I see this incorrigible mask. I know it's not me, but I'm stuck with it. Perhaps it amounts to the same: you might be *anybody*. Which means I have the makings of an actor too. But not the gift.

How could you describe her face? There was no other word for it: it was full of *life*. So full of life. I think she was beautiful, but that is not an objective statement. I think she was beautiful because she was *her*. Because she was Ruth. She had brown-green eyes and a way of smiling and laughing with them before even moving her lips. Off-stage, off-screen, people always found her smaller, slighter than they had imagined. She had this—naturalness. Yet she was an actress. But isn't that what actors seek—naturalness?

There was this space that was always hers, just hers; this magic, mobile space. There were these audiences who claimed her, but there was always this space that was hers alone. And back in the days before she was famous, when she was only Girl Number Three . . .

Romantic, impossible love. The student and the chorus girl. The scholar and the actress.

She cut the process short. She couldn't bear, or bear that I should bear, the coming disintegration, which, on that February day, by some inner gauge that very sick people have, she must have known was about to begin. I can't think of any other reason. No, I can't think of any other reason.

It's wrong, of course. Suicide. My father was wrong. Ruth was wrong. I— But I'm still here. We don't have the right. To take ourselves from ourselves. And from other people. It's cowardly. It's selfish. The mess it leaves for others. But there would have been mess anyway. It's vain: a last bid for posthumous limelight; a staged exit. "I have immortal longings . . ." A form of death not so uncommon among actors. Though they aren't supposed to. They are supposed, by the sheer force of their personalities, to make miracle recoveries and so inspire us all. They are supposed to turn their inexorable demises into brave, grotesque performances on behalf of medical research funds. We look to actors and actresses—don't we?—to show us how to act.

You keep saying to yourself (trying to dismiss the thought, trying to give it your utmost attention) there will come a last time for everything. A last time to do this, a last time we do that. Simple, inconsequential things. A last day, a last hour. Then, when the last time comes, you don't realise it's the last time. She wanted to sleep. She slept all that afternoon. It was during these increasingly frequent periods when she slept in the day that I would begin, then immediately abandon, the exercise of trying to imagine the world without her. It was a fine, cold, clear day. I looked out towards the end of the garden. Beyond the trees on the other side of the field, the silver tip of a silage tower, hidden in the summer, glinted ruddily. Huge shadows barred the glowing folds of the Downs.

She didn't wake till dark. I remember that she said she'd meant to wake before it was dark, and she gave a little, half-asleep, worried look. That same night, according to the findings of the inquest, she died, by her own hand, between the hours of three and five in the morning.

And I will never know whether she made up her mind suddenly, waking that night while I slept, or whether the intention was there even as she woke that afternoon. Even before then. And I will never know—it is an absurd, hypothetical question—whether, if I had had the choice, I would have wished for such a cruel, merciful blow or would have preferred her to linger on for more precious weeks, perhaps months, becoming less and less like the woman I would want to remember. A matter of recognition. I have the contrast, now, with my mother: a wasted figure, sprouting tubes in a hospital bed, resolutely letting her own death run its full course. Could I have borne to see Ruth like that?

But my mother was seventy-eight. And "resolutely"? I wonder, now.

I came down the stairs. Her body was lying on the sofa. Not "she"; her body. The difference sinks in. There were the pills; the empty tumbler on the coffee table. Cliché props.

"Our wooing doth not end like an old play; Jack hath not Jill."

It's not the end of the world. It is the end of the world. None of the arguments, none of the catechisms work. There was a time—don't you remember?—when you never knew her; you lived without her then. No amount of grief ever brought anyone back. You wring your heart out over the death of one woman; but thousands die every hour, every minute. Well, I'm sorry. I'm selfish, I'm feeble, I only have heart enough for one.

Life goes on. It doesn't go on. Yes, yes, I know, all we want in the end, we living, breathing creatures (am I still one of them?) is life. All we want to believe in is the persistence and vitality of life. Faced with the choice between death and the merest hint of life, what scrap, what token wouldn't we cling to in order to keep that belief? A leaf? A single moist, green leaf? That will do, that will be enough. What do the dying cling to in their final moments? Sunlight through a curtain, the sound of a tennis game, the noise from a Paris street?

Good God, I am surrounded by leaves! But only Ruth will do. She represented life to me. I know that, now she is dead. She was life to me. And that isn't just vain hyperbole, is it? She was an actress, wasn't she? It was her job: to represent life to people.

I picked up the note. It was meant only for me, but it had to be submitted as evidence to the coroner. "I never could stand drawn-out farewells. . . ." I stooped over her body. It is almost inspiring, almost uplifting, at first, to be in the presence of such a momentous event. Later the madness, the helplessness, but first the gravity of the situation. I stooped over her body, as if I had rehearsed it all before and knew exactly what to do.

Romantic love. Romantic love. The first, flustered kiss on a wet night in a taxi to Girl Number Three. The last kiss, at the break of dawn, to the Queen of Egypt. "Now boast thee, death, in thy possession lies a lass unparallel'd."

And in between? Happiness. Yes, I commemorate it. Happiness ever after.

11

So Matthew married Elizabeth, in Burlford church on 4th April 1845. And on that April day John Pearce would have presented the couple with the clock he had lovingly and expressly made for the purpose.

Quite possibly Matthew was in league with his father over the clock, since the Latin inscription on the brass backplate, though a perfectly apt motto for the young couple, also conveyed, being a quotation from Virgil, a sly tribute to the Rector, whose chief recreations were the Roman poet (he laboured on his own translation of the *Aeneid*) and bee-keeping—complementary passions, as anyone will know who has read the *Georgics*. And perhaps the Rector, touched by the gesture, even more touched by the union of this sweet couple, which he himself had consecrated, refrained from ever pointing out (he was no pedant after all) that the Latin was the popular misquotation, the word order being inverted in the original—as was only characteristic of the Virgilian style and, in any case, required by the scansion.

And the marriage must have been blessed and happy and Matthew's animal nature must have been nothing lacking, because between 1847 and 1853 Matthew and Elizabeth produced four children: John, Christopher, Felix and Lucy. And when in 1854 he began his Notebooks, after the death of Felix, Matthew would refer to this whole period as "the ten happiest and most fragile years of my life."

I see Matthew tiptoe from the side of a cot. Of two cots . . . I see him blow out candles; open the little brass plate and wind the clock. He watches Elizabeth at her dressing-table as she loosens her hair. She smiles at his watching smile in the mirror. And he resolves once again—though by now, perhaps, the resolve has become a reflexive, unconscious, continuous thing—not to tell her, to lock up his thoughts. It sometimes seems to him that that very smile of hers is like a warning finger raised to her lips (the way she does it with little John and Christopher), bidding him not speak, not spoil things. She brushes her hair. He feels a tug, like an anchor-chain, at his heart. And beyond the window, in the middle distance, hidden now in the dark, is Burlford church. If Elizabeth is the anchor, there is the harbour wall. And every night now (for they are living at Leigh House, on the edge of Burlford village) the chimes from the solid old tower steal across to them over Rectory Meadow.

No, I don't believe he ever told her about that afternoon in Lyme. He kept quiet, as the Rector kept quiet about the misquoted Virgil. Perhaps he *meant* to tell her. Many times, perhaps, especially in those months before they were married—to get it over with, to exorcise the ghost!—he would have looked for the right moment. But his mouth would have been stopped by her innocent unsuspecting-ness, then by the innocent unsuspectingness of John and Christopher, and by the simple safety of silence. So that the *not* telling became in the end a duty for *her* sake, for her protection, a measure of his devotion. And, anyway, how did you *begin?* An ichthyosaur . . . And with each non-disclosure the eventual utterance became less prob-able, less plausible. The more it hung back from his lips, the more it receded from the front of his mind. And perhaps that was all that was necessary: Don't talk about it, don't think about it, it will go away.

4th September 1855:

What a good-hearted, muddle-headed old soul is my father-in-law. He understands—why should he be disposed to understand?—so little of the matters I have now begun to raise with him. How we forgive narrowness of mind, when it accompanies largeness of heart. Yet no breadth of intellect exonerates want of feeling. I could thank for ever my darling Liz and my darling little ones for opening my heart, even to the emaciation of my thoughts. But hungry thoughts sooner or later must feed. . . .

And the good-hearted Rector, in those days before Matthew's "thoughts" began to fatten, may even have suffered some small disappointment that his son-in-law was not quite the vigorous whetstone to his own blunted faculties that he had hoped. To put it plainly, happiness seemed to take away some of the man's bite. Well, well, he could hardly complain of that. His trivial loss was a measure of his daughter's gain. He could scarcely grumble if preoccupations domestic and professional (old Makepeace duly retired in 1848, and Matthew was his own master) left his son-in-law with little time for stimulating debates in the Rector's study on the relative merits of the Classics and the Sciences in fitting a man for life.

And, as the Rector baptised grandchild after grandchild, there was plentiful comfort and even relief to be drawn from watching Matthew mellow before the age-old influences of matrimony and procreation. Well, well, a man settles down and finds out how his heart truly lies, just as he, Rector Hunt, had done some thirty years ago. Once— he was to confide this much to Matthew, and then, as it happened, during an exchange of some heat in his study —he had wanted to be a missionary. A more daring and pioneering undertaking, surely, even than laying a railway line from London to Land's End. But instead of finding himself among the savages of Africa, he had settled for a rectory in Devon, and the role had fitted so like a natural skin that even his aspirations to further preferment had somehow evaporated. It would have been agreeable, of course, if a little chafing from his son-in-law had shown that some sharper, keener, more venturesome man still lurked within this skin. But it would have been disagreeable if, under the test of the young man's provocation, nothing more had emerged than that he was what he was: an amiable, amenable husk of a man.

Yes, when you got him alone, there was something strangely muted and docile about his son-in-law, for all his fine, vigorous qualities, something almost—the Rector would not have seen it at first, then berated himself perhaps for overlooking the obvious, while simultaneously adjusting to a not unflattering irony—something almost suppliant. Of course! It was Matthew who looked to *him*. It was the younger man who in these changing times, in a profession which exposed him to so much modern upheaval and innovation, looked to the older man for guidance and certitude. As why should he not to one approved as a spiritual father?

But perhaps it went further than this. Gilbert Hunt could not have helped noticing, as the years passed, how Matthew's links with his own father grew thinner, how his visits with Elizabeth to Launceston grew more infrequent and how John Pearce, even with the incentive of becoming a three-fold, four-fold grandfather, seemed to shy away from the close-knit atmosphere of Burlford. The Rector perhaps put this down to some wary residue of Methodism.

Later, he would have revised his opinion. Later too, Elizabeth would have perhaps confided in him that there had been some difference of feeling between Matthew and his father: something to do with Matthew's not advancing himself further in the world. So, Burlford parish was not far enough in the world for the former apprentice of Launceston, and all Matthew's attainments failed to sate the clockmaker's pride? Matthew was not doing badly. He had advanced far enough in the world for a God-fearing man—and advancement, in the world or in the Church, was a ticklish thing. . . .

In any case, before this point was reached, it would have seemed to the Rector that Matthew had transferred onto him from his own father a paternal status that it was difficult not to accommodate. And, remembering that sanguine young man he had first encountered in John Pearce's premises, he could not have imagined the almost prostrate state in which Matthew would come to him, ten years later, yes, in the Rectory study, after little Felix had died, and demand an *explanation*, a *reason*. Nothing less.

He uttered the usual formulae. He spoke of God's will. What else could he have done? God knows, his own heart was afflicted cruelly enough by his little grandson's death and he grieved for both parents, though it was Elizabeth who seemed better able to bear this loss of one quarter of her issue. God knows, he found it hard enough, in this thick glut of family tears, to keep his own eyes dry and remember his priorities as a clergyman. And yet (could he ever be forgiven?) he could not deny that thrill of pure joy when (God's will not seeming to suffice) he had put his arms round Matthew in a silent, receptive embrace, while a voice inside him uttered the equation: he has lost a son, I have found one.

And that was when the trouble really began. If that scene

ever really took place (I imagine, I invent), then how deluded the older man was. He could not have guessed how this son-in-law, who had so far failed to be his friendly sparring partner, would one day become his earnest antagonist, on terms beyond any he could have predicted.

I see Elizabeth turn from the dressing-table, put down her hairbrush. I don't believe that these Victorians were really, when it came to it, so Victorian. So demure and strait-laced. I don't believe they were a different species, who propagated their kind by some method less intimate and passionate than ours. John, Christopher, Felix, Lucy. The atmosphere at Leigh House in those early days was surely ripe with love; as sticky, as fertile, as any pullulating little patch of ground that Matthew would have stooped over with his magnifying glass and collecting bottle, ready to trace yet more evidence of nature's astonishing irrepressibility.

For that was how the villagers of Burlford must now and then have come across him, on Jacob's Hill or in Loxley Wood, though not yet with the haunted and furtive looks he would later display when discovered in this way. Far from it. Like as not, he would wave to you and give you the time of day and tell you something savouring rather of one of Rector Hunt's harvest-tide sermons, about how all creatures were exquisitely adapted to their purpose in creation. Which was obliging of him.

To be sure, he had his scientical fancies, did the Rector's new son-in-law—beetle-hunting and the like. But he was a good sort, for all his being a Cornishman larded over with Oxford learning. He made a fine picture with his young wife at church on a Sunday and said his Amen as loud as anyone, and any man who could marry the Rector's favourite daughter with the Rector's own blessing was good enough for Burlford and should hold himself, what's more, a privileged mortal. He didn't put on airs or hide the twang in his voice. All in all, he seemed to have his head set square on his shoulders and his feet square on the ground, and everything as it should be in between, judging by results. More to the point, when he stopped jawing about bugs and caterpillars, he could lean against a gate with you and tell you all that was worth knowing about the field in front of you, just by looking. Which showed he had a care for those who lived by the land and wasn't just a lackey to the folk in Tavistock who got rich quick (and poor again just as quick, no doubt) by burrowing about underneath it. . . .

Happiness quells thought. And work quells thought. And Matthew did not lack for work. I see him, as his neighbours saw him, riding off over the hill to a world that was changing even more rapidly than his father-in-law's misgivings could encompass.

Who has heard of the copper rush of southwest Devon (you see, Potter, I have done my homework), which came and went over a century ago? Forget your Klondikes and your Californias. Who has heard of Josiah Hitchens of Tavistock, "King of Copper," who in 1844, the same year that Matthew Pearce encountered an ichthyosaur and also happened upon Elizabeth Hunt, discovered in a wood in the Tamar valley a copper lode so rich that it would form the basis for almost two decades of the biggest copper mine in Europe and within two years return its shareholders eight hundred per cent. The "mine"—that is, a chain, a family of mines (Hitchens must have regarded them as his children), which multiplied themselves along the course of the lode: Wheal Maria, Wheal Fanny, Wheal Anna-Maria, Wheal Josiah (naturally), Wheal Emma . . . Collectively known as Devon Great Consols.

Then there were all the lesser, hopeful ventures spawned by Hitchens' discovery—including the Wheal Talbot mine, in which a certain James Neale would have a dominant interest. Then all the attendant enterprises (all work for Matthew): quays on the lower Tamar (ore out; coal in), canals, pumping systems, even the Consols' own railway.

Under the guidance of his moribund senior partner, Matthew would have acquired the sought-after skills of a mining surveyor and watched the sinking of shaft after shaft. Beneath the day-to-day bustle of it all, the uncanny irony must surely have struck him. That he should be plunged, so literally, so nakedly, into the realms of Geology. That he should be lowered—for sometimes it must have been required of him—into those subterranean zones from which no one returns without having their view of life on the surface modified. When he rode back over the hill to Burlford and took in the timeless cluster of rooftops and church tower, the rookeried beeches behind the Rectory, how did it seem? Like a welcome refuge? (After all, he and Elizabeth might have chosen to live in Tavistock itself.) Or, more and more, like some piece of brittle, nostalgic scenery?

24th June 1856:

I perceive the Rector apprehends the literal undermining of his parochial security. Tavistock marches outwards—underground! Says: "My dear Matthew, I fear there will soon be nothing left of our familiar surroundings but a precarious crust. When you ride into Tavistock, do you not expect at every moment your swift descent into the lower world?" Answer, to the point: "I assure you, sir, we surface dwellers are in no such danger." Do not say: "But the picture we cherish of our familiar world may be a thin crust for all that."

And then there was the railway. By 1849 it had reached Plymouth, with further track laid in Cornwall. A little matter, in between, of spanning the Tamar estuary at Saltash: it would take ten years. Matthew worked on the Ivybridge-to-Plymouth section and on the projected Tavistock branch line, and, as early as 1848, would have been involved in the preliminary surveys and geological soundings for Brunel's great Saltash bridge. It was during this time that Matthew himself was first introduced to Brunel (these little glimpses of the great—you can see why Potter is keen) and came under the spell of the engineer's mixture of practical genius and formidable energy.

18th August 1854:
   . . . I have grasped the meaning of I.K.B.'s perpetual cigars: he *must* have them, as furnaces must have chimneys—they are lit from *within.*

(So Brunel was a smoker too.)

And it was during this time which marked the high tide of Victorian endeavour and the high tide of Matthew and Elizabeth's marriage that the couple, like true devotees of the new age, travelled to London (by express train, naturally) to see the Great Exhibition.

11th September 1855:
   I remember—but four years ago—how we journeyed up to see the Exhibition. I do not think there could have been two happier people. It was her first journey of any length by train, and she was full of the astonishment of the thing—how it could not be possible that the cattle and the hedgerows and barns and millponds passed by so quickly and smoothly, as if *they* moved, not us; and how London, which she had never seen, was surely too *far* a place to be reached so rapidly. And I was full of

how it was all, indeed, quite possible, giving a reprise—
she acknowledged it—of my observations on that day we
first met, and expounding the further mysteries of gra-
dients and viaducts and cuttings and tunnels, until she
threw up her hands and said, "Stop it, stop it, please! I
would rather admire than know!" Whereupon I said,
continuing to tease, "I grant you the joys of ignorant
wonder, but, to quote your father—that is, to quote one
of his quotations: *'Felix qui potuit rerum cognoscere cau-
sas'*" (giving a fair imitation of the Rector's best scho-
lastical style). Whereupon we laughed like children out
of school, apologising, in his absence, to the good man.

Then she said suddenly, "Why—that is it! We should
call him Felix!"—for she was then newly with child for
the third time. "Is not that a *happy* name?!" "So it is
another boy?" I said. "Of course," she said. "And how
can you tell?" "I simply can. Was I wrong with John and
Christopher? You see, my dear Matty, in this case *I* know
and *you* must admire."

And a boy it was. And I will never forget how her eyes
sparkled, how we laughed, with the countryside rushing
past us. And those words still ring in my ear: "I would
rather admire than know."

The green valley, the church, the ivied Rectory, the
huddled cottages, the copse, loud with rooks, behind the
churchyard. An image out of a picture book of ye olde
England, but it still exists. I should go there, perhaps (in
my condition?). A sort of pilgrimage. A legitimate piece of
field research. I can imagine it. There will be chicken wire
in the church porch to stop birds nesting—there always is.
And there will be a little, charred, utilitarian enclave in
one corner of the graveyard, with a heap of grass cuttings
and discarded flowers and an ancient, rusted incinerator.
There always is. And *they* will still be there. Or some of
them. Not Matthew, of course. Nor the elder brothers. Nor
Lucy. But the Rector, and Mrs Rector. And Elizabeth. Real

people, real bones (not this cast of characters). And, with a headstone older than them all (the graves of infants are always affecting), Felix.

22nd April 1854:
  Today, after falling ill of scarlet fever on Sunday night, our darling Felix died, beyond the doctor's saving, at half-past six in the morning, aged one year and ten months.

I don't understand him. I never sought him out, I could do without him. But there he is, washed up before me: I have to revive him.

  I don't understand him. The Notebooks don't begin until 1854, with the death of his son. And they end in 1860, with the departure of Matthew from Burlford and from his wife and children for ever. And throughout that six-year period Matthew must have lived, to the world at least, the life he had always lived; must have ridden off every day over the hill to his work, and slipped into bed beside Elizabeth and sat with her in their pew on Sundays, as if nothing had changed.

  The Notebooks must have been secret, even from the Rector, to whom his "thoughts" were not. The entries are sporadic—whole months go by with not a word written. And at any time during those six years (but how many times did he *do* this?) Matthew might have looked around him at all that he had and said, indeed, What is the difference? What difference does it make? And even on that very last day—it was a fine June day: he even found time to note the fleecy clouds and the roses in the Rectory garden—he might have walked up on to Jacob's Hill, looked down at his house, at the village, at all that sweet, unaltering make-belief, and, with a simple turning of a switch inside him and a sealing of his lips, returned to embrace it.

22nd April 1855:

Is there not in our minds, no less than in physical nature, a power of regeneration and renewal? Are we not lopped and smitten only so we will grow again? I thought it so once. "Heaviness may endure for a night, but joy cometh in the morning."

9th August 1856:

Such a lovely day, blessed day. Unbroken sunshine and the breeze not bringing in clouds but seeming to sweep and cleanse the air. In the evening, at the imprecations of Lucy, who seemed to decide that today she must be my constant consort, took the gig and made a brief excursion with her round and about the village. Such a sweet evening, such a rare light over the valley, and the tops of the trees in Rectory Copse stirring as if with a consciousness of delight. On such a day why should we resist what we credulously call the "evidence of our senses"? "And the firmament sheweth his handywork"! Coming back, Lucy fell at once fast asleep, even in the jolting gig. Had to be lifted, still sleeping, from it. Observed how in her sleep she passes the back of her hand deliberately across her eyes, just as her mother does. Thought how a future husband will treasure that gesture just as I treasure it in Liz. No thing, perhaps, is truly separate from another. What right have I to make hostages to my conscience my children, my wife and all that is dear to me? When I know, truly, I would lay down my life, on the instant, for my daughter and her brothers and their mother, why can I not do the lesser thing and make a sacrifice of my doubts?

24th October 1856:

Raise again with the good Rector the question of Extinction. N.B., not Death—Extinction. The Rector would have it that I confuse—because he himself, perhaps, confuses—the two, and that my discoursing on the latter is merely the old cavilling at the former. I am not so foolish as to take issue with mortality. I will bow to Divine Will—however volatile that Volition—in the individual (have I not done so?). But in the species?

These fossils of mine, quips he, are fast becoming the "insuperable bone of our contention." But I will not be jested into submission. Question: Is the Creator to be viewed as a mere Experimenter? Why should the Maker who fashioned Noah, and gave him such provident instructions, make what he unmakes? He answers: Being the Creator, he would have every right. I answer: Yes, but what reason? He answers: Did not God repent of his Creation? Was not the Flood sent to punish all flesh with destruction, saving only the seedstock in the Ark? And might not these creatures (viz. "my fossils") be the remains of those living things destroyed in the Flood, their shapes "monstrously altered" by that great Catastrophe? Answer: Anatomy not so flexible, nor distortion so uniform. And, in any case, "these creatures" were extinct (by any reckoning) *before* the Flood.

But he does not care to be launched again on the question of Time. He looks at me, indeed, with the scowl of a man who begins to feel I take up too much of his. Yet he once, not long ago, gave it freely enough. He was once not a little glad that, after some ten years his son-in-law, I opened up my thoughts to him and put him, in his words, "on his theological mettle." We should not, he says, from the small vantage of our private grievances, call to task the universe and its governance. No, no, perhaps. But we regularly, it seems, do the opposite thing and suppose, from our private contentments and the smooth running of our local affairs, the compliant disposition of all things. Example: I am a surveyor; I go out with my yardstick to measure the field. I am told by Lyell here, whose *Principles of Geology* rests at my elbow and whom I do the credit of re-reading, this time *with my eyes open*, that the universe is a thing beyond all known calculation. No matter: in order to measure the field it is not necessary to measure the universe, and I will swear, for all Lyell can tell me, that the field I tread today, after diligently perusing his work, is the same field I trod yesterday and that three feet still make one yard.

25th October 1856:

If Lyell is right, and I cannot—without shutting my eyes—pronounce him wrong, then the Book of Genesis is not a history but an allegory—and an imperfect one —and my father's frail chronometers are of little avail in estimating the immense periods of Geological Time. Suppose that aeons elapsed before the Creator made Man, before the world became such as we see it to be, and that the six days of Genesis are properly to be counted in *millions* of years; then the entire record of human history is as a wink in the world's duration. And if the world existed so long without Man upon it, why should we suppose that futurity holds for us any guaranteed estate and that we occupy any special and permanent place in Creation?

29th October 1856:

Walked with the Rector before dinner over Jacob's Hill. Fine autumn weather, the bracken turning. Ventured—with caution—to raise again above questions. Answers: Bah! Who but the Almighty could have raised mountains and levelled plains? I answer: Lyell could tell him. Offer to lend copy.

Question rather is: Why should the *Almighty* have been so *slow*? If He ordained for us a privileged position between the brutes and the angels, why did He place us there so *late*? Anticipate the Rector's answer: God not to be reckoned by temporal gauges; all is one *sub specie aeternitatis*; "a thousand years in thy sight are but as yesterday," etc., etc.

6th November 1856:

Dined in Tavistock with Neale, who will be chief venturer in Wheal Talbot, and Mr Benson, a visiting acquaintance of his, a Manchester man and something in cotton. Neale a sound enough fellow. Mean to invite him some day to Burlford. Benson harder to fathom. Proposes: (1) to acquire of Neale, and similarly of others, the exclusive right to refine the arsenopyrite waste from Wheal Talbot, which can hardly be objected to by Neale, who would otherwise have the task of its disposal; (2) to export said arsenic to the American plantations to curb the American boll weevil, thus benefiting—"a pretty chain of consequences"—not only the planters but the economies of Devonshire and Lancashire.

Asks (Neale having told him, doubtless, of my "bug-hunting") whether I am acquainted with the boll weevil—"a prodigious devourer of cotton." Answer: "No, I am not familiar with that species, but is there not a blight upon the cotton trade more detrimental than the boll weevil? I mean the blight of slavery." Answers: "Indeed, sir, there is much sentiment aired nowadays on the subject of slavery, much of it, I observe, by those who do not object to wear cotton on their backs or who fondly suppose that slavery is an evil unmet with in our own happy land. You do not know our Lancashire factory hands. You would find them also an interesting species. I assure you that were you to view the conditions under which the mass of them exist, you would consider the miners here in Devon to be blessed in comparison. It would be an interesting experiment, would it not, to remove one of your negroes from his shackles in the Carolinas and set him down, a free man, in the din of one of our Manchester mills? Would he thank us, I wonder, for our Christian mercy?"

9th November 1856:

Estimation: from one mature oak tree, in a seed-bearing year, some 20,000, or, say, two bushels, of acorns. (This from calculations upon my own observation of the oaks in Loxley Wood.) Of which but some hundreds will root as seedlings (failure in germination; eaten by birds and animals). Of which again barely some ten per cent (nibbling by animals; want of light—your bracken is your enemy of your oakwood) will remain after the first three years.

Estimation: A hen salmon of ten pounds from our Tamar will deposit, say, 10,000 eggs, of which perhaps only a quarter are made fertile and of these the vast bulk will be destroyed as eggs, in the larval stage or as parr. For this (being itself one of the lucky survivors) it performs, unstintingly, its gruelling and eventually fatal yearly journeys from the sea.

Estimation: The pheasant (this from Wilson, the gamekeeper) will lay, say, twelve eggs in a year. Of which (assuming no vigilant and protective Wilson) some three or four will be lost as eggs to weasels and other nest-robbers—not counting the frequent destruction of whole clutches—and of the surviving nestlings some three or four again will fall to predators or, as young birds, to the trial of their first winter.

The same pattern, if the margin of waste narrows, among the higher animals. If we suppose the human species to be above the harsh husbandry of nature, then we need but look to our own systems of economy (N.B., Benson's factory hands). Two minutes in the company of our copper miners will prove that they are Toms, Dicks and Harrys; but are they not perceived as so many man-units, quantifiable (and expendable) at cheap rate?

Conclusions. (*a*) Bad: That nature is a pitiless arithmetician and gross cozener, hiding behind her bountiful appearance the truth that the greater portion of Creation exists only as a tribute to Destruction.

(*b*) Good (but conditionally): That nature is indomitable in her promulgation of life. *What expense will she not spare* to maintain her own? But this the tenacity of the blind. If disposed by the Almighty and All-seeing, why not with more *thrift*?

10th November 1856:

"And herb for the service of man"? If the cotton plant were created so we might not lack for clothing, why the boll weevil? And all the nations of *pests*.

The Rector has returned my Lyell. Confesses he has
progressed so far but found it bewildering ground. It is
the ground *under our feet!* Concedes he will not judge
what he cannot pretend to have studied. A humble way
of wishing the subject closed. But I perceive a kind of
challenge in this embargo on further parley. I have spoken; he has heard me. This is the gist of it. He has allowed
me, for so long, to be the *advocatus diaboli* in his study;
he has answered me with patience, with sympathy, even
with pleasure in the envigoration of the exercise—but
now, if I truly mean to persist in all this, would I consider
very carefully the consequences?

Meanwhile, under this enforced truce, he does not
shrink from outfacing me indirectly. He pre-empts me
from the vantage of his pulpit and counters me in his
choice of text—I am sure these things are intended especially for me. This Sunday's sermon: "Therefore will
we not fear, though the earth be removed; and though
the mountains be carried into the midst of the sea."

And still I go and sit in our pew and listen while he
thus dares me before the unwitting congregation. And
still I kneel and pray, and my heart is uplifted by the
words of the Bible, which I cannot believe, no, no, are
mere fancy, mere poetry, like the Rector's Virgil. Dear
God, I do not want to hurt the dear old man. And only
when I put on again my Sunday hat, do my "thoughts"
return. Only at the church gate does my conscience meet
me once more and charge me with desertion.

I trust—I know—he will not speak to Elizabeth. Is not
that the true measure of my hypocrisy? That I keep from
my own wife what I impart to her father, wishing to spare
her, being her father's daughter, the full pain of disclosure, when I daily injure and perplex her with my furtive
preoccupation; and she, dear Liz, patiently supposes that
periodically I must wrap myself in weighty but necessary
"studies." Surely she suspects. But surely if I were to tell
her all, she would only commend me to her father's counsel. Surely, one day, taking the matter into her own

hands, she will speak to her father. And there will be the poor Rector in a fine state of contortion.

6th July 1857:

My dear little Lucy! Such a sweet mixture of trustingness and forwardness. I confess she has become my favourite. I endeavour to instill in her what, increasingly, is absent in me and to teach her to see what I discern less and less: an immanent Divinity in all things. As this morning, when we passed a memorable hour in the sunshine, observing the butterflies on our buddleia bush. I had thought she had no mind for her lost little brother, but today, when I explain how short is the life of the butterfly, she pierces my heart by remarking: "Poor things, like Felix."

"This is the Large White," I say, "and this is the Tortoiseshell—you see, each wears its own apparel—and this the Red Admiral, who is called admiral not because he is a naval gentleman but because he is to be admired: do you not agree?" She asks: "But why should each kind be dressed the same?" A big question. I answer. "Why, so we can recognise them and tell one kind from the other and know their names." Answers: "But that is silly, Papa, they cannot all have the same name. I would rather they had names of their own, like you and me."

20th August 1857:

To the Rectory for dinner. The first such occasion for some time. I observe the Rector cannot altogether restrain the animosity formerly confined to his study, though his good wife and Elizabeth mark nothing more than an unwonted testiness, for which they chide him, and he, good soul, is duly contrite. I introduce the subject of Brunel's bridge, the first great truss for which is to be positioned next month; whereupon he adopts the popular stance of fearful and scornful incredulity. "But surely," he exclaims, "the thing is *impossible*!" I see his drift: he will not attack me, not before Emily and Liz, but he will attack the bridge, which I defend, for its unholy presumption. "You tell me," he says, in the manner of an *ipso facto* denunciation, "that the distance to be spanned is nigh on a thousand feet, and each truss will weigh over a thousand tons!"

How we human beings are so easily dismayed by effects of *scale*. The Saltash bridge is indeed a thing of vast proportions, but it is no less practicable, no less conformable to the laws of physics, than one of my father's quietly ticking clocks. With a sketch or two and some mathematics, I could show—I offer to do so, but the Rector forbids such dinner-table science—how such a mighty thing is achieved. To be sure, there are many who take the immensity of I.K.B.'s schemes as a measure of his vainglory and as an omen of his ruin. But it is their calumny which inhibits his success, not the man's own scrupulous calculations.

I confess that I too, on first meeting I.K.B., had my qualms. I shuddered—not only at the fierce effluvia of his cigars but to encounter one so plainly marked out, so *naturally* prepared for *exceptionality*; and my awe converted itself into that unthinking and superstitious suspicion that in some way he transgressed.

Transgressed what? Nothing more, I would say now, than the bounds of *normality*. Why are some picked by fate and some not? Why are we not *all* Brunels? That is the conundrum out of which we construct the false charge of impious presumption. And how much more, for me, was that mystery deepened by my observing, on further acquaintance, the ordinary human limits of the man. He is no sorcerer. He has sacrificed his health for his work, which only proves he is flesh and blood; and though he is beset by a thousand obstacles and is prey to a thousand practical anxieties, I do not believe—I do not assert this out of pride—that the roots of his soul have ever been rocked as mine have been or that he could have achieved what he has without the ballast of a steady conscience.

To build a bridge! Is not that one of the noblest of man's endeavours? To link *terra firma* with *terra firma*; to throw a path across a void. The ignorant say it defies nature, yet it rests upon her co-operation. And I might profess to the Rector—if only I might still believe it—that such an enterprise only bespeaks the work of Him whom he serves. That our science attests a greater omniscience; that the Almighty has given to the humblest bird the gift of wings with which to perform the same feat, but only to man has He given the power of Design, which is the first principle of His universe.

6th January 1858:

Illogicality of nature. Lavishes attention on the individual (fall of each sparrow?) but sacrifices individual to species. Cares only for continuation of the stock. Should result in uniformity and conformity. Yet nothing more apparent in nature than diversity, differentiation, distinction. Why this?

Answer. (*a*) Bounty and inexhaustible resourcefulness of the Creator. So Creation may be wonderful in the sight of man. So we may rejoice in the skill of Him who made us and know Him thereby. "O Lord, how manifold are thy works! In wisdom has thou made them all: the earth is full of thy riches."

Objection. We see only what we are pleased to see and are too apt to find in nature's variety, in the infinite invention of her forms and colours, an aesthetic inspiration. We observe the butterfly but not the grub. We lament its brief, gorgeous life, but not that of the worm snatched by the bird. And what of the pretty plumage of the redbreast and the chaffinch as they go about their murder?

Answer. (*b*) Diversity makes possible *interdependence* of creatures, i.e., one *would not be* without the other: e.g., the spider, the fly; the bee, the flower, etc.

Objection. Makes of all creatures predators, plunderers or parasites—or victims of the same. Even-handedness or blindness of nature? Cares for the field vole *and* the buzzard?

Further illogicality of nature: Man. Uniformity and conformity firm principles *within* the species. A crow is a crow is a crow—for all his lack of insignia. Why, then, does individuality and the sense of individuality so pro-

foundly imbue the species man? When I behold a crow
I see only a crow. I do not feel the loss of one crow in a
score, and it makes little sense to me to speak of a crow's
"identity." Yet when I look at my little Lucy I see a
creature whose identity, I know with absolute conviction,
is unique and cannot be replaced. And this would be true
even for the man I may meet in the street tomorrow and
never see again.

Why in the human species should *reproduction* so belie
its name? Why—*argumentum ad absurdum*—should not
all human beings *be the same*? And why should the re-
semblance between offspring and parents, which we like
to think of as so strong, be, in fact, so imprecise and
tenuous?

Answer. Because this is the palpable proof, registered
in our innermost being, that we are elevated over the
beasts, that we partake of the divine, that we possess a
soul.

Objection. But why should the divine express itself in
the imperfect? Since, if the essence of speciation is true-
ness to type, the species man is infested with randomness.
Not a useless randomness, perhaps, since it equips us for
a complex social existence in which, as we say, it "takes
all sorts"; since it gives us our Brunels as well as our
blacksmiths, and allows us all indeed (oh, misnomer!) to
feel "special." But would it not be the grossest piece of
fabrication, to construct upon a condition so shifting and
fickle—upon the chance mutations of progeniture and
the lottery of identity—the notion of what is eternal, immutable and godlike in our nature?

Hamlet's mother says to Hamlet, "Why seems it so particular with thee?" What is the difference between belief
and make-belief? What makes us give to any one belief
(since it is only a matter of shifting, tuning the mind) the
peculiar weight of actuality? "For there is nothing either
good or bad but thinking makes it so." Little Felix was

barely two. Ruth was forty-nine. A child of two, one has hardly begun to know. And an *ichthyosaur*. An ichthyosaur.

Who lets a Big Question upset his small, safe world? When matters reached their head, Rector Hunt, who still clung, perhaps, to the belief that that "inner man" in him, that former would-be missionary, might save the day, must have cursed Charles Darwin, not for his assault on religion—that could have been dismissed, he could have consigned the man to the realms of irrelevance so far as his congregation was concerned—but for timing the publication of his outrageous work so as to clinch his son-in-law's apostasy, bring scandal on his family and parish, and smash for ever that image of himself as a spiritual champion. What was Darwin to him? What is Matthew to me? "What's Hecuba to him or he to Hecuba?"

"Seems, madam? Nay, it is. I know not 'seems.' "

And, for contrast and to go back to where it all seems to have begun (what was an ichthyosaur to *anybody*?), consider the life of Mary Anning, of Lyme Regis, who was only twelve years old when she stumbled on that first thirty-foot fossil skeleton.

Was she horrified? Was she shaken? No. Was her universe turned upside down? No. True, she was only a child. But she was a shrewd enough twelve-year-old. She sold that first skeleton for twenty pounds. She went on to discover not only more ichthyosaurs but the first specimens of plesiosaur and pterodactyl, and she made a living and a name for herself out of her flair for fossils. Lyme Regis enjoyed a tourist boom. Renowned and learned men came to call. These included, one day, no less a person than the King of Saxony, to whom Mary is supposed to have remarked, pertly but without falsehood: "I am well known throughout the whole of Europe. . . ."

Perhaps all her life Mary only saw herself as a successful

purveyor of wonders, a dealer in Mesozoic freaks. Leave others to ponder the meaning of her treasure trove. Was she happy, this daughter of a humble carpenter (she buried him when she was eleven and dug up a monster when she was twelve), who lived her life and found fame among bones? It was not a long life. When Matthew came to Lyme and, quite possibly, met her, she was forty-five. She would die two years later, of breast cancer. Would she have wanted (silly question) some other kind of life? Did it please her to know that posterity would not forget her? Did she ever reflect that her fate was little different from that of that unsuspecting ichthyosaur, that particular ichthyosaur, that expired long ago in some embalming lagoon, little knowing that after millions of years it would be resurrected by the touch of a twelve-year-old girl into the amazed consciousness of another race of animals, and be placed on show in one of their great museums?

Alas, poor ichthyosaur . . .

And everyone has this saving counter-logic, this belief in make-belief. Yes, that may be so, but—it's not the end of the world.

I see a graveyard scene. Not Hamlet juggling a jester's skull. A family group. Two are no more than infants, and there is a third child, not present, who is too young even to know what has happened. There is Elizabeth and there is Matthew. And there is the Rector, performing manfully one of the more testing duties of his clerical career. Pale spring sunlight on the hummocked turf, the tiny coffin.

What do I know of Matthew? I conjure him up, I invent him. I make him the protagonist (a touch of Potter's TV temerity) of this "dramatized version." I drag him into the light. He might have been no more than the bland words on a mossy gravestone. Sleeping inscrutably beside his wife and little son. Instead of which.

If he hadn't married a rector's daughter. There might have been no terrible rupture, he might have spoken without destroying, without being condemned. The day might never have come, fifteen years later, when he stormed out of the Rectory, leaving the Rector, head in hands, in his study and still in that ridiculous bee-keeping garb, and walked back to confront Elizabeth—who might, on that June evening, have picked up the clock, the clock of their union, and smashed it against the wall: there! If all creation was at fault, who cared about a little clock? But she didn't. Plainly she didn't.

The rescue of his marriage becoming a trap. But what was the trap? He loved her and she loved him: the world was good again. And wasn't that the case, wouldn't that be just as true—a question even a rector's daughter might have put to him—whether it was God's world or not?

12

He didn't have to tell me. He didn't damn well have to say a thing. All he had to do was keep his mouth shut. He'd kept it shut for forty years. And if he'd bided his time just a little bit more, prolonged the dilemma just a little bit further, the matter would have been settled in any case by that fatal rendezvous in a Frankfurt hotel.

And I might never have found myself, in this den of learned inquiry, compelled to pursue yet another line of research—one with nothing of the academic about it, and one, you may judge, rather more germane to *me* than the notebooks of Matthew Pearce.

You might have supposed that my mother's death—the equity of mutual widowerhood—would have settled all scores between my late stepfather (and dearly remembered benefactor) and me. What stored-up venom of guilt and blame, what recriminations that remained from those far-off days in Paris, might have been annulled by the amnesty of bereavement. The fact is that, following my mother's death, Sam became afflicted with an attack of conscience, an agony of duty, a positive seizure of moral responsibility. Hardly the Sam of yore. Hardly Mr Plastic. Hardly, either, the Sam of a Frankfurt hotel. But you never know, it seems, the people you thought you knew.

A not so uncommon symptom of grief? But I don't think Sam was so sorely stricken. You have to remember that my mother was seventy-eight. People do die at that age. I would have said (though I know now there was more to it) that it was simply the *fact* of death—how to deal with it, how to get away from it as quickly as possible—that implanted that look of terror on Sam's face when I emerged, that glowing evening, from my last meeting with my mother. Fear, yes; grief, I'm not so sure. As to the hole that his wife's death left in his life, Sam had a simple and well-tried expedient for this, one that he had been applying, in fact, for a considerable time before my mother breathed her last: substitoots. It was in the embrace of one such substitoot (not to say prostitoot) that Sam himself breathed his last, some nine months after his wife's funeral. And if I were asked to describe in a word the bereft husband's demeanour and behaviour at that sad ceremony, I would have to say: shifty.

On the question of grief in general—but with particular reference to mine—Sam was obliged to adopt a cool and unsentimental line, in keeping with the realities of step-fatherhood, with the circumstances of his entry into my life all those years ago in Paris, not to mention with the role he had unwittingly been playing, of Claudius to my Hamlet—"Fie, 'tis a fault to heaven, a fault against the dead . . ." Thus his ability to bury my mother and carry on with life with a minimum of morbid fuss merely proved his consistency and demonstrated, moreover, how I should have behaved with Ruth.

But, in fairness to Sam, his world was neither as regular nor as callous as this. *My* grief undoubtedly troubled *him*. It gnawed at him; isn't that why, to take the kinder view of the deed, he had me moved in here? My picture of things is—fuller—now, but it seemed that that shiftiness at my mother's funeral carried an element of apology. As if he were saying, comparing his scant powers of mourning to mine: I'm sorry—it's the best I can do.

And along with the hint of apology there was a measure

of genuine, vaguely envious incomprehension. No, he didn't understand it, this—romantic love. It was some other sort of glue, a durable, serviceable and remarkably flexible glue, that had held him and my mother together for so long. But if pressed on the point—I never did press him on the point; I should have tried that last day I saw him—Sam might have admitted that this marriage to my mother was itself a kind of long-term, plausible "substi-toot": Ruth and I were the real thing.

You never know the people you think you know. How could I have foreseen that my arch-enemy Sam, the man who had pronounced such merciless judgement on my future, would one day take me to one side and, with a halting attempt at a wink and a nudge, want to know what my "secret" was? *He* should have spoken about secrets. How could I have known, during those rampant days in Paris, that this man who had the run, to say no more, of our apartment, would one day complain to me, as if I were some chafing fellow, free spirit, about this woman (my mother) who seemed so unfairly and stubbornly unwilling to let him go out to play. (Not that she actually *stopped* him.)

But by the time that these confidences occurred, I had done what Sam would never have believed of me. Gangling, sulky, flat-footed, ungrateful bookworm, I had married an actress. I was all set—or this was how Sam pictured it—to become a playboy myself.

She was seventy-eight. He was sixty-six. There would always have come a time when that age gap between them would tell. In the early days there was of course that element of expedient confusion in Sam which enabled him to adopt with me a brotherly stance while craving from his own wife a maternal indulgence. But he would discover that you cannot expect maternal indulgence without reckoning also on maternal authority, and you cannot expect maternal anything if you yourself aspire to (pseudo-) paternity.

The old delusion, the old foible of stepfathers: that in the fullness of time, their new-found charges will come to view them as the genuine article. It was a challenge that Sam, being a man of bold and competitive spirit, could not decline: to become my father, to achieve (masterwork of substitution) that synthetic breakthrough. Somewhere along the line, Sam and my mother must have broached the question of children of their own—and shelved it. I was a barrier—I see it now—to such future issue. If Sam was ever to have "real" offspring, he had first to make me his child.

He failed, of course. That day when I refused the inestimable boon of Ellison Plastics and he cut me off, as if I were his true son and heir, set the seal on his failure— though it did not stop him trying again. How obvious it all was, how easy to confound him. The more he tried, the more I rejected him. The more he strove, not being my father, to become my father, the more I resurrected, like a shield, my real—

"You see, pal, your ma keeps a tight rein. . . ."

It is a summer afternoon in the late Sixties. Years have gone by. They have loosened some of the fixed positions of the past, hardened others. Every so often, under a flag of uneasy truce, I go to see my mother and stepfather in their new and opulent retreat (the Tudor mansion with all mod cons) in Berkshire. All this, I am still proddingly reminded, might have been mine. But the challenge Sam once set himself has not been met; I have not repented; and the time for real fatherhood, for growing up and begetting real children, is long past—my mother is well over fifty. So Sam has reverted to his own childish dreams, meaning, now, fooling around with secretaries, taking dubious foreign business trips and generally indulging in part-time good-time. He has the money for it and the opportunities—all around him he sees now visions of rising hemlines and lapsing morals—and he has still, let's not be uncharitable, the looks.

There he sits on a sun-lounger by his very own swimming-pool, clearly a man who has not yet decided the time has come to make prudent arrangements with his body, since he wears only a pair of skimpy, powder-blue shorts, the waistband of which is not excessively at odds with his belly. The hair on his head, it is true, is receding, but the thicket of hair on his chest is set off by his smooth, solarium tan. A further dark pelt runs downwards from his navel into his shorts. He smokes a cigar; cradles a tall drink; sits amid the attributes of wealth.

He has everything, it seems. Except—poor man—the unqualified licence of my mother to do just as he likes. He has not yet—this will be a later phase, and anyone looking at him now might find it hard to credit—succumbed to those fantasies of old-world, pedigreed patricianship which will have their unlikely fruition in the discovery of John Elyson, once of this College. But he already sees himself as a lord of the manor with limitless *droit de seigneur*. The reality is that he is still subject to my mother's infinitely subtle methods of manipulation, still the victim of her maternal sway. Still in short trousers.

He takes the cigar from his lips, then clenches it again more tightly in the corner of his mouth. The fabric of the shorts bites into his thigh. The man—he can't help it—has an outsize, unflagging but anxious libido that requires regular attention. Moreover, though he has never enjoyed the gratifications of true fatherhood, he has not been spared its pains: even a stepson's manhood threatens his own—even a bookish, sulky, flat-footed stepson.

"A damn tight rein."

As if he would have me believe he never transgressed. Or as if the fact that she kept a tight rein was a justification of, a tacit testimony to his (actual and numerous) transgressions.

The blue water of the pool wobbles listlessly. The trouble was I always liked him. He resettles himself on the lounger. This is Berkshire, not Bermuda, but on this Sunday afternoon even the temperate hills and genteel lawns of the Home Counties are blessed by flagrant, sub-tropical heat. We sit by the pool, just the two of us. My mother is indoors, taking a siesta. She favours, these days, an afternoon rest. She will emerge soon, in a summer frock sensibly yet becomingly attuned to her advancing years, bearing a jingling tea tray.

Tea on the lawn. English correctness balanced by American looseness. I don't think she had any complaints. She had struck her bargain. She had had, perhaps, the chief pleasures. Now there was the secondary but not to be underestimated pleasure of making Sam suffer for his own pleasure. To have forbidden that pleasure outright would have been to prevent hers. Ever the pragmatist. And there were, besides, the consolations of being lady of the manor. Tea consumed, she will don gardening gloves, fetch a trug and proceed to patrol the flower beds. I will still half expect her, as she does so, to burst into latter-day, long-suppressed song. (I have learnt to ration, to gauge carefully, the accounts I give of Ruth's success.) Sam will light another cigar. She will wield the secateurs.

But now, while she lingers within, and after a sombre,

uncomfortable silence has encroached at the pool-side, Sam suddenly draws confidentially towards me, little slicks of sweat appearing in the creases of his belly.

"Can I ask you something? Just between ourselves. How'd you do it? How'd you swing it? With Ruthie. What's the secret?"

He never could quite believe it. Or rather, his disbelief and his envy were always chasing each other in bemused, teasing circles. That I, a little squirt, a little studious runt, should run off with a night-club performer. Even the noble founder of Ellison Plastics (UK), who had once banished me from his sight, had to admit that this showed some gump, and was an action, furthermore, not a little after his own heart. And then the little runt goes and marries the night-club performer. Who turns out to be an actress. Who turns out to be a famous actress. And year after happy year he lives in married harmony with a star of stage and screen, and there is not a sign, not a whisper, of the thing breaking up. I don't know which affected him more: amazement at my initiative, respect for this miracle of constancy, or jealousy at my entrée into a world (as he saw it) of fabled adulterous opportunity.

"Come on—you can tell your Uncle Sam. Things still sweet between you two?"

As if his own opportunities had been, by this time, so few or so little seized upon. You see, pal . . . (I summarize, I paraphrase the little heart-to-heart that followed his pool-side inquisition, in reply to which I was not able to give him much enlightenment.) You see, some of us like to put all our eggs in one basket and some of us like to hedge our bets. You see, a little adultery makes this adulterated world go round, as well as love pure and true. . . .

I might have told him, but I didn't (and now, anyway,

it seems it wasn't so simple), that it can also bring the world to a pretty smart halt. Or had he forgotten that spring day in Paris?

Why did he have to tell me? He rings me up, here in my Fellow's fastness. He wants to come and see me. There is something he wants to talk about. He won't say what. His voice, on the telephone, is not quite the voice of the Sam I know, and I picture, accompanying it, a cloudy, untypical constriction of the features. When, finally, he climbs the staircase to my room and I open, to his knock, my impressively sturdy oak door, the countenance I see before me—somehow I am not surprised, if I am nonetheless unnerved, by this—directly recalls the countenance of Sam some eight months before, about to have his last interview with his wife. It is the face of a man about to go into battle; and just for a moment, though it has nothing to do with the proceedings of this day, I am palpably sure I have seen, in the face of the sixty-seven-year-old Sam, the face of the nineteen-year-old Ed—trying to summon up saliva, shifting in his cockpit.

His car pulls up at the college gates. He dismisses his chauffeur for several hours. There is every reason to mark the occasion in style. This, after all, is one of the college benefactors entering the College for the very first time. A welcoming party; an invitation to high table. But by some prior arrangement (and much as he might have revelled in it), he seems expressly to have vetoed such ceremony. This is a personal visit, on private business; he is travelling incognito. A correct porter, in bowler hat, leads him to my staircase (I am watching all this from an upper window that overlooks the court). He follows, looking around him uncertainly. He is wearing, of course, his best traditional, sober English suit—which doesn't suit him. When I hear him mount my stairs, which are of ancient, spiralling stone and have an ecclesiastical smell, I imagine his footsteps to have a penitent's faltering heaviness.

You see, I think, astonishing as it seems, that he is coming, after all these years, to *apologise*; to make a clean breast of it: not bidding me go to him, but coming and knocking humbly on my door. My mother is dead. He has had time to think it over. He is here (Claudius at his prayers) to atone for his part in my father's death.

It is a bright, smiling day in the early part of May. The sunshine frustrates him. He has envisaged, perhaps, a certain austere solemnity appropriate to his plainly serious purpose, aided by what he supposed would be the monkish atmosphere of an ancient college. He had not imagined windows flung open and sparrows chirruping under the eaves. And, there, from across the court—scarcely has he entered and had time to survey, with a mixture of respect and dismay, my scholarly chamber—comes the plain sound of a female giggle. He says, as the curtains billow and warm air sidles in: "Look—er—can we take a walk or something? Why don't you show me around this place?"

So we wander through the adjacent colleges: around cobbled courts and vivid lawns, through shadowed archways and sun-pierced passages. He waits—and waits—for his moment, while I play the part of the patient guide. He is duly impressed, even awed (this is the latter-day Sam) by the air of treasured antiquity, of sacred space. So this is where he has put me. This is where—out of spite or charity—he has had me interred. "They treat you okay here?" he says, as if we are in some grand hotel and, depending on my answer, he will have words with the manager. About his whole bearing there is something parodically suggestive of the munificent father coming to see

———

165

his son at some high-class boarding school. And yet it is Sam who, for all his years, has the look of a timorous boy.

We walk, skirting carpets of greensward, by the willow-hung, punt-cluttered river. The scene is a vernal idyll. This is the time of year when academic cussedness dictates that the youth of the university should shut itself away to swot for exams, just when its young blood should be pulsing to the joys of spring; and when the youth of the university naturally defies the injunction. There is a general sprawling on grass; couples fondling; flimsy attire; river-borne frivolity. Sam takes this in too. No, he hadn't expected these—distractions. It seems to make it so much harder for him to get to his point.

Then, in a flash, I revise my theory of his unspoken purpose and chide myself for being so obtuse. Of course! Everything around us is spelling it out. These ancient confines; these young limbs. This other-worldliness; this earthly delight . . .

He is going to tell me he is going to remarry. It doesn't surprise me. I wonder who. But does it matter? Some creature less than half his age who has her hooks firmly into him and whom Sam doesn't mind, not in the least, being hooked into by.

January—and May.

And, of course, he would feel guilty about it, doubly guilty—my mother barely eight months dead: "the funeral baked meats . . ." He would feel that announcing as much to me would be like putting his head right on the block.

"Sam—," I say, to try to shorten his misery.

He registers my tone. He looks me suddenly straight and pityingly in the eye. Then he says a most un-Samlike thing.

"Can I ask you a question? A serious question. Do you think people kill themselves for love?"

A volley of laughter from a passing punt greets this inquiry. We are on one of the bridges, leaning against the balustrade. The river beneath us is a rippling ribbon of mirth.

"Sam, why are you asking me this?" I have a strange, cold feeling in my legs.

He looks at the water. "I'm talking about your pa, kid." An American tourist, about to take a photograph at the centre of the bridge, turns and smiles heartily in our direction, no doubt having heard Sam's Ohio tones. "But why don't you answer the question?"

We move off the bridge.

"How should I know the answer?"

He looks at me. "If you don't, pal, who does? Who the hell does?"

We are not far from the Fellows' Garden. I remember that I have the key in my pocket. Without telling him, I guide him (needing guidance myself) towards the little ironwork gate. ("You got your own garden too?") And it's there—it's here—that, in a fever of clenched-faced, uninterruptible disclosure, it all comes out. It's here, under the bean tree, that he spills all the beans.

"I mean they don't *do* it, do they, pal? Not in real life. Why do you think your pa did it? Because he found out about Sylvie and me, and it was all too much for him, and he couldn't bear to go on living? If he cared that much, why didn't he take me aside and kick the shit out of me? Why didn't he point that goddam gun at *me*? And let me tell you, if he *had*, I'd've *run*, I'd've got the hell out of there fast. You wouldn't have seen me for dust. You wouldn't be talking to me now. It was just a fling—Sylvie and me. If it wasn't for— You think your Ma and me were *made* for each other? You think I wanted the old guy out of the way so I could pick up the winnings? That's what you've always thought, isn't it? But you're wrong. It was just a fling.

It just happened to end up lasting forty years. You see, pal, some people are just flingers. Just flingers. You see, I don't believe in this there's-a-girl-for-every-boy-and-a-boy-for-every-girl stuff. It's just who you get thrown against in the trolley-car, and there's more than one trolley-car and more than one ride. Hell—I haven't even got to the main item. You haven't heard anything yet."

He looks around at the sun-filled garden, as if it's in his power to bring a shutter down on all that he sees. He gulps for air.

"I don't have to tell you this. I know that's what you're going to say: 'You didn't have to tell me this.' But I'm going to tell you this. You see, I figured it was up to her. And I figured if she told you, I'd soon know about it. Then, after she died, I figured I'd give it time, in case you found something among the stuff she left you. Yeah, yeah, you found those notebooks you told me about. I'm glad you found those notebooks." He gives me a soft, solicitous look. "Well, I've given it time. You see, I figured she might have meant to tell you. But she couldn't *speak*, could she? She couldn't damn well speak. So I figured it was up to me. It was damn well up to me. And don't think I haven't thought, over and over: I don't have to tell him this, the kid need never know. But I'm going to tell you, because it's the truth. The truth. And you have to tell the truth, don't you, pal? You see, he found out. Your pa found out. Of course he found out. Were we *careful*? And there was this helluva bust-up between him and Sylvie, and in the middle of it Sylvie tells him—and afterwards she tells me she's told him—that you weren't—that you weren't his son. She tells him that to his face. And two days later your pa—who isn't your pa, who never was your pa—well, you know this, pal—he goes and shoots himself."

I stare hard at Sam, whose face has the dissolved, transparent look that people have when they wish they had the power of disappearance, or when they would be very grateful if, for a few minutes at least, they could be someone other than they are. I suppose, in a different way, this is my look too.

The first thought I register on receiving Sam's words is a perfectly empirical observation of the state of the world around me. It hasn't altered. Spring sunshine, with a little flutter of a breeze, caresses the flower beds. A pigeon waddles nonchalantly on the lawn.

The second is the sudden, headlong, insane thought that the blenching, familiar but transmogrified face I see before me is the face—of my father. But this, of course, is impossible; this would be entirely irrational.

So I say, in a voice that surprises me with its rationality, its steadiness, its cool, unpanicking pertinence: "So, if my father wasn't— Who—?"

"It's okay. It's all right. He's dead. He was dead when Sylvie told him. He was killed in the war. He's dead."

I stare at him, not comprehending his propitiating tone. He can't refuse me more information.

"I think she said he came from Aldermaston. But I guess he was always on the move. . . . He was an engine-driver, pal. Would you believe it? She had this thing going, back in the Thirties, with an engine-driver. On the main line west."

13

The word "innocence" lodges in my mind. A teasing, a fugitive notion, easiest to gauge by its loss. In this metamorphosed condition in which I find myself, in this state of stunned divorce from my former self, it sometimes seems to me that innocence is the very quality of which I have been entirely drained. Self-slaughter, even bungled self-slaughter, is, I believe, a sin. A mortal sin. And yet, as I sit in these paradisiacal surroundings, it seems to me, equally, that innocence is precisely what has been rendered unto me, as if my return to life—if I can call it that—has restored me, but without expunging my memories, to a condition prior to experience.

Innocence. So insidiously close, in sound and sense, to "ignorance." Not knowing something, we are "innocent of it"—so we say. Yet, from another point of view, only the truth is, truly, innocent. So when Matthew determined to know the truth, was it Matthew who was the foolish innocent, or was it the rest of the world, happy in its worldly credulity? And what of this place right here—this hub, this Mecca of knowledge? Are we innocent other-worldlings, cut off in our cloistered confines from mundane erroneousness, or are we really the arch-villains of the piece? A proper little gang of Fausts? Are we the ones *to blame?*

I told myself, of course: it doesn't matter. What should I do? Nothing. What should I say? Nothing. How am I changed? In no way. The fiction of my life (if that is what it is) may as well serve as the fact. I am my father's son, meaning my father-whom-I-once-knew-as-my-father's son, by whose death my life has been so irreversibly moulded. I am who I am. I am Bill Unwin (there, I declare myself!). I am Hamlet the Dane.

Innocence. Innocence.

What I am about to relate occurred only three days after Sam's annunciatory visit. Yet I don't think that on that Tuesday morning I was in any particular way altered. Three days had passed, it might be said, since the passing of my innocence. But against this, I maintain, I actually *felt* more innocent. To discover that for fifty years of your life you have been labouring under a massive misapprehension is a fair enough reminder at least of your *capacity* for innocence. It puts a sort of childlike hesitancy into your step and a dazed, receptive smile on your face. It makes you feel—as though you have swallowed some initially tranquillizing drug—really quite *good*.

It was another fine spring day, though there had been rain and, in contrast to the day of Sam's visit, there was a slight chill in the breeze. That is, I think the chill was in the breeze, not in me. But perhaps what I am struggling to avoid saying is that on that bright May morning, which began with my routinely making my way (always carry on as normal), like a good scholar, from college to library, I felt the first shadowy premonition of what I am now.

For the scholar on foot, the way to the Library (I mean the University Library, not our quaint but incommodious college library) lies along those very paths which Sam and I had trod, on such different business. Over humped bridges, by flowery verges and through budding groves (the veritable groves of academe). There is only one road to cross; then a further, less sylvan path leads to the looming bulk of the Library.

It is hard not to see in this layout an allegorical significance: the Palace—the Citadel—of Knowledge approached through the meads and thickets of Dalliance, along the by-ways of Beguilement. And anyone can be beguiled, even the worthiest pilgrim of Learning. For there, on this spry spring morning, was Potter. Or rather, there was Potter's easily spotted and meant-to-be-conspicuous car—a red Audi—drawn up at the edge of the road (the Highway of Worldly Traffic) which the good pilgrim must cross. And there, leaning in at the passenger window, was one of the pilgrims. At least she was dressed in the sombre hue of a votary—black skirt, black sweater, black tights, short, pixyish black boots. But such a funereal outfit on a girl of little more than twenty has a way of suggesting not solemnity, not mournfulness at all.

I recognised her as Gabriella, from that evening at Potter's.

I could see that Potter was leaning across from the driver's seat and that his hand was extended through the open passenger's window and was grasping hers. Or rather—which was a crucial difference—he was not grasping her hand, he was grasping her wrist and pulling at it. And it was clear from the tension of her body that, if she was not exactly pulling away, she was resisting his tug. There are only certain limited circumstances in which this sort of contact might occur between a man and a woman (just as there are only certain circumstances in which a woman might stroke, not just touch but quite deliberately, coaxingly stroke, a man's unsuspecting forearm).

I thought of slinking off—into the Thickets not of Dalliance but of Discretion. But as is often the case when you stumble upon an awkward situation, evasion is more obvious than holding a steady course. I walked on.

Potter saw me first. I'm sure he didn't wish to see me. I'm sure these were the last circumstances in which he would have wished me to appear on the scene—I admit to savouring my advantage. But then he didn't know how much I had seen—least of all that I had observed Gabriella in his clutches before, the clutch being then not to the wrist but to the buttock. He let go his grip. She turned: a furl of dark hair; a face, in the gleaming brightness reflected from the wet road, of startled Latin loveliness. A smile—I couldn't tell exactly—of pleasurable recognition or of flustered gratitude at my timely intervention. She took the opportunity, at any rate, to depart without more ado, moving round to the back of Potter's car and waiting in the road for a gap in the stream of traffic. I thought: she is going my way, to the Library; I should continue in that direction too. Then Potter, still leaning across towards the passenger window, exclaimed, "Ah, Bill—just the man," as if he had been expecting me all along. Then he added, opening the passenger door, "Get in."

"I'm going to the Library," I said. My eyes may have flickered for a moment to where Gabriella was still standing, waiting for the chance to cross.

"I know. Get in," he said, in the peremptory tone that gangsters in films use, often reinforcing their words with a gun. Come to think of it, with his eyes hidden by a pair of thick-framed dark glasses, Potter looked, intentionally or otherwise, not a little like a gangster. I had the feeling of having happened on him at his most absurd and desperate—caught in some outlandish charade. Perhaps he realised this. I was glad his eyes were hidden. Perhaps he merely wanted to prevent me from joining Gabriella on the walk to the Library. Perhaps he was trying to save the situation by an apparent seizing of the initiative.

Like a fool, I got in.

Gabriella had crossed the road and was about to disappear from view. The black sweater almost eclipsed the black skirt. He stuck his head out of the driver's window and shouted *"Ciao bella!"* in her direction. She didn't turn. Perhaps she didn't hear. As we drove off, he said, "I think you've met Gabriella. Research student. From Verona. Sweet kid. Sweet kid."

He looked at the briefcase lying on my knees.

"Where are we going?" I asked meekly.

"Oh—just for a ride. A ride, a spin, a chat. Lovely morning like this. Don't worry, the Library won't go away. You're working on the Pearce manuscripts?"

"Yes, as it happens—"

"And how's it coming along?"

I shrugged.

"You can't do it, Bill. You can't fucking do it!"

"I can't?"

"You don't have the background."

"I'll find out. That's why I was—"

"Why should you spend a year researching what I could tell you right now?"

There was an answer to this, not an easy or a scholarly answer. But this was no time to give it.

"They're my notebooks," I said.

"It's my field."

"It's my business."

We stopped at traffic lights. He groped for a cigarette and roughly offered me one. Inside the car there was still a faint trace of scent. The seat was warm. How casually we human beings exchange places. Then I noticed on the shelf in front of me, beneath the dashboard, hidden from Potter by assorted clutter, a small, cylindrical bottle of perfume. So (the evidence of a hasty exit): while they had "had words," she had coolly taken out her perfume and dabbed herself, perhaps serenely eyed her compact mirror as well. Then, the words getting more heated, she had got out and slammed the door, having absent-mindedly flung the perfume bottle beneath the dashboard. Then she had remembered and reached in through the window—"My perfume"—and he had grabbed her wrist.

These little scenes . . .

He turned to light my cigarette. The glare of the sun, as it had set off Gabriella's limpid complexion, showed up his tired features. Minor celebrity-dom has not become Potter. As his TV face has acquired definition, so his private face has become blurred. Perhaps it is exposure to the studio cameras which has given him, in the light of day, the worn-but-defiant looks of a faded matinée idol. The hair, which affects a tousled nonchalance, is betrayed by the crinkled brow. The eyes, when not masked by the raffish sun-glasses, have their own shadowy nimbus. Every so often they have this vexed expression, as if a serious man were trying to get out from the guise of a clown.

"What were you going to look up?"

"Lyell."

"The *Principles*?"

"Yes."

"Which edition?"

"What do you mean, which edition?" I said ingenuously. I knew perfectly well that Lyell published more than ten editions of the *Principles of Geology*, three with significant revisions, and that the edition I should use—the edition which Matthew would have lent to Rector Hunt and which the Rector failed to finish—was the 1853 (revised) edition.

"You see, this is just the sort of thing I mean. Lyell published a dozen editions. He revised the thing several times. His thinking changed. Are we talking about the 1850, the 1853 . . . ?"

"Oh—I see. I think the 1850."

"And are we talking about the *Principles* or the *Elements*? You know the difference?"

(Matthew had both. Companion volumes. He lent the Rector both. Over a thousand pages.)

"Ah—"

The lights changed. We drove off.

"It's my subject, Bill." The voice took on a more frenzied note. "The spiritual crisis of the mid-nineteenth century is *my subject*!"

Uttered in the late twentieth century and emanating from that dark-vizored, cigarette-clenching face, these words, if they had not carried such urgency, would have had a comic splendour. Perhaps he realised their preposterousness. We careered round a roundabout. Why should a man whose principal interests seemed to be a dubious bid to become a TV personality, and the exploration of ever-varying female flesh, care at all about scholarship, let alone the spiritual crisis of the mid-nineteenth century? But then why should I—?

"You have a monopoly?"

"You have credentials?!"

If he hadn't suddenly started to drive like a madman, I might even have begun to feel sorry for him. I had encountered him at a bad moment. He had had a lovers' tiff, poor man, and been witnessed in the process. Now, with me as a hostage to his spleen, out was coming all his deeper discontent.

And why was I so immovable? If I owned the Notebooks, did I own Matthew? I might have said, "All right, stop the car," and handed over the briefcase. I admit that on this bright morning, three days after my interview with Sam, I came close to doing just that. "Here you are"—with a sweet and compassionate smile—"What does it matter? If it means so much to you."

And how does anyone find "their subject"?

We had driven out of town and turned on to a minor road that led across flat, glistening farmland, threaded by willow-fringed ditches. It was then that he began to behave like a frustrated rally-driver. Admittedly, there was a virtual absence of traffic, and visibility was perfect, but there was the problem of the sharp bends the road took, after long straights, round the corners of ancient, inviolable fields. Also the problem, on occasion, of an oncoming car. I clung, reflexively, to my briefcase. I thought: he means to scare me into surrender. I fleetingly but seriously indulged the fantasy that all this was a deliberate exercise: Plan B, or Abduction. I was being whisked away to some secret hide-out, where the price of my release would be the contents of my briefcase. I would be found, a day or so hence, wandering dazed and dishevelled by the roadside.

But there was a moment—I swear it—when all speculation seemed beside the point. As we headed towards a right-hand bend which the expression on Potter's face seemed grimly to disregard, I thought: he means to kill us both, him and me, on this spring morning. He could really do it. And as we hurtled towards this possible outcome, I was conscious of the vibrant green of the fields, of little, individual larks trilling somewhere, unseen, above us, and I had a distinct vision of the ghost of Matthew Pearce (he wore a black frock-coat and was wondering just what it was he had started) coming to visit the scene of the crash, coming to ponder these two dead men who had died locked in mortal argument over his own lifeless remains.

"Why don't you stick to poetry, Bill?"

"The terms of the Ellison Fellowship," I jabbered, "clearly allow me—"

"Fuck the Ellison Fellowship. The Ellison Fellowship's a fucking joke. You know that."

"Michael, I think you should slow down."

"What do you *want*, money or something?"

"I think you should *slow down*."

"You want to sell the Notebooks, is that it?"

"I think you—"

"Okay, okay—"

He slowed down, braking hard and just in time for the bend. A cold smile squeezed his lips. He drove with exaggerated caution and gentleness.

"There's no need to hang on to that briefcase like that I need my hands for the wheel, you know."

I had to admit this was so.

We took a turn back towards town. I felt the blood in my veins, the air in my lungs. He could have done it. He lit another cigarette. I refused. We reached the centre in stiff silence. How strange, how incongruous is an ancient university city. These age-grimed walls, these modern people; this hoarded learning, this mindless sunshine.

The traffic thickened. Posses of cyclists weaved around us.

"So—the Library, then," he said, with sudden, bizarre amiability. "Let's take you to the Library. It won't have gone away." Then he added, as if we were back at our point of departure, as if the last twenty minutes simply hadn't occurred: "Yes—a sweet girl, Gabriella. Does this and that for me. Very bright. Very—hard-working. You know—" he turned and glanced at me "—if ever you need a research assistant."

He watched the denimed rump of one of the passing cyclists.

I thought: Plan C, Seduction by a Female Agent.

Then, as we came to a halt in the line of cars, he said, "Christ!"

I had seen her too, at almost precisely the same moment—Katherine, walking towards us on the opposite pavement (carrying that straw bag), so far not having spotted us. He was plainly caught between the incriminating hope that she might not notice us at all and the difficulty of justifying to me why he should let his own wife walk right by without greeting her. We were at a standstill and—for a variety of reasons—I considered making a quick exit. Then Potter lowered his window and called out, with a sort of clotted brightness: "Katherine!"

She stopped, gave a perplexed smile, then, since her side of the road was clear and we remained stationary, walked over towards us. At some point she took in the fact that I was sitting beside Potter, and her smile became more perplexed. She stooped by Potter's door.

"Hello," she said. "How was London? Hello Bill."

"Fine," Potter said. "London was fine." The repetition seemed to come sideways out of his mouth, expressly for my benefit. "Thought I'd drive back early. Beat the traffic. I bumped into Bill here on the way in. Just giving him a lift to the Library."

Katherine looked at me. Her puzzled smile turned into one of undisguised intrigue. "But you're a long way from the College, Bill."

"Exactly," Potter said, quick off the mark and seeing his escape route. "What is our Bill doing on the other side of town so early in the day, yet supposedly on his way to the Library? A question he hasn't answered." He darted me a look. Then he said to Katherine as the traffic began to move, "Why don't you hop in? You're on your way home? I'll take you there, after we've dumped this reprobate here."

Katherine got in, scrambling across the back seat. Then she leant forward, a hand on each of the front seats, so that her face was almost between us. She seemed suddenly all alertness and amusement, as if this chance encounter had brightened an unpromising day.

"Well, Bill," she said. "Aren't you going to tell us?"

Plainly, the joke was on me, and, plainly, Potter was relishing the twist in the situation. I might have been more discomforted if it hadn't been for the little bottle of perfume still lying under the dashboard (and for a kind of dazed thankfulness for still being in one piece). I thought: it is quite simple. All I have to do is nothing. All I have to do is leave the bottle of perfume just where it is. But I couldn't do it.

"You'd be surprised if you really knew," I said. I gave a quick sideways glance at Potter.

"Ah—a man of mystery," Katherine said.

I don't think she had seen the bottle. She sat back. I shifted in my own seat in such a way as to make my brief-case slip, as if by accident, from my knees. Leaning forward to retrieve it, I contrived at the same time to scoop up the bottle, then transfer it, hidden in my hand, to my pocket. Potter glanced from the road ahead to me. Maybe he hadn't seen it. I don't think so. Maybe the moment of my secreting it was the moment of his realising it was there in the first place. I couldn't tell, with his eyes hidden by those glasses.

"Hang on to the goods," he said, with a slight touch of gall.

Katherine leant forward again, grasping the back of my seat. "How's it going?" she said, looking over my shoulder.

"Oh—fine." I gave the briefcase a meaningless caress.

"No," she said, in a softer, more solicitous, more all-embracing tone. "I mean—how's it going?"

181

It was strange. It was like a question spoken out of her husband's presence. Her lips were almost in my ear. It was as though at any moment she might have ruffled my hair or put her arms round my neck. Potter looked at us both, like some foxy chauffeur. To my surprise, I found myself suddenly glad of the briefcase lying across my lap, screening the state of things between my legs. Maybe none of it mattered. Maybe it wouldn't have mattered if she had seen the bottle of perfume. Maybe she *had* seen the bottle of perfume. Maybe that's how things were.

"Oh—okay," I said.

We headed back towards the Meadows of Dalliance and the True Path of Knowledge. Potter slowed down near the spot where he had hijacked me earlier. The day had warmed. The wet road was now a dapple of damp and dry patches. It would not have surprised me if, as I made to get out, Katherine had suddenly kissed me or pinched my cheek—like a mother saying goodbye to a son departing for school. Instead, she sat back—not bothering to move into my place beside Potter, giving me a sort of bold-but-beleaguered look.

"Bye, Bill."

"Happy hunting," Potter said.

Whoever designed our University Library must have known what they were about. It is variously likened to a fortress, a prison, a power-station. Alcatraz. Fort Knox. It stands in geographical and architectural scorn of the cosy huddle of colleges some half a mile distant across the lawn-fringed river. And the inference, I suppose, is that it will continue to stand so—with all those books, all that compacted civilization, still safe inside—when the fragile colleges and tranquil lawns are no more. Even inside, it is not exactly inviting. You have the impression that books are stored here as ammunition is stored in readiness for some awesome, cataclysmic conflict. All day long, along mysterious passage-ways and up and down secret lift-shafts, they are shifted and trundled like shells in the bowels of a vast dreadnought.

I sat, belatedly, at my desk, Lyell's 1853 edition in front of me. Also before me, the 1855 (enlarged) edition of the *Elements of Geology*. Yes, I knew, all right, which were the proper editions. But I couldn't concentrate (any more than the Rector). I couldn't feel whatever it was Matthew had felt. What was I doing, a hapless civilian in this arsenal of learning? I fingered the phial of perfume in my pocket. Yes, I admit it, I took it out, unscrewed the gold cap and sniffed. It is as well that library-goers are generally used to each other's eccentricities.

She would be here, somewhere in this building. The girl in black. Gabriella. I should find her, return the bottle. This, after all, was the classic way in which Romance began: the misplaced article, the trinket retrieved. This, after all, was the way life worked, the way it took its chances and began again, especially on a May morning when sunlight penetrated even the thick bulwarks of the University Library and fondled the dusty racks of books. What was I doing in this necropolis? What was I doing, bent over a book about the antiquity of rocks?

We are prepared, therefore, to find that in time *also the confines of the Universe lie beyond mortal ken. . . .*

A simple matter. All I had to do was wander the premises. The History section was a good bet. I would happen upon her, as if by chance. We were, after all, half introduced. I would whisper, in this place meant for whispering, that perhaps, if she could spare a moment from her studies, a cup of coffee . . . Better still, a bite of lunch . . . Over coffee, or lunch, I would venture a disclosure or two (why not?) about the Pearce manuscripts. She would say (let it go, let it pass) how much she had admired Ruth. Then, at a certain point, with the deft timing of a practised intriguer and wooer of women, I would produce the bottle of perfume: "I think this is yours. . . ."

It didn't happen, of course. That is, I didn't find her. So how do I know, if I didn't find her, that—?

(But how could it have happened?)

A library is equipped so that any book within it may be located precisely; but people—that is a random matter. And, of course, in so vast a complex as our University Library, it would be perfectly possible for two people, wandering independently along different routes, to elude each other for ever. I toured the building. I patrolled the corridors. I peeped along shelves and at the hunched forms at rows of desks.

A mad aberration induced by my having survived my ride with Potter? (He could really have done it.) A portent of things to come? This other life; these leases of life.

January and May.

I loitered on stairs and by the populous Main Catalogue. At the exodus for lunch I lingered by the main entrance, sun streaming through the tall doors. Gabriella. A name like a flower. And from Verona. Balconied city of love. The name was inseparable in my mind from something dark-haired, dark-eyed and slender. I couldn't imagine a blonde called Gabriella. I couldn't imagine Katherine being called Gabriella.

When I returned to my college room I still possessed the little bottle. I put it on one of the glass shelves in my

bathroom. It is still there now, a source of perpetual speculation, I imagine, to Mrs Docherty, who cleans for me.
But then its curiosity value has been far surpassed by other,
recent events. It was Mrs Docherty, after all, accompanied
by a porter, who "found" me. In the "old days," she has
since comfortingly told me, college cleaners were regularly
stumbling upon suicidal inmates. There is something
about this contemplative life. But she herself had never
had the misfortune . . .

I could have thrown it away. But then it was not my
property to dispose of, and in theory the opportunity might
still have arisen to return it to its rightful owner. Though,
had I done so, it's true, the little bottle might by then have
lost its strategic charge, the aura of cunning gallantry that
it had possessed for a few, fond hours on a bright spring
morning. So it stayed on the shelf.

It was on that May afternoon—only two months ago—
as I put the perfume on the shelf—a gathering rain-cloud
was squeezing the last rays of the sun over the college
rooftops and onto the tiles of my bathroom—that I realised
with sudden acuteness how little trace there was of anything feminine, let alone of Ruth, in these new rooms I
inhabit. I had brought my two favourite photographs, one
or two other things, that's all. Besides John Pearce's clock.
A sort of self-denying instinct had made me not wish to
embarrass others, or myself in front of others, with too
many icons of remembrance.

And perhaps I clung to the illusion that I would go back.
These rooms were only a temporary expedient, therefore
deserving a sort of Spartan, bachelorly restraint (how many
Fellows before me? How many muttering old fools?) When
the lawyers and accountants had sorted things out, when
this short-term shelter, courtesy of Ellison Plastics, had

served its turn, then I would go back—to my former life. Like some soldier completing a tour of duty, I would return home. It would all be as it was.

I would never go back. This is what I realised, standing in front of the mirror. I was in my place now. A place which wasn't my place. I was institutionalised. I had been in it for nearly a year. This was where I was.

In the roseate light of the bathroom I unscrewed the cap and once more lifted the bottle to my nostrils. He really meant to— A young girl's perfume. I sniffed its little released world. Then I put it back on the shelf.

14

And how do I know? And why should I believe it?

The College notepaper is a godsend. A tasteful ivory, with the College crest lightly embossed in blue, top centre, and (only available to such as me) the words "Senior Combination Room," for extra swank, in Roman capitals, top right corner. The sort of notepaper that must surely command respect and compel an answer, even as it is evasively passed, as I'm sure it will be, from desktop to prevaricating desktop in the warrens of Whitehall.

I haven't a clue whom I should write to. I don't know if there exists, in the bowels of officialdom, any functionary appointed to deal with inquiries like mine. But who am I to turn to, a poor orphan, committed to the (temporary) fosterage of this goodly college?

And the College motto (embossed scroll under the crest) is auspicious and encouraging, not to say downright optimistic: *Qui quaerit, invenit.*

So I compose a "Dear Sir" letter, imagining, as occasionally we all do, that this "dear sir" really exists—a seasoned, ashen-haired figure, authoritative but kindly, long-suffering but fair-minded, on whom there presses the weight of many a more onerous matter, yet who is moved, as is only proper, as is only right, to give our particular little plea his heartfelt and painstaking attention.

Dear Sir,
    I am writing with reference to my late father, Colo-

nel Philip Alexander Unwin, DSO, MC, formerly of the Hampshire Regiment, subsequently seconded to extra-regimental duties, who died by his own hand on 8th April 1946, in Paris, while on attachment to or in the full employ of the diplomatic service.

At the time of his death, my mother, Sylvia Jane Unwin, and I were temporarily resident in Paris with my father. I was nine years old and an only child.

My age naturally restricted my acquaintance with the facts. However, it has never been a secret to me that my father died by suicide and that his death occurred (by gunshot) during working hours in the office where he pursued his duties in Paris. This I believe to have been in an annexe of the then British diplomatic mission in the Rue St. Dominique. I assume the matter to have been filed in the appropriate records.

On the authority of my mother, together with the findings of the inquest, I have always accepted that the motives for my father's death, in so far as they could be scrutinized, were personal, if never wholly clear. However, following my mother's death, eight months ago, information has come into my possession which prompts me to reconsider the matter.

I do not anticipate that official records, such as they are, will necessarily assist in a question of private concern. However, any further light you may be able to shed on the circumstances in which my father died would be greatly appreciated. . . .

The language that we use! The postures we adopt! A little ingratiating mimicry of those whom (we think) we are dealing with? Or is this stuff *me*?—the professorial blather (the infection well advanced); the palpable signs of fogeydom. No, not the moody Prince all along, but prating Polonius. Three "howevers" and an "in so far as." The craven guff into which we slide in order to settle the most intimate facts of our lives. "Information has come into my possession." Well, yes—and no. And "personal"—his motives for suicide "were personal." What the hell else should they have been?

15

What did it was the bees. The Rector's innocent, Virgilian bees. It began with dinosaurs, but what brought things to the breaking point, to their final undoing, was the humble, humming bee.

You have to picture the scene. Matthew does not detail every moment of that June afternoon—though he makes it clear enough that this was the genuine, the irrevocable denouement. It seems that the Rector issued an ultimatum; and perhaps nothing less, in the end, would have satisfied Matthew. Perhaps the pitch of his conscience, so long attuned to its own dilemma, was such that it required and desired another's pronouncement of judgement. Or, to put it another way, the Rector was part of Matthew by now: if he hadn't existed, it would have been necessary for Matthew to invent him. You could say that when Matthew called at the Rectory that afternoon, he was only knocking at the door of his own soul. Except that that, of course, is the wrong way of putting it. Precisely the wrong way. What he was about to do was evict his soul from the premises, to send it packing. What he would have to say henceforth would be: My soul? My soul? I do not possess such a thing.

24th June 1860:
    . . . and, amidst everything, I still ask myself, did I will it to have fallen out thus, or was the hand of chance still my final arbiter? If the latter, it would not be inappropriate; since I am committed now—oh, committed!—to a random universe, the seeming capacity of which to

present to our eyes instances of omniscient purpose only deludes us. What I ask is: did I truly set out this afternoon—I cannot remember now my exact feelings, it seems such an age ago—prepared, by my own determination, to take upon myself the consequences which now, indeed, I must accept; or was this to have been, at worst, but another addition to our stretched chain of "disputations"? But then was not, increasingly, the very drift of those disputations towards precipitating, in the heat they generated, what I myself could not in cold blood initiate?

Cold blood! Is my blood cold? It rushes now round my veins with such animal tumult. Did I not, like some spiteful heretic, like some cowardly deserter to the devil's side (such phrases!), repeatedly tempt the good man to deliver his thunderbolt? As if, so long as he failed to do so, I might draw the mean and furtive satisfaction that, as I was a doubter of my faith (doubter—I must say now "abjurer"!), so he lacked the courage of his calling.

Well, I cannot charge him with that now.

And if, indeed, my intention, all along, was so resolved and adamant, then circumstances could not have been better disposed to dissuade me, to mollify me. Did this seeming perversity only spur me on? The sweet midsummer weather. Sailing clouds and the scent of hay. Dog roses in bloom. And the good Rector so eager to be examining his hives that he quite neglected his normal air, on my calling, of testy forbearance, quite failed to prepare himself for weighty altercation. Thus was I like the bringer of bad news who comes upon a household in a state of happy levity and is compelled, in spite of himself, to reciprocate the good humour.

"Come, come, my dear Matthew, you must assist. Surely you have noticed—you with your eye for such things—there never was such a year for clover. The combs will be oozing." And, so saying, in the full holiday mood of his enthusiasm, he bade me don a spare pair of his long-sleeved gauntlets and one of his long-veiled straw hats—oh there was comedy in the tragedy! And in this clownish costume I came to my final declaration and he to his final fulmination, not because such was at first the tenor of our discourse, but because he would not have it that a system so wondrously disciplined as the society of the honey-bee, or a structure so ingenious as the honeycomb, not to say a thing so delectable as honey itself —surely the veritable manna from heaven—could exhibit anything other than the work of a benign and intelligent Creator.

"I only urge you," I insisted, "to read what Mr Darwin has written on the subject in his chapter on instincts. How even a skill as consummate as that of the hive bee in making cells may be arrived at by a gradual modification of instincts which other species also demonstrate, if less perfectly. How instincts, no less than organic structures, are the result of an adaptation of nature's *random variations*. And the only principle behind this process is neither the will of God nor, indeed, as you will have it, the work of Darwin's master, the devil, but, in Darwin's phrase"—I confess I had begun to shout, the flapping veil before my eyes seeming to smother my words—"the continual and irrepressible *struggle for existence!*"

Whereupon the Rector cried, with a force that seemed to take even him by surprise, "Damn your Darwin! Damn your detestable Darwin, sir!" There was a moment when I thought he might add, "And damn you, sir!" But he did not do this. He strode up the row of hives, striking with his gauntleted fist the trunk of one of the apple trees, then strode back to deliver upon me his verdict, his anathema. Was there ever such a strange priestly garb for the purpose? Though who knows if it were not those outlandish masks—neither of us could clearly see the other's face—that made such terrible words possible?

And, truly, even as I received my sentence, part of me still saw with the old man's believing—credulous, I should say—eyes. Had I not once, too, drawn short at the great mystery of the instincts? Had I not, like the Rector, taken the industry of the honey-bee as one of the sublimest testimonies to the hand of Providence, demonstrating, moreover, like the milk of cattle (oh milk and honey!), that the chief care of Providence was the good of mankind? And if this were illusion, was it not a sweet and benign illusion? And was not exposing it but an act of wanton destructiveness—as if, there and then, I had lifted up the wooden roof of one of the hives and, upon a mindless whim, dashed to pieces the little insect Jerusalem within? See, it is as nothing!

(And yet—invincible instinct!—they would have repaired it at once.)

And even as the Rector spoke, I could not help thinking of the many pounds of the Rector's honey we have consumed at Leigh House, and how, in the days when I was still her mentor in such things, I instructed Lucy in the "miracle" of its manufacture, holding it up to her as something to wonder at and reverence: "So, my dear Lucy, the honey we eat is made from flowers—does it not taste as sweet as a flower looks?—and the magician who performs this trick is the bee."

She is asleep now, or so I hope. So I hope are they all. I am alone in the house with my children. Asleep or awake, they are frightened, and must all face the morrow. They are none of them so young as not to ask, in their own way: What will become of us?

And my dear Liz has departed for the Rectory. I do not know—there have been so many alternations of anger and tears—whether to remonstrate with him or to take his side (his "side"!). I do not know when, or if, she will return. Yet her children are here, she did not think to bundle them with her—I cannot therefore be such an ogre. For them, at least, she must return.

"How could you do this? How could you do this?!"— I will always hear her repeated cry. As if all this too were only a perverse, destructive whim. The little honey-hive of our home. The nectar of our happiness. Fifteen years!

I said nothing of Neale. It seemed to me that to make such a reference was inadmissible, though more than once I thought her look challenged me, even desired me to do so. To make this domestic drama no more than one of those familiar, sordid upheavals by which households fall apart. When she had stopped raging, I put myself, as resolutely as I could, at her mercy: "If I am no longer to make my home here in your father's parish, then I ask you to choose between your father and me. If the former, do not suppose I shall cease to provide for you." "Oh," she said, eyeing me fiercely and tossing her head, as if she would turn this into some common jilting, "do not suppose I shall not be taken care of!"

She is gone. The night is still and starry. And the chimes from the church tower—one, two o'clock—seem to tell me she has made her choice.

I cannot sleep. I cannot move. I keep company with this notebook. This book! This book! What have I become, that I have parted from my wife, but I still keep company with this book?

Do we have souls? Do bees? Did Matthew have a soul? If not, why should he have written, over a period of six years, those pages in which it is no misapplication of a well-worked phrase to say he "laid bare his soul"?

But then the Notebooks ceased on that June day in 1860—or rather, a little later, when he had left wife, children and home. And they were, by his own description, the record of his life as a fiction: "the beginning of my make-belief." From now on, he would be "real"—he would live according to the way things truly were. But if the soul is a fiction, why should a book—a few ideas set down on the page—make so much difference to the world? Did people have souls until 1859, when Darwin published his momentous work, then suddenly cease to have them?

And if the soul is a fiction, and it is all just a struggle for existence, why do we ever reach beyond ourselves to the existence of others, not to say beyond existence itself? Why do we think of the dead? And why, and for whom, did Matthew write the Notebooks at all? For some all-viewing, all-reading witness (like God in the sky)? For some "kindred soul" in the audience of the future (oh yes—an avid theatre-goer) who unexpectedly "identifies," as the saying goes, with the plight of this "character" up there on the stage of the past?

Why do bees make honey? They say it will last, uncorrupted, for a thousand years. People have eaten honey from the tombs of the pharaohs. They say it is as good as gold.

I see the two men in the little apiary at the far corner of the garden. I see Ruth pacing beside the tumbledown fence, learning her parts. They stoop over the first hive. They have an observer (as well as God in the sky): the Rector's wife—let's suppose she was watching, watching quite intently, from a rear window of the Rectory. She knows that something is in the offing. She knows that the two men do not see eye to eye. It is some while since she has indulged the fond notion that Matthew is like a son to her husband (there have been regrettable developments by this time, with Matthew's own father). And her former motherly soft spot for her son-in-law (who, after all, scarcely had a mother of his own) has hardened of late. It is high time the Rector took things firmly in hand. And now here is Matthew again, showing up with his face like the calm before a storm. And here is her husband employing his usual blustering, stalling, side-tracking tactics.

The sky is heaven-blue. The hives hum like little generators. Dressed in their grotesque costume, as if for some strange form of martial art, the two men bend over their peaceable task. The Rector has lit his curious, home-made smoking-device. They proceed to the second hive. The Rector removes its roof. They seem to confer. Then there is a distinct pause. The two men pull themselves upright.

An evident disagreement. Some difference of opinion on the finer points of apiarian practice? Hardly. The exchange is more fraught, more passionate, than that. There is a pacing to and fro and flinging of arms—the older man waves his smoking-device like some useless gun. The inspection of the other hives is forgotten. More gesticulation. Then the gentle Rector seems suddenly to wax apoplectic. He throws aside his smoker: the smoke indeed might be issuing from his head. He shouts something at his companion, marches off to the very edge of the garden, delivers a blow to one of the apple trees, stands stiff and intent for an instant, like a man taking a final look at a cherished view, then turns.

You have to picture the scene. You have to reconstruct the moment, as patient palaeontologists reconstruct the anatomies of extinct beasts. If it were not for Matthew's Notebook, nobody might have known it had happened at all, it might have been as though it never was. So what, on the part of this unforeseen testifier, is a little bit of creative licence? A little bit of fiction? The place: a rectory garden in Devon (it is like the setting for some vapid period piece—of course, Potter's TV "realisation"). The time: a June afternoon in 1860. The persons: Gilbert Hunt (the Rector); Matthew Pearce, his son-in-law; (off-stage, Emily, the Rector's wife). I don't know what they really said, but all around them, like some counterpoint—it's the same sound now as it would have been then—was the undesisting drone of bees.

. . . RECTOR: But look, look again at the contents of this hive! Look at the combs! You are aware that they are constructed upon a principle that is geometrically perfect. Geometrically perfect! Is it not astonishing?

And you are to tell me that this is some freak, some stroke of chance? Have you no spirit of *wonder*? You may as well say that a rose is an ugly thing that stinks!

MATTHEW: I do not question the wondrousness of things—only that God made them so.

RECTOR: So, so. Then how comes your very wonderment? How comes your capacity to behold, marvel and inquire? How comes, Matthew, the marvel of your marvelling brain?

MATTHEW: In just such a way—I cannot tell exactly—as comes the marvel of the bee and the honeycomb.

RECTOR: Indeed! And you may as well have a honeycomb for a brain! Do you hold yourself as no more favoured than a bee?!

MATTHEW: That is no simple question. A bee, had he my faculty of speech, might profess that I lacked his faculty of flight, and his unrivalled ability to build in wax.

RECTOR: Do not joke with me, Matthew.

MATTHEW: I don't joke. I say only that creation—I use your word—favours no species save as it adapts successfully to its means of existence. A million fossils tell us that nature discards as well as promotes. The bee and mankind are just two of her ventures.

RECTOR: I see, sir, I see. So we may as well shut the book of nature, and give thanks to no one when next we spread a little honey on our bread? And what of Holy Writ? We must have it out now, sir, it has come to this! What of the words of the prophets and evangelists? Come, speak your blasphemies!

MATTHEW: Poetry! Poetry! Like your precious Virgil, who so extolled the genius of the bees. Admirable, inspired and inspiring, and composed by those, I do not doubt, who believed what they set down. But poetry—fiction!

RECTOR: And your Darwin—who has had the bene fit of the world's judgement for a little less time than the Bible—he only lacks the poetical inspiration to found a new creed?! By God, sir, by God, I charge you now to repeat *your* creed, here, before me, a minister of the church. And if you cannot—if you cannot, Matthew, if you will not—then, by God—

But I do not know, I cannot even invent, what the Rector said. I falter in my script-writing, just as the Rector himself, perhaps, faltered on the verge of his imprecation. Did he say, wavering desperately at the last moment, "But can you not *pretend*?" Did he utter, thinking of the scandal about to unleash itself on the quiet backwater of Burlford, only what an inner voice had uttered to Matthew for six years? "I give you one last chance. I bid you go back now to your home. I bid you say nothing of this to Elizabeth, nor to anyone. I bid you go through the motions—yes, if it must be so for you—of a God-fearing man, of the husband of your wife and the father of your children. And if you cannot do this, then never darken my church door again, nor this rectory, nor, with my blessing, the home of my daughter! Go sir! Choose your way!"

Did he compromise his own faith sufficient to beg another man to play false with his? Or did he, indeed (Matthew failing to recite his creed), draw himself up—in his bee-keeper's hat—to his full anathematical height and thunder: "Then never henceforth, etc., etc. . . ."?

The June afternoon still blooms. The bees still go about their summery business. The Rector stands alone among his little congregation of hives. Beyond the garden is the green flurry of the beech copse. Beyond that, the hedged languor of fields; warm, unavailing hills.

And if we do not have souls, why should we have these—feelings? These moments that rack and enrapture us and take us by storm. Why should things *matter*?

He stares, in his quixotic outfit, at the little gate, set in the hedge, leading to the churchyard, through which Matthew has departed. He has shouted, twice: "Matthew!" For a moment, the sweetness of the afternoon turns to sheer nightmare around him. He sees himself in some medieval vision full of demons and terror. He is before the walls of some beleaguered city in which the pious cower for safety and he, their champion, is beating back, with the intrepid zeal which once he hoped to bring to the darkest corners of the earth, the ravening beast, Darwin. Then the vision melts into the mocking familiarity of Burlford church and its quiet churchyard, its trusting retinue of gravestones, and the immemorial murmur of bees.

> *At genus immortale manet, multosque per annos*
> *Stat fortuna domus . . .*

Poetry! Fiction!

How long does he stand there? The Rector's wife watches him. She knows that something extraordinary has happened. She has seen Matthew leave abruptly, not by the way he came but by the garden gate, and has watched the Rector watch him walk—retreat (so she pictures it)— across the churchyard and so out by the lych-gate to the street.

Well, and about time too. A few sharp words. For his own good. She feels a moment's bristling solidarity with her husband, a moment's pang for a stronger man she once knew.

But the Rector does not move. He stands there stock-still. At last he turns and walks slowly towards the house. He has quite forgotten to replace the roof on the second hive and quite omitted to inspect the remaining hives. And, as the Rector's wife well knows, if you do not attend to the combs when the bees are in full production, then you will have trouble, you will have swarms. Not to mention the need to extract the honey—the golden honey which, for years now, it has been her proud custom, with a little sweet glance to her husband, to press upon guests for tea at the Rectory: "Now, you are not to go without tasting some of Gilbert's celebrated honey. . . ."

The Rector walks towards the house, though not to speak to his wife. There is a French window in his study which opens directly on to the garden, and he makes straight for it. He does not remove his bizarre accoutrements—the gauntlets and hat. It seems that whatever it is that has happened out there has made him more than usually forgetful. Then the Rector's wife sees that the wide-brimmed hat with its attached gauze curtain is still performing a useful function—the same function that her veiled black bonnet, and Elizabeth's too, performed at little Felix's funeral. Her husband is shaking with tears.

16

Qui quaerit, invenit. I wonder.

I received a letter from a Major Pilkington, whose exact function and status remain far from clear to me, but who appears to be the final clearing-house for any awkward but unignorable inquiry from the general public. I have tried to picture Major Pilkington, this man who (in a manner and language so different from Sam's) has been the bearer of such significant if belated news. The name suggests some buffer of the old school. I see him therefore as a grey-moustached, reddish-cheeked, chubby-jowled figure, long since past his military zenith and thus edged into this dead-end, dead-letter job, which a sort of tendency to fat in his character enables him to perform with the appropriate cushioning tact. He looks (I imagine) more like a headmaster of the patient, understanding sort, or an inured but genial family doctor, than a major. "Now, what seems to be the trouble . . . ?"

Then the image fades into that of some crisp, sharp-faced, still youngish high-flier. This, after all, is a responsible, if unspectacular, position: access to records, the handling of "sensitive" matters. And if it is a job in which our zealous career-maker has no wish to linger, then the best way to be shot of it and be picked for better and greater things is to carry it out with conspicuous diligence and the minimum of bureaucratic dither.

Dear Mr Unwin,

Your letter of 19th May has been passed on to me through various departments and it has been necessary to trace the relevant records. I apologise for the delay in this reply.

The records relating to your father's death on 8th April 1946, and to his career from March 1945 until his death, are governed by the strictures regarding classified information. I am therefore not at liberty to enter into details. However, in view of the personal aspect of your inquiry and of the fact that, subsequent to your mother's death, you yourself have received new information on the matter, I am authorized to make the observations below, while trusting in your absolute discretion.

Immediately following your father's death, an internal inquiry was conducted into its circumstances. Your father was cleared of all suspicion of pressure brought to bear on him relating to a breach or endangering of security, and I must emphasise that his professional record remains that of an honourable man. However, it emerged from the evidence of colleagues and superiors that your father may have harboured, since the final months of the war, a growing aversion, on conscientious grounds, to the nature of his special duties, which, conflicting intolerably with his considerable dedication and ambition, may ultimately have contributed to his suicide.

The records show that your mother was interviewed during the inquiry and, beyond recognising that they involved secrecy, appeared to have had no knowledge of the sensitive aspects of your father's duties. Indeed, she adduced the "personal reasons" for your father's suicide, which I assume are those referred to in your letter and which I will not, therefore, comment upon further.

It was deemed necessary for the purpose of the inquiry to inform your mother, in the strictest confidence and in the barest terms only, of the nature of your father's recent duties: that is, that from the spring of 1945 he was engaged in liaison activities with our wartime allies relating to the development of atomic weapons.

You will appreciate that it was essential that none of this should emerge at the public inquest. Your mother was charged to repeat nothing of what had been disclosed to her and it was agreed that she should adhere to the aforementioned personal factors, which, I hope you will forgive me for observing, served very fortuitously the interests of secrecy. It would appear from your letter that your mother kept her word, with commendable compliance, up until her death.

I regret that I am not empowered to enter into any further correspondence on this matter, and I must remind you that, although they date from over forty years ago, the records referred to herein remain subject to rules regarding public accessibility.

I trust, however, that the contents of this letter are sufficient to answer your inquiry, and I offer my sincere regrets for any distress caused by the necessity of withholding information. . . .

So, he was a spy then—of sorts—after all. A reluctant, a regretful, a squeamish spy.

And it seems that my letter must have been taken as in some way loaded, double-edged ("information has come into my possession . . ."). They thought I *knew* something. Ha! And it seems we have got our wires crossed. Hopelessly crossed.

And look how I obey Major Pilkington's stringent admonitions. I copy out the text of his letter right here for everyone to see.

(Everyone?)

But none of it matters, does it? Because he wasn't my— Was he? What does this phantom that Major Pilkington has conjured up out of his files matter to me?

The night mist swirls round the battlements of Elsinore. Shapes loom on the guard platform. "Who's there?" Did ever a play so palpably and so troublingly sound its note?

"Angels and ministers of grace defend us!"

But even when he was alive, he was no more than the ghost of my father. "An honourable man" . . . "conflicting intolerably" . . . when you are out on an adventure . . .

So why should I—?

"Armed, say you?"—"Armed, my lord."—"From top to toe?"—"My lord, from head to foot . . ."

And what good, in any case, is Hamlet's long-deferred and juvenile revenge, now that its spur, its object—my dear old wicked uncle Claudius—is dead . . . ?

For one thought that did not occur to me as Sam delivered his fateful message, here under the bean tree, was that I was looking at him for the last time. Barely six weeks later he would be dead, and news of his death—and of its nefarious circumstances—would reach me only days, in fact, before Major Pilkington's dispatch came winging towards me out of the even more nefarious circumstances of an earlier death.

Death! Death! You think it is elsewhere, but it is suddenly all around you, like a mist, a tide. It springs up like overnight mushrooms, it descends like the ghostly parachutes of secret agents, slipping behind enemy lines.

Was that it, then? He somehow *knew*? Sam knew. I didn't know, but he knew. Something some specialist had gently broken to him. The old ticker, it's not what it was. . . . Or just some unquellable premonition. After Ruth, after Sylvie. Brother Ed's old coral-boned tug at his sleeve . . . My turn is coming. My last chance, maybe. So—do I tell the kid or don't I?

Except he didn't know the half. And now I'll never be able to face him with it, ask him (a reversal of his confiding visit to me—and a flagrant contravention of Major Pilkington's orders): Sam, I've got to tell you. . . . Sam, did you ever know what my father—I mean my— I mean what he *did* . . . ? Sam, will you take a look at this . . . ?

Why is it that it is Sam's features and not my father's (my whose?) that float before me as I read and re-read Major Pilkington's studied words? The clean, unfadingly tanned smoothness of his skin, which even at sixty-seven (the man *really* thought he didn't have long?) looked so incongruously unlived-in. The doggish eyes.

"You have to tell the truth, don't you, pal?"

We might have continued our discussions, resumed our topic. Further visits, further colloquies, here in this contemplative domain. Mr Plastic in the purlieus of knowledge. A subject worthy of philosophic debate: Do people kill themselves for love?

"Tis here!"—"Tis here!"—"Tis gone . . ."

That she did or didn't know I was another man's son.

That she would or wouldn't have told me in the last days, hours, of her life.

(That Sam should have kept his mouth shut.)

That he killed himself because of my mother and Sam —i.e., for love. (And Major Pilkington never knew the half.)

That he killed himself because of his "conscientious aversion," and she really knew it.

That she didn't know it, and the explanation given by the inquiry must have seemed to her like the perfect gift. But she couldn't use it, could she, because she had to keep quiet? (My mother—keep quiet?)

That she told him he wasn't my father (a monumental row, the heat of the moment, out it all comes) never thinking the revelation might kill him.

That she told him he wasn't my father, knowing that the man was primed, in any case, to commit suicide.

That she was a murderous bitch.

That he really was my father and she told him he wasn't. A lying, murderous bitch.

But then why should she have told Sam?

That she never told him he wasn't my father, but she told Sam she had told him he wasn't my father, to take upon herself the full blame for his suicide and spare Sam's incipient guilt.

Not such a murderous, and only for benign motives a lying, bitch.

That Sam in all this was a complete innocent?

That he wasn't my father but she never told him he wasn't my father and invented the story of telling him he wasn't because it was (a) a way of confessing a long-suppressed and burdensome truth, and (b) it effectively masked (Major Pilkington would have been proud) the real cause of his suicide.

That . . .

That . . .

Felix qui potuit . . . I doubt it.

17

I was born—in the week that lovelorn King Edward renounced his throne—in the county of Berkshire, between the valleys of the Thames and the Kennet, not so far, in one direction, from the little Thames-side township of Pangbourne, and not so far, in the other, from the quaint and sleepy village of Aldermaston.

Now, Aldermaston, in those days, was wholly innocent of the sinister connotations it would later have. Its modest but ancient main street climbed up to the gates of Aldermaston Court, a Victorian pile in the mock-Tudor style, which nonetheless looked back to its real-Tudor avatar (visited by Henry VIII and Elizabeth I) rather than anticipated the days when an Atomic Weapons Research Establishment would occupy its grounds. Toiling horses, not yet ousted by the automobile, would still have hauled the occasional cart up Aldermaston Hill. And below Aldermaston, a mile or so from where the road bridge crossed the old Kennet River, barges, bound for Aldermaston Wharf, would still have plied their trade on the new (meaning hundred-and-fifty-year-old) Kennet and Avon Canal.

But as I grew up, in those far-off days, I saw myself as a child of the future. I was enamoured—little thinking that the object of my passion was doomed, too, soon to become an anachronism—of that roaring, hurtling, up-to-the-minute thing, the steam engine. And, hardly appreciating that my wish was the oldest wish in the book, I wanted to

be, as every little boy was supposed to want to be—ha!—
an engine driver.

Since I lived not only between the converging Thames
and Kennet but between the diverging arms of the Great
Western Railway (northwards to Didcot, southwards to
Newbury) as they emerged from Reading, it was not surprising that I should feel this call of the rails. Boys will be
boys. Even my hypothetical grandsire, Sir Walter Ralegh,
was once an anonymous scamp obeying the truant instincts
of his kind—scurrying down, if we are to believe the leg-
ends and Millais' famous painting, from his Devonshire
home to the sea-shore, to spy the passing ships and sniff
the beckoning air. There he sits, hands clasping his drawn-
up velveteen knees, like some child in a Victorian nursery,
while a whiskered, brawny mariner straight out of stage
melodrama, flings a histrionic arm towards the horizon.

The first stirrings. The call of destiny. When you are out
on . . .

But I was not born within scurrying distance of the sea.
I was born in the soft-bellied, landlubber's county of Berkshire. So what could I do but pedal down to the railway
line (half an hour to Pangbourne, half an hour to Aldermaston Wharf) and there spy those galleons of iron and
steam, sailing on their way to Oxford, Bristol and the far
south-west?

But always better, it seemed to me, than to loiter in some
hemmed-in station, where the great machines, in any case,
slowed down to tamed, frustrated versions of their true
selves, was to find some private look-out point in the peaceful yet tremulous countryside along the margins of the
track—to throw your bike down in the grass and await the
full, spectacular effect. The rattle of the signal wires. The
whispering of the lines. The first distant, pistoned bellow-

ing, then the full-throated fury as some mighty express—the Ocean Mail! the Cornish Riviera!—cleaved the landscape.

Between Aldermaston Wharf and Midgham, where the Reading-to-Newbury line clipped the side of the hill and entered a short cutting—a favourite spot for these enthralled vigils, so limply known as "train-spotting"—I could look out on a vista which might have formed the model for one of those contrived scenes in a children's encyclopaedia, depicting the theme of "Old and New." River, canal and railway line were all in view. At a single moment it would have been perfectly possible to see, in the background, the old water-mill on the Kennet, with a horse working the field before it; in the middle distance, a barge on the canal; and in the foreground, a train racing for the cutting; while no less than three road bridges provided a fair opportunity for some gleaming motor-car (complete with an inanely grinning couple in the front seats) to be brought simultaneously into the picture.

I must have seen it once—many times—that living palimpsest. And no doubt I should have been struck by some prescient, elegiac pang at the sight of those great expresses steaming only to their own oblivion, and taking with them a whole lost age. O West Country world! O creamy, bucket-and-spade summers! O thatched cottages and smugglers' coves! O nestling market towns! O green dreams! O Mendips! O Quantocks! O England!

But I didn't have such thoughts. Any more than I gave thought, as it shadowed my infancy, to the Second World War, whose historic rumblings occurred, so far as I was concerned, off-stage, and whose ending I recall, not for any joyous feelings of deliverance, but because it was in that summer of '45, while the trains of the GWR reverted to their regular schedules and peacetime colours, that I was first allowed to cycle off alone on train-spying missions—a considerable and perhaps ill-advised privilege for a boy not yet turned nine, which owed much to my mother's blithe libertarianism ("Don't get knocked down, there's a good darling") and her husband's absence. But thus my passion—and vocation—bloomed.

What a manly, mettlesome, rugged little imp I must have been. No poetry or ballet-dancers in those days, only engine drivers. And the great thing, of course, as the mighty engines sped by, was to catch a blurred and exalting glimpse of those heroes of the rails. To leap up in a frenzy of adulatory, emulatory waving, hoping for the magic return wave.

And one of those knights of steam, though I never knew it, one of those lords of the footplate (might we have waved, all unwittingly, to each other?) was—my father.

I should track him down, shouldn't I? This mystery man, this nameless entity. My flesh and blood. I cannot picture him. I see only this generic, child's-eye caricature: an engine-driver, for God's sake! Worn blue jacket, twisted neckcloth and greasy cap with a flint-black peak. His eyes are screwed up against the slipstream, the obligatory pipe is clamped in the corner of his mouth—and he is mounted, appropriately enough for my surreptitious begetter, on a giant phallic symbol. I see him careering round the countryside, siring bastard after bastard. Sometimes I think he is grinning at me, leering at me—oh yes, he is waving, all right—as he rushes unrecognisably by.

But he was "killed in the war"—so how could I have waved to him in the summer of '45? Dead even then. My very own father. Dead and beyond recall. But Matthew is dead. Matthew is even deader. . . .

And how far away, how beyond recall, seems even that train-mad infant, perched in his grassy observation post beside the railway line. He is nearer—though he doesn't know it—to Matthew's world than he is to me. When he grows up and comes of engine-driving age, there will be precious few steam-engines left for him to drive. And in just three years' time that Great Western Railway, with all its heraldry of chocolate and cream and its hundred years and more of service, will be nationalized into extinction. But under the blue skies of the first months of peace, it is still, in fact and name, the same Great Western Railway that, a century before, Matthew helped to forge. And that other line, the Didcot line, snaking out along the Thames to Pangbourne, is still, though it no longer favours his famous broad-gauge track, the original, pioneer line west, built by Brunel, whom Matthew once knew.

18th August 1854:

To Torquay, where I call upon I.K.B. He is much changed since his days on the South Devon. But the eyes sparkle and he is as high-spirited and chaffing as ever—though he does not omit to commiserate upon poor Felix.

The usual clouds of cigar smoke. I do not think that during the whole afternoon a cigar was ever out of his mouth, and I recalled Brereton's remark that he could perfectly well sleep and smoke at the same time. Naturally, I am offered one, and I decline, observing that I have refused such offers before. "Ah yes," says he, "but I never lose hope of converts."

He is inclined to make light of our little problem beneath the Tamar—the extraction of the impacted oyster beds. I remind him—an unwarranted digression—of the inveteracy of the molluscs and the crustacea, how they have formed whole strata, whole landscapes, where no trace will be found of a creature with bones.

"I had forgot," says he, "your taste in palaeontology. I will own, at least, to a taste for oysters."

There is a demon in him, for all the easy gaiety: it is as certain that this man will consume and destroy himself as that he will erect monuments to his undying memory. I have grasped the meaning of I.K.B.'s perpetual cigars: he *must* have them, as furnaces must have chimneys— they are lit from *within*.

The Great Western. An iron tentacle stretching from the capital to Cornwall, in which the bridge over the Tamar would be the last and most prodigious link. But more than that. More than just a railway. The very name suggests an idea, an aspiration, an epic, insatiable yearning. London, Bristol, Plymouth and— Why stop at Land's End? Even before the railway had reached the Thames valley, and while Matthew was still a student at Oxford, the steamship *Great Western* (designer, I. K. Brunel) had docked for the first time in Manhattan. As if, stepping off the platform at Paddington, one could be propelled, in one continuous movement and by the same stupendous force of burning coal and hissing steam, from the old world to the new. As if all those expresses that hurtled by me, while I watched from the embankment, really brought with them, after all, the tang, the ozone-tug, of the ocean.

Perhaps Brunel, like old Sir Walter before him (another tobacco man), was irresistibly drawn by the siren call of the West. The inexorable direction of destiny. The sunset way. The realms of gold.

Fuel, fire, ash. The famous photo of Brunel taken in Napier's Yard in Millwall in 1857. He stands before coils of colossal chains. Top hat; rumpled frock-coat; muddied boots; jaunty pose; hands in pockets; cigar in mouth. He looks like anything but a serious engineer. He looks like an impostor, a charlatan—a circus-owner, the proprietor of a gambling saloon. As if the trick of fame is to be something other than you really are, to know that you have come into the world only to play a part.

He has two years left to live.

Local legend has it (I read up on Brunel) that Brunel died by jumping in despair from his Tamar Bridge. But this was not so. The bridge was opened, after ten years in the building, by the Prince Consort in May 1859. Broken in health by overwork (Matthew was right), Brunel was not there. But Matthew and his in-laws were there—and so was Matthew's father. And Brunel himself was not, in the end, denied one last look at his masterpiece. With no cheering crowds or waving flags or royal guests, and lying on a specially prepared truck, he was pulled slowly, as if on a hearse, by one of the GWR's original broad-gauge locomotives, under the massive piers and ironwork, over the glittering river.

Si monumentum requiris . . . It still stands, it is still there, still bearing its designer's name, and still bearing the (diesel-powered, narrow-gauge) expresses into Cornwall. To build a bridge! To span a void! And what voids, what voids there were. He would never know. Need never know. These happy bridge-builders, these men of the solid world (these level-minded surveyors). He was safe. Safe in his sunset glory. Safe within the limits of an old, safe world. Only seven months after his bridge was opened and only two months after his death, Darwin would publish (some come to fame by building, some by—) his *Origin of Species.*

2nd May 1859:

. . . The occasion a strangely subdued one, compared with the triumph two years ago (I.K.B. then in splendid command) of the positioning of the first truss. Adorned by royalty and all the pomp of celebration, but marred by the sad absence of the presiding genius; and marred, quite spoilt—I must say it—so far as our little family outing was concerned, by the unhappy presence of my father.

Inexcusable! Unforgivable! And yet I forgive him, I forgive him. He had as much right as any of us to be there, to be lending his voice to the public applause—and, to be sure, he was not alone in finding the occasion worthy of a bumper or two. But it was inexcusable of him so to have sought us out, quite purposefully, among the crowd, in such a flagrant state of inebriation as must have offended grossly my whole family and the Rector and Mrs Hunt, not to say have humiliated me utterly before them all. And if his intention had been to humiliate me (though I do not think it truly was), then he might have been more consistent than to proclaim to the whole company that, but for my want of ambition and excess of circumspection, I might surely have been as famous a man as Brunel—when circumspection and a sense of proportion were once, so I recall, the very watchwords of his paternal counsel.

Yet who am I to admonish, let alone disown, my own father, when his plight is perhaps not so far, not so very far, from my own? Dear God, along the road of life we are destined to lose so much, the absence of which we can never make good! "Is not Brunel," he ranted, "one of our greatest men?" "A great man," I answered, as pointedly as I was able amidst the embarrassment, "and also a very forlorn one. They say he is dying." Whereupon I noticed a visible flutter pass over his expression before he continued, for all to hear, pretending not to have marked my words, and actually clapping my back, "And yet I'm proud of the boy! Proud of the boy!"

The boy! Yet I do believe he meant it. I do believe that in his mockery he was expressing his pride.

And so our day was clouded—ruined. And henceforth, no doubt, I shall have to withstand ever more vinegared inquiries from the Rector as to my father's "health." A neat means he shall have for deflecting the usual direction of our conversations. What a trifling matter is a great and triumphant feat of engineering (not to say the question of ultimate causes), that it can be overshadowed by a family quarrel. And poor I.K.B., not long for this world. And yet his bridge will remain, surely, long after he and I are gone (and I am quite forgotten), a lasting memorial. . . .

I read up on Brunel; but I do not research my own father. I summon up Matthew, but I do not try to know my own father. My nameless, engine-driving, killed-in-the-war father. And why should I, when I never got to know the living, breathing man whom I took to be—? What difference does it make? The true or the false. This one or that one. The world will not shatter because of a single mis-conception. . . . There I sit on the embankment above the canal and the railway line, and I do not spare a thought for him. He is far away, as it happens, on the far side of the Atlantic, and if he were at home, he would soon put an end to these bicycle rides. I am thinking of the roving, heroic lives of engine drivers. And I am so ignorant of how the world is changing, will change. Of how already like clumsy dinosaurs are these quaint, cacophonous steam trains, which, as they split the summer peace, fill me with such a sense of unsurpassed power.

He did it because of me. Because of me. Because there I was; and I wasn't— I was the last straw. He did this thing: I know it can be done. He wanted—I see it now—to be something other than he was. He wanted all the deathly, death-defying magic of recognition, renown. This road to fame; these valleys of death. But he couldn't pretend, he couldn't turn the blind eye. It makes a difference. Oh it makes a difference! If I had known.

Look. The age of steam trains is already over—devoured by the ruthless age of ballerinas. I sit in the little *école*, mouthing some rigmarole from La Fontaine, with the April sun dancing at the window, and only streets away— if I had known—he is coming to his decision. This cancelling of the self by the self. To be or— Pull the trigger, then it won't matter any more. April in Paris: surely this isn't the end of the world? The patter of typewriters, the smell of coffee. But he really does it, he isn't pretending or playing Hamlet. Little pieces of his hot, bright skull scattered across the floor. My father! My father!

18

He left Burlford in 1860. He never wrote another word in the Notebooks. But he didn't throw them away, didn't destroy them. Why? What were they for? Who was supposed to read them?

These notebook-keepers. This jotting urge. This need to set it down.

Is it possible that in the midst of his torment of soul (his what?) one tiny corner of Matthew's eye was aimed at posterity? Some reader hereafter. Some unknown accreditor. ". . . and I am quite forgotten . . ." A small plea, after all, for non-extinction. A life, after all, beyond life.

Is it possible, in other words, that he was thinking of *me*?

And what did he suppose that I should think of him? Did he consider, being a one-time fossil-collector, that he might turn into just another fossil himself? That his spiritual torment might become just another thing of the past, and future generations would shrug at the meaninglessness that once so appalled him?

(Shrug! All the pills in the bottle.)

And Elizabeth? And Elizabeth. It must have seemed to her such a simple and terrible thing. It must have seemed to her that nothing, least of all the mere thoughts in a man's head—albeit her own husband's head—could counterweigh that undeniable, years-old possession of love, that palpable access to happiness. And did he suppose that the death of Felix was something she hadn't felt too? That she didn't nurse too that aching, child-sized absence, which only made more precious, nonetheless, the treasure they *kept*? What did it matter what he had or hadn't faith in (though she wouldn't have put it this way to her father), so long as he had such still-remaining happiness (was the whole stock ruined?) before him? And if it mattered so much that he rejected it, then it must mean that he'd never truly valued it. That he was pretending. That *he didn't really love her.*

That's what it must have felt like when she woke at night to an empty space beside her and knew that he was still down there at his desk: that he was deserting her. She must have thought of ways to get him back.

Who is Elizabeth? What is she? I see her as a warm-hearted, trusting, perhaps rather brittle girl, emerging suddenly from the chrysalis of life at the Rectory into the full bloom of womanhood. Any man, perhaps, might have been the touchstone; it happened to be Matthew. It was her fortune, and her misfortune, to marry Matthew. And strange that this robust and outgoing man, to whom she had looked to lead her, some way at least, out of the sheltered existence that she could admit now had been hers, should himself slip so easily into domesticity and family-hood, should choose to settle, after all, right here in Burlford, under the eye, as it were, of the Rector and her mother, should even seem now and then to need a sort of shelter himself. It must mean he was happy; that she made him happy.

She has soft brown eyes and the smile of newly awakened, newly indulged instincts; the clear conscience and undissipated emotions of a clergyman's daughter. What did she think of her husband's "interests"—the specimen-collecting, the reading-up in learned tomes and journals? Perhaps they seemed, at first, endearingly, if vexingly, like her father's interminable devotion to Virgil. Men seemed to need these "enthusiasms," which rapidly became so all-consuming. She had thought, perhaps, that her own sex, with its needlework, sketching and piano-playing, was lacking in this respect. But now, watching little Christopher at play, watching the earnestness with which he went about it—a furrow in his brow just like one in Matthew's—she would have felt more of concern than envy for these curious menfolk. But she would no more have dared knock on Matthew's study door and urge him, for his own sake, to stop, than she would have dared ask her father (though perhaps she had the subversive thought) why he, a minister of the Christian church, should spend so much time in the company of a *pagan* poet.

She has deep-brown hair and a soft, ripe bosom. And she is perfectly capable, now that she has discovered her instincts, now that she knows, beyond all girlish dreams, the full extent of her power to give and receive love, of concurring absolutely with that motto (what if they *were* the words of a pagan poet?) which Matthew's father had had inscribed for them. Yes. *Amor vincit.*

2nd March 1860:

Neale here again for Sunday dinner. And playing very merrily afterwards with John and Christopher and offering them fine exhortations as to how they are almost grown men now, with "places to take in the world." Cannot help supposing that these visits are encouraged by Elizabeth in collusion with her father, so as to preserve our Sundays from the animosity that now so often springs up between myself and the Rector following our church-going. Suspect also that the Rector has had private words with Elizabeth about the parlous state of my father's affairs—how, in plain terms, if I do not have a care and desist from lending my father money, the taint will spread to my own reputation.

Neither of these suspicions becomes me. Yet suspect also that Elizabeth wishes, out of an understandable and not uncharitable motive, to put Neale before me as an example of what *I* should be, and, indeed, once was before my falling off of these last months. That is: sanguine, cheerful, dependable, steady in my responsibilities and successful in my affairs. Yet cannot, for the life of me, see myself in Neale (or him in me) at all. Distrust my former liking of him. Despise my own distrust and upbraid my own seeming want of character. Should perhaps be simply jealous and act the plain part of jealousy. Nothing, in fact, might better restore me in my Lizzie's eyes —proving I was a creature still of direct and vivid emotions, and not the remote occupant of my own incapacitating thoughts.

Yet I disdain to be—even as I become the very thing —the pallid husband resenting the vigorous interloper. And I disdain (pride! Oh, pride!) to engage in matrimonial histrionics, when it is indeed my "thoughts" which are the nub of the matter.

Neale asks, in seeming candour or in seeming tact, after my father. Wheal Talbot fares well. Neale, in truth, is a rich man, an eligible match, slow to take his pick, and the story goes that he pays court to the fair daughter of one of our reduced gentry—or, rather, that she pays court to him. He observes that Benson (do I remember our "scourge of the boll weevil"?) does well enough out of his arsenic licence, and wittily remarks that while he extracts the "cordial" of the mine, Benson extracts the poison. Adds that Benson may be obliged shortly to interrupt his war against the weevil, if the States, as seems almost certain, go to war themselves. Might advise him that at such time it would be opportune to buy back the arsenic rights and thus secure, against future vicissitudes, another basket for his eggs. Might remind him also that Wheal Talbot does not command the richest section of the lode, and he would do well to sink exploratory shafts for tin while there is time and capital. But this perhaps would be only my "circumspection" speaking—who now sees any perils in the copper market?—and I do not wish Liz to suppose that I resent Neale's success.

But these pages should not be a furtive laboratory in which I analyse my wife. God forbid that she should think that that is the object of these "studies" of mine. Truly I believe that—still—she would never dare touch a single page of these notebooks without my permission. Yet, while I closet myself repeatedly in their fellowship, has *she* not a right to be jealous?

What would I do without her? What would I have become without her? What price should I not pay not to lose her? I do believe she would forgive and forget all my strange humour of late, if I would only, as she once, so warily, entreated me, call upon my better nature and "be myself again."

"Better nature"? What, in any of us, is our "better nature"? And what does it mean—is this what we love and respect in each other?—to "be oneself"?

So what are we supposed to believe here? Forget what Matthew, by now an almost confirmed non-believer, believed or didn't believe. Consider the facts. Matthew left Burlford (and Elizabeth) in July 1860. Under new laws—imagine the Rector's mortification—Elizabeth obtained a divorce, on grounds of desertion. I am working now from data outside the Notebooks (I have done my background research), which stopped with Matthew's departure. Elizabeth married James Neale in November 1862. Neale, with his lucrative stake in a copper mine, and something of a charmer, had been on the scene at least since 1856. So what are we supposed to believe? That from 1854 until 1860 Elizabeth held out, the mystified, forbearing, loyal, loving wife, until it was all up? And then, and only then—?

Let's read between the lines. Let's be brutal and modern and take apart these precious Notebooks—this precious marriage of Matthew and his Lizzie. Forget his numerous avowals. Forget that last letter from Plymouth. Hogwash! Eyewash! When it comes down to it, Matthew was just another disillusioned idealist, an over-reactive Hamlet type—couldn't take it that the world was real. See how he lapses into whingeing sentimentality. What price would he not pay not to lose her? But he did lose her. He left her on a July day in 1860. Though she had left him, perhaps, long before that.

And while we're about it, we may as well ask the big question: which came first—the failed marriage or the ideological anguish? Which would Potter go for in his TV production? The fully licensed historical protagonist? The tortured man of his time? But think of rooms and beds and breakfast tables. (Think of the private life of Michael Potter.) Let's face it—for at least six years they were in a state of marital shut-down. The good husband confides in his wife. Matthew kept it all to himself. Reason: some day he might just come out of it all, and there would have been no point in telling. But that way he dug a deeper and deeper pit for himself, and when he finally crawled out of it to tell her, can you blame her for feeling cheated—for having already made her contingency plans?

What was she supposed to have done? An Ophelia routine? Talked to the flowers?

So, have I got it all wrong? I invent. I imagine. I want them to have been happy. How do I know they were ever happy? I make them fall in love at the very first meeting, on a day full of radiant summer sunshine. How do I know it was ever like that? How do I know that the Notebooks, while they offer ample evidence for the collapse of Matthew's marriage, were not also a desperate attempt to keep alive its myth, and that even when he seems most honest Matthew, with much display of fine feeling, tender conscience and wishful thinking, only beats about the bush of an old, old story?

An old story. Cuckoo! Cuckoo! Happens all the time. The way of the world. Even a clergyman's daughter. Even a Victorian clergyman's daughter. *Così fan tutte* (and *tutti* too). God damn it, it was how you were *born*.

And Ruth. And Ruth? No, I don't believe that she ever— But suppose, suppose. In the days before I became her manager. Her minder . . . The freedoms of these theatrical folk, the way they touch and kiss and hug, and slip in and out of roles . . . No, I don't believe she ever really— But what if she had? What if she had? Would she have been someone other than Ruth? People aren't defined by other people. We have to be ourselves.

Talk to the flowers. My prerogative, here in this garden. There is a buddleia bush, a clump of buddleia bushes, over there at the far end of the herbaceous border, assigned the rather lowly function of screening a compost heap. And buddleia bushes must still have the same properties they had more than a century ago, because even now, even from here, I can see, against the floppy purple flowers, the intermittent wink of tiny wings.

10th July 1857:
    The enigmas of our buddleia bush! To which, while this fair and butterfly-breeding weather lasts, my little Lucy—as the butterflies are attracted to the florets—seems irresistibly drawn . . .

He wrote the Notebooks for *me*?

Perhaps it was Lucy who persuaded her to keep them. If persuasion were needed. Perhaps it was Lucy who, long before that, persuaded her to keep the clock.

The third (surviving) child, the only daughter, and the youngest. She would have been only seven when the news rocked Burlford. The children, of course, made it worse. How could he do it? His own flesh and blood! The downright perversity of it! He laments the death of one, then abandons the others. He heeds the exhortation of Scripture—"Be fruitful and multiply"—then denies Creation. The man must have been mad. Neale's verdict, no doubt, and others'—disguised under the easy rant of outraged piety and, in Neale's case, the rectitude of sexual triumph.

But Neale must have considered what he was taking on. The guardianship, the stepfatherhood of three children, all, presumably, in a distraught state of mind. It says something for the attractions of the former Mrs Pearce that, an unencumbered bachelor up to this point, he should have accepted these charges along with her. And it says something, perhaps, for Neale's own position on the fruitfulness and multiplication question, or for the scruples of the second-time wife (Elizabeth was thirty-six), that no little Neales issued from his marriage.

I make no glib comparisons. Even though there is an entrepreneurial similarity between James Neale and the late Sam Ellison, and both acquired the waifs of scandal. But, of course, Neale *chose*. As far as the scandal went, perhaps it redounded to his credit—to be the saviour of this damsel in distress, to step in where that godless wretch had left off. Rich businessmen have a penchant for being judged virtuous; abandoned mothers of three need charity.

Of the Pearce children, both the sons were to throw in their lot with their stepfather and go into copper. No, I make no comparisons. We are talking about real ore hewn from the depths of the earth, not factory-made synthetics (though, as it turned out, John and Christopher might have been better off with the latter). Lucy seems to have made a break from the family, over which, by then, new shadows had fallen, when she married in 1872 and moved to London. Yet she took the clock with her. I know this. It is the fact that Elizabeth decided to give it to her (thus inaugurating a tradition) which makes me think that it was Lucy who perhaps persuaded her to keep it in the first place. And, of course, by that time, by 1872, that gift of the clock would have meant so much more. . . .

With Lucy, my mother's reluctant and not necessarily reliable recollections come into play, along with the faint tug of my remote consanguinity with Matthew. For it was Lucy's daughter, Alice, who in the early years of the century married the talented but ill-starred surgeon, George Rawlinson, inventor of the Rawlinson Forceps, and thus became herself the recipient of the clock. The fact that Lucy chose to pass it on suggests that her own marriage, of which I know very little, may have been a happy affair. All Lucy's woes, perhaps, lay in the memory of her suddenly blighted childhood and in the tribulations that her own daughter, seemingly so well set up, would bring her. It is strange to think that "little Lucy," she of the evening gig rides with her father, died only some dozen years before I was born, living long enough to contend with the surgical catastrophe that ended her son-in-law's career and the ensuing marital débâcle. In fact, it was probably these things that finished her off.

My mother decried her father's hubristic ambition. But George, perhaps, was only a man who made mistakes. One was that dreadful slip of the scalpel. Another, so it proved, was to have married, in his middle years, a woman substantially younger than himself, with a robust will of her own. It was Lucy's daughter, Alice, possessor of the nuptial clock, who responded to her husband's ruin by rapid and brazen flight to the arms of another man—a Latin lover, no less, called Salvatore. Whether this was the expedient of the hour or whether something had been going on for some time already is anybody's guess. I think my mother's somewhat unfilial guess would have been for the latter. Poor George really had it coming to him.

We seem to have been this way before. This butterfly love. January and May. Cuckoo! Cuckoo! I do not say that history repeats itself. Or that my mother learnt from her mother's example. I do not say that the beneficent clock was fast becoming a curse. My grandmother hung on to it, as part of the spoils of divorce, following which event, my mother's relations with her mother were understandably tenuous. We are moving into that vexed period when my mother (discovering her gift of song) and her brother became unhappy dependants upon my great-uncle Ratty's grudging and tortuous whims—while my unrepentant grandmother seemed to be having a high old time, much of it cheerfully out of the country, in such places as Monte Carlo and Capri. Remarkably, my mother seems never to have held this against her. Perhaps it secretly inspired her. And, indeed, the runaway Alice showed up, at least, for her daughter's wedding (to the consternation, I can imagine, of the stiff and military bridegroom)—which is how my mother became the next proprietor of the clock.

As for the Notebooks, I don't know if they came from Lucy to my mother via George (and/or Ratty) or via my grandmother. In any case, it's plain that they were simultaneously preserved and overlooked. I can't imagine they would have been of vital interest to Alice, while Uncle Ratty would have dismissed them as having nothing to do with the Ralegh hypothesis. But I can envisage my grandfather, man of science, after all, grey-matter specialist, being strangely drawn in his last, lonely, woebegone years (what am I *saying*?) to Matthew's sceptical lucubrations.

I don't know if my grandmother turned up also for my

christening (that *dubious* ceremony). I suspect not. At any rate, she was never to be a presence in my life. Two years after my birth and only some two years before my uncle Jim met his end (yes, death sometimes comes a-knocking with a vengeance), she and her erstwhile lover, now husband of some years, died simultaneously in a car accident on the corniche road of the Cote d'Azur ("Tragic, sweetie, but a stylish way to go"). One should resist the thought that my grandfather may then have settled more easily in his own grave. One should resist these poetic pay-offs, these dramatic strokes and flourishes. Life isn't a theatre, is it? Life is a back-stage business. A struggle for existence.

But to return to the West Country and the mid-1860s. It is clear from Matthew's farewell letter from Plymouth that the days of the "Kingdom of Copper" were numbered. Matthew had been right. Neale should have hedged his commercial bets. It seems that scarcely had the Pearce brothers been co-opted into the mining business by their stepfather than the copper market, booming for some twenty years, fell crashing around them. Neale never bought back his arsenic licence and, having pushed the boat out to impress and provide for his new wife (I imagine some white-fronted villa, a gravel sweep, a backdrop of dark, shielding trees), must have thrown himself on Benson's mercy. Benson, we may take it, weathered the interruption of the American Civil War, which, while it reduced the human population, presumably allowed boll-weevils to thrive. He must have looked smugly yet pityingly on Neale. What saved them all, as it saved many an ailing copper mine, must have been arsenic. They were kept alive by poison.

I know little of the subsequent history of the Wheal Talbot mine. My mother, speaking out of the dim recesses of family lore, never used that name and only referred to it contemptuously—as if her great-uncles, Lucy's brothers, were never more than doomed adherents to a lost cause (crazed, unshaven prospectors)—as "some wretched little tin mine in Cornwall." My mother was capable of getting facts wrong. But I like to think that in that confusion of metals there was a degree of truth. That the brothers recalled their father's insistence that tin deposits almost certainly lay beneath the Wheal Talbot copper and that Neale should dig for it while he could. Did they miss their father—his sound surveyor's advice, his nose for geology, his feel for the secrets of the earth?

But if they found tin they would not have enjoyed its benefit for long. Tin was to crash in the early Nineties. Even arsenic slumped at the turn of the century. Wheal Talbot was abandoned. Elizabeth Neale, formerly Pearce, née Hunt, and by this time a widow, died in 1906, unaided by poison, but assisted, quite possibly, by the gall of memory: those days at Burlford; those days of honey and constancy, when this world, this other world of deceitful metal, lay all beyond the hill.

And the Rector? The would-be missionary who had come to a quiet Devon valley, seen the village, the church and the rectory and seen that they were good, and seen as the only shadow upon a comfortable living the onus of being an Anglican cleric in Methodist-infiltrated territory, could little have guessed at the changes he would witness in these seemingly unchangeable surroundings. That the little nearby town of Tavistock would become, depending on how you looked at it, a modern Eldorado, a satanic gambling-den in which the stakes were dividends and miners' bellies—a crowded enclave of avid, abused humanity. That in his old age it would be part of his pastoral charge—the would-be missionary indeed—to visit the dismal hovels of the starving and cholera-ridden.

Did his fears persist of that undermined world, waiting to collapse into infernal darkness? Did he have thoughts akin to Matthew's?

19th March 1856:

These toiling masses of our mine-workers trouble me. Because in the habitat of their workplace they do indeed appear as so many termites labouring in the dark and occupying a literal subexistence, we convert the appearance into substance. But by what perverted definition of common humanity do we pronounce that they are brutes and not we?

And what, in the end, would he have judged to have been worse? His son in-law's defection to the forces of godlessness? Or his daughter's rush—with his blessing, oh yes, with his politic blessing at the time—into the arms of Mammon, that false god that it was his duty to denounce in his sermons?

And what comfort had it brought her?

This search for buried treasure. This fever of the mines. The hills and vales of the south-west are still, apparently, sprinkled with the forlorn chimneys, the ruined engine-houses and overgrown waste-heaps of old mines. With the wind sighing around them, they have acquired, no doubt, a soulful effect, like the rusting hulks of old locomotives.

This alchemical quest to turn base metals into pocket-able gold. This search, if not for the real thing, then for the substitute thing, the thing that, perhaps, will do just as well. The money. The money. First copper, then tin. Then—O heir of the Ellisons! O fully lifelike model fresh from the factory of the dead!—plastic.

And Matthew? And Matthew—gone on his soulless way? Throughout these years—or for part of them—in which the market in ore peaked then fell, we must assume he was living in Launceston, where he ministered to the ailing John Pearce and weaned him off the bottle. A Christian enough picture for a man who had forsaken Christianity. Did he attempt to revive his father's neglected clock-making business? Did he—could he?—practise still as a surveyor? Did he endure a barrage of gossip, both on his father's account and on account of his former, dissolved marriage; and did his father, who at one time, in his cups, had rebuked his son for not having become a famous man, ever chuckle over the rueful joke that at least they were reunited, now, in mutual ignominy?

He never wrote another word in the Notebooks. Not one word. But he preserved them. Why? Did he ever show them to his father? No, I think not. Not to the man who had once kept him ruthlessly at his school books and who only in his last hours yielded up a supposedly lost Bible. They both had things, this father and son, they thought it best to keep from each other.

And when John Pearce, creator of the original, ticking wedding gift, breathed his last, Matthew kept the Bible, as well as the Notebooks. Both were with him when he wound up his affairs in Launceston and travelled to Plymouth, thence to voyage to the New World. Then on that last night, as the Atlantic drizzle drenched Plymouth, he sent the Notebooks to Elizabeth, but held on to the Bible.

Question: did she or didn't she—with Neale, even before that afternoon of the bees? The birds and the bees. Question: did she stop loving him, as (so she believed, let's suppose) he had stopped loving her? Or did she love him still, even as the price of copper plummeted, even as Matthew looked his last on England?

Forget the other stuff. Stick to the love-interest. The ever-popular love-interest. What the audience wants.

When all is said and done and the meaning of the universe has been fully squeezed dry, Hamlet sees Laertes usurping Ophelia's grave (these dramatic strokes), picks a fight with him, spikes himself on a rapier and so achieves in the heat of the hour what he might have achieved, with a bare bodkin, after much exhausting philosophical deliberation. Matthew quits Burlford, to return to his birthplace. And Elizabeth quits Burlford, to marry into copper. Years later, she receives a package.

She kept them. (What did she do—hide them from Neale?) She kept them, persuaded or not by Lucy. And kept the letter too. Would she have replied? But he left no forwarding address. He wished to disappear. And he did, he did. So would she have kept them anyway, or was it only that other news, that would have reached her not long afterwards—news not from but of her former husband—that decided her?

For the bare fact is—I have done my additional research: a simple matter of consulting shipping registers—her former husband never reached the New World. The *Juno* went down on 14th April 1869 in a storm some miles west of the Scillies (what final terror, or acceptance? what revelations, confirmations—wrenched-out prayers?); and among the list of those who perished was Matthew Pearce, surveyor, of Launceston.

But there he sits, for now, on *terra firma*, in *terra cognita*, pen in hand, in his lodgings in Plymouth. The rain, a gentle, enclosing rain with no hint of fury to come, patters at the window and induces in him seafaring, far-ranging, spacious thoughts. By the light of the oil-lamp, he fills the page, as once he filled so many pages in his study at Burlford. This need to write it down. To describe it, to know it: this strange land of the living. He describes the rain. He describes the gaggles of displaced miners who mill round Plymouth in the spring of 1869. He says he will go to take one last look at Brunel's bridge. Memories, and memories of memories, flood in.

A New World. A new life—a new name. Forget it all. Start again. Is it possible? There will always be what remains. He loved her. He wrote it down: that flimsy, romantic thing, a love letter. And Elizabeth? She kept the letter, she kept the Notebooks. She loved him still.

19

I have dipped into Darwin. It's heavy going. The prose thick, grey and formidable, like porridge. It is hard to see in this sober stodge the bombshell which tore apart Matthew's life and horrified Victorian society. Perhaps this proves Darwin's point. Species *adapt*. Yesterday's cataclysm is today's absorbed fact. Yet it is equally hard to see, behind these plodding, scrupulous, epoch-making words, the man who wrote them. To picture the young Charles Darwin who set sail one day from Plymouth just as Matthew did, though this would have been nearly forty years before, when Matthew was only a boy of twelve, trying to absorb the recent cataclysm of his mother's death. And the voyage was somewhat longer.

New worlds. New life. Matthew perished barely a day from port. Darwin returned, safe and sound, after five years' roving, with the inklings of a new picture of the universe.

So was he the adventurous sort? A budding Sir Walter? Hardly. Seasick, it seems, all the time. And comes back not exactly with a booty of rattling yarns. But not, at one time at least, such a dull swot either. A dab-hand with a shot-gun. Footloose, outdoor type. His father, alarmed at his son's idle ways, steered him first, abortively, towards medicine, then, of all things, towards the Church.

Was there a compartment in Darwin's later fully freighted mind—a subsection of his own Theory of Natural Selection—which gave due consideration to the question of how individuals who undertake momentous undertakings—are selected? Did he ever ask: but why me? Why *me*? The captain of the *Beagle*, an amateur phrenologist, nearly rejected Darwin as a suitable shipmate on account of the shape of his nose. And it is a well-recorded fact that the great Theory, some twenty years in the forming, was only rushed into publication because someone else—a fellow called Wallace—seemed to have got hold of the same idea. Were it not for the mutual reasonableness of the two parties (not typical, I can vouch, of your rival men of learning) and for the fact that Wallace was tied up at the time in the Celebes, we might have had Wallace's Theory of Natural Selection—Wallacism, Wallacists and Neo-Wallacists.

But what's in a name?

So what became of the feckless duck-shooter (and prospective priest)? He signs on, more by chance than design, as naturalist with the *Beagle*. Voyages for five years to the far corners of the earth. Then ends up a studious and sickly recluse, writing endless notes in a house in Kent. So, he had seen the world? The rest was contemplation? To challenge the universe from a house in Kent!

No, not the adventurous sort. A sufferer, most of his life from mysterious, possibly psychosomatic ailments. And hardly one of your showmen among men of genius. No top hat, cigar and thumb poked in waistcoat pocket. The frontispiece of my copy of *The Origin of Species*, a late-Victorian edition published within ten years of Darwin's death, shows a brooding, oracular figure, all flowing beard and thought-furrowed brow, seated on a rickety wicker chair. He looks like the original Hoary Sage. He looks a miserable old codger.

So did he want fame? Was it important, after all, that it was his name on the bombshell? He always maintained that he worked only for the elucidation of truth. Witness those years of painstaking toil before he was finally induced to publish. Did he reflect on the desirability of the elucidation of truth? Did he consider what the effect might be on lesser mortals (was he some greater mortal?) like Matthew Pearce? On the big question, the God question, he seems to have maintained—this one-time candidate for orders—a careful reticence, a curiously bland open-mindedness, an obtuse bewilderment. Reading Darwin, you sometimes get the feeling that the man was—dim. It was not his business to settle questions of final causes; it was his business only (only!) to elucidate the truth.

And where did it get him, this devotion to the truth? A gnarled and lugubrious septuagenarian in his creaking wicker chair, author of hundreds of pages of meticulous, fatiguing, world-shattering prose.

I pick at the *Journal* (this magpie scholarship), struggle with the *Origin*, home in on the letters and the *Autobiography*. There is a passage in the latter where the author laments the gradual loss of all taste for poetry, likewise, virtually, for music, painting and fine scenery, and speculates (ever the man of science) on what has caused the atrophy of the relevant parts of the brain. Is he trying to tell us something? In 1858, the year before the *Origin* appeared, and before, presumably, the "atrophy" set in, he wrote, while on one of his numerous "cures" in the country, to Mrs D. (with whom, by the way, there was never a rupture, and with whom, for all his ill health and monumental toil, he begat seven children):

> *The weather is quite delicious. Yesterday, after writing to you, I strolled a little beyond the glade for an hour and a half and enjoyed myself—the fresh yet dark green of the grand Scotch firs, the brown of the catkins of the*

old birches, with their white stems, and a fringe of dis-
tant green from the larches, made an excessively pretty
view. At last I fell asleep on the grass, and awoke with
a chorus of birds singing around me, and squirrels run-
ning up the trees, and some woodpeckers laughing, and
it was as pleasant and rural a scene as I ever saw, and
I did not care one penny how any of the beasts or birds
had been formed.

These great men of ideas, they get turned themselves
into ideas. So Darwin becomes a kind of abstract condition,
a sort of irrevocable tinge that settled on the world around
the middle of the nineteenth century. The world before
Darwin, the world after Darwin. Who thinks of Darwin
the man? Was he a man or a mind? Who thinks of Newton
the man? Save, of course, to picture him in that legendary
reverie, not unlike Darwin's idyll (Darwin in nature's play-
ground!), ensconced beneath an apple tree—a reverie shattered by the Law of Gravity. The apple, of course, provides
a resonantly Edenesque touch. These men of knowledge.
These meddlers with the universe. Darwin, they say, was
the Newton of biology. If Darwin was the Newton of biology, then Einstein was the Darwin of physics.

In the red-brick village of Aldermaston, there used to be
a little tea-shop, of the welcoming but unassuming kind
(a cool, oaky demureness, even on a hot summer's day)
now virtually vanished from rural England; and there, one
day in the first summer of peace, my mother took me and
told me about the William's pear.

We must have come in the new Armstrong-Siddeley:
one of her madcap drives—hands fluttering over the
steering-wheel—through pulsing tunnels of trees, hazy

troughs of heat and the dry, ropey smell of harvest time. I don't remember if we stopped on the railway bridge—completing that child's encyclopaedia picture—to watch a train billow through beneath us. And I still don't know (I certainly didn't know then) whether this outing to Aldermaston held for her some special, extra *frisson*. But I remember the blatant fact that as we took our tea (lemonade for me) the top three buttons of her blouse were undone—there was a little sheen of sweat at the base of her throat—and I remember thinking (the first time, perhaps, I had had such thoughts) that this fact was not only remarkably compelling in itself but also remarkably complex, fraught with unsteadying repercussions, such as: did she know that the buttons were undone, and if she did, why didn't she do anything about it? And was it more proper for me, as a gentleman, to point out this little omission or to say nothing?

The blouse was cream silk (even in those war-pinched days). A white strap, thin and shiny like a ribbon and lifting from her skin where it crossed her collar-bone, was visible. The just discernible fringe of the garment to which it belonged had a filigree tenuosity, curiously evocative of the doily that bore our angel cake and macaroons.

Who now connects Aldermaston with the William's pear, first produced there in seventeen hundred and something by a local schoolmaster? But in those days it was one of Aldermaston's little claims to fame and it was the done thing, in season—and this year they had ripened early—to buy them while you were there. My mother had bought two ("a pair of pears"), wrapped in a brown paper bag, and, for some reason, over our sticky and crumb-strewn tea plates, she chose to give a brief lecture on the local genesis of this distinguished fruit.

At that time (aged eight-and-a-half) I had no conception

that pears might be *made*. As far as I was concerned, they grew on trees. And I couldn't tell a William's from a Conference or a Comice—I am still hazy on such things. But my mother, who was no doubt proud of her little scrap of knowledge and who would now and then have this curious urge to be my instructress, took it upon herself to enlighten me.

And yet—do I remember this correctly?—having launched eagerly into her subject (I picture the old schoolmaster as rather like the rector of Burlford—with one it was bees, with the other, fruit propagation), she drew herself up suddenly on the brink of a tricky discourse on cross-fertilization, and said, "Oh well, never mind." Perhaps I had protestingly voiced my thought—"But pears can't be *made*!"—and she had said, "Oh yes, they can!" At any rate, she cut short the lecture. Then she proposed that we eat our pears.

It was, of course, the riddle of hybrids and cross-breeds that set the Sage of Kent thinking.

Outside, the afternoon was a hot, chalky glare. A canvas awning kept it at bay. An arc of black lettering on the window, above the little skirt of lace curtaining, proclaimed in reverse the name, which I forget, of the premises within. Spoons clinked. A fly-paper twirled slowly beneath the ceiling. Doubtless, there were other tea-takers at other tables and, doubtless, there was some bustling proprietress with a sugary smile, and a flustered teenage waitress. I don't know—why should I have noticed?—if any of them were giving my mother looks. I don't know if she still had, in the reckoning of country villages with limited horizons but long memories, a certain reputation. . . .

And only now does an extraordinary thing occur to me. I can pinpoint, after all, the date and the purpose of this little jaunt exactly. My father (let me call him that) was, as he had been for most of that summer, away. Some of the wartime secrecy of his whereabouts had been lifted and I knew for a fact that he had gone to Washington.

Not that this meant much to me. I now recall an earlier and more ambitious lecture of my mother's, which aimed at nothing less than a brief history of the world, or at least the New World, a concept quite beyond me, since I was still at that stage of infancy (Paris would end it) when I vaguely suspected that the existence of foreign countries was a clever adult fiction. Washington, apparently, was called Washington because of George Washington, who had made America American. But, before that, America had belonged to us—it was really British. There was also something, to add to the confusion, about a cherry tree. These great men and their trees.

August 1945. August 5. It was my mother's birthday. That was the point of this tea-time excursion. I was "taking her to tea." My father was in Washington, and it was my mother's birthday; and, as it was her birthday, there was a chance he might telephone at any moment. Think of that—a phone call all the way from America. (But would that prove—I was sceptical—that America really existed?)

By lunchtime no phone call had come (my scepticism increased). But apparently there was still plenty of time. You had to remember that over there they were only just having breakfast. A likely story. Perhaps she saw my disbelief, and perhaps rose to the challenge of another lecture —but thought twice about it. Waving the whole matter aside, she said, "But what a *gorgeous* day! Where are you going to take your mother for her birthday treat?"

The past, they say, is a foreign country, and I fictionalize (perhaps) these memories of that afternoon. But then my mother is dead. With all the others. She doesn't exist. And fiction is what doesn't exist. Did she really, right there and then in the tea-shop, hold up before her by its stalk her William's pear, as if inviting me to snatch it, or as if she might suddenly let it fall? A small age seemed to pass in which it dangled between us, like a hypnotist's watch, and in which my mother, her eyes swimming in and out of focus, seemed like a woman I was just beginning to know.

Then she bit, voraciously, into the plumpest part.

A lesson in gravity? Or in levity? Eternal levity. She couldn't have known, any more than I, that in a far-away foreign country, where it was several hours later than us, where night had already fallen, they were about to drop a bomb. That for ever afterwards she would share her birthday with the anniversary of the last pre-atomic day.

She took a bite, a good, lip-splaying bite, out of the pear. Juice ran—a drop, a splash or two of pearly pear juice in that baffling opening of her blouse. Her tongue made slurpy noises, her eyes wallowed.

"Mmmm, darling—divine."

20

The sun is beginning to sink. The shadow of the bean tree creeps over the lawn. Across the river, the towers and turrets, the little twinkling arched and latticed windows, take on their evening aura. These ancient walls. These hallowed groves. So ripe with the steady defiance of time, with the presumption of mind over matter. So evocative of the King of Navarre's other-worldly schemes, of Berowne and Longaville and Dumaine: "a little academe, still and contemplative in living art . . ."

"*Worthies, away! . . .*"

It was my mother who first warned me, invoking the examples of vainglorious grandfathers and great-uncles, against the ruinous desire to outwit mortality. And, having heeded her advice so far as to rush, spontaneously, into death's arms and having returned from its apparently escapable embrace, what can I say about this old and terrifying bugbear, *mors, mortis*? That it turns you (surprise, surprise) into a nobody. That my little bout with it has left me with a ghostly disconnection from myself—I am wiped clean, a *tabula rasa* (I could be *any*body)—and a strange, concomitant yen, never felt before, to set pen to paper.

O death-defiers of this world! O luminaries, O immortalists! To leave one's mark! To build a bridge, christen a theory, name a pear, write a book. The struggle for existence? Ha! The struggle for *remembrance*.

So I am in it too, this race for posterity? I succumb, just

like Matthew, to the jotting urge. But who are they for, these ramblings? And who am I, to seek to go on record? I don't even have Matthew's agony of conscience (and why should I envy him that?), which is as obsolete now as that ichthyosaur he met up with on his summer hols.

"Let fame, that all hunt after in their lives, live registr'red . . ."

But it was she who wanted fame, not me. I was content to be the happy stagehand; I could attend rehearsals. Yet who doesn't want to leave behind some token, some trace, some reminder, some plea? Usually, it's children. But we had no children. Too busy finding fame—or just happy without them? But, in any case, it's not so simple—so it seems—this begetting of children.

Who am I? Who am I? A nobody. An heirless nonentity. What's more—a bastard.

Consider, for contrast, my fabled ancestor, brave Sir Walter, born long before Providence was declared invalid, setting sail from Plymouth (him too) with never a qualm. By my time of life (is that the phrase?) what had the little lad of the sea-shore not achieved? Discovered new lands, founded a colony, won queenly favour, tackled the Spanish Armada. Been soldier, sailor, discoverer, explorer . . . "Exposing what is mortal and unsure to all that fortune, death and danger dare . . ."

Ah, what a thing is man.

Actually, what *was* he doing, aged fifty-two-and-a-half? He was cooped up in the Tower of London. I make no comparisons. These ancient walls: the storied stones of the Tower. But what does he do with this forced confinement? Makes a virtue even out of incarceration. Puts pen to paper. Writes a *History of the World*. No less. From Adam and Eve until— And schemes and dreams. Of Eldorado. No less. Of a land of gold, an earthly paradise in the far, far west. O brave new world!

And ever mindful of his image, of how caged lions draw the public, takes care to show himself now and then, like Napoleon on the *Bellerophon*, to the awed citizenry of London. There he walks on the battlements, the old, proud sea-dog, in the years that Shakespeare's tragedies were first staged: the "last Elizabethan," the one-and-only Renaissance man, living proof that anybody can be *any*body, since this fellow was *every*body: discoverer, explorer, colonist, courtier, scientist, historian, philosopher, wit, dandy, ladies' man, physician, chemist, botanist, tobacconist, potato merchant . . .

And poet.

> *Our mothers' wombes the tiring houses be*
> *Where we are drest for this short Comedy . . .*

Life after Darwin: As You Like It, or What You Will. But even those long-vanished Elizabethans, who'd never heard, poor ignoramuses, of Newton, Darwin or the splitting of the atom, and whose history books began with the Creation, were not so sure of the Life Eternal that they did not invest heavily—and profitably—in that other eternity: fame. A bumper crop of fine old worthies. The age was thick with them. And the poets! Never so rich a hoard. An Eldorado in verse. Poetry. That still other, verbal eternity. The so-called divine spark. That thing for which Darwin lost all taste.

It is true (we know now) that we are descended from the apes. And it is true that an ape, set before a typewriter and given a time-scale of infinity and an eternal factor of randomness, might eventually bash out the sonnets of Shakespeare. But, by and large, it is just as well and a good deal neater that Shakespeare appeared when he did to do the job. Which leaves a host of questions still wide open. How Shakespeare came about in the first place (why he didn't go into sheep farming or die, aged two, of scarlet fever), and why, though Shakespeare is all things to all people, we cannot all be Shakespeares. Why some are poets and some are not. And why not all poets are also explorers, adventurers, courtiers, etc.—all things in one. And why there should be this stuff called poetry, to begin with, which strikes our hearts at such a magic angle. And why there should be certain things in this random universe which cry out to us with their loveliness. And why it should be poetry that captures them.

> *Full many a glorious morning have I seen*
> *Flatter the mountain tops with sovereign eye,*
> *Kissing with golden face the meadows green,*
> *Gilding pale streams with heavenly alchemy . . .*

Why is *anything* special? Either everything is special, which is absurd. Or nothing is special. Which is meaningless.

10th July 1857:

How we flatter the humble *nymphalidae*—and delude ourselves. The Peacock. The Painted Lady. The Red and White Admiral. The Purple Emperor. How we clothe them in splendours they cannot heed and wrap them in tender sentiments they cannot share: how sad, that they open their gorgeous wings but to die. The Purple Emperor, who seems to us such an illustrious fellow, wears (as my little Lucy unwittingly reminds me) but the common garb of his tribe, and takes no thought for the hereafter. Can there be heroes and worthies among the *lepidoptera*? Surely not, since it is only the knowledge of death that breeds the desire of its transcendence. *Timor mortis conturbat me.* So one might say our need of distinction follows from our fear of extinction and all our dreams of immortality are but the transmutation of our dread.

It is getting cooler. I feel the coolness—being a convalescent invalid, having felt death's chill fingers. It is always a problem: when to go in. Sometimes, despite the coolness, I have lingered out here in the garden, my upturned tray on my knee, till it is almost impossible to write. . . .

And maybe it's not posterity I seek at all. Since I have already essayed the dread bourne, whereas, for most, posterity is the goal that looms, cryptically, on its other side. Maybe this *is* posterity. Maybe for me it is the other way round. Maybe it's anteriority (if such a thing exists) I'm looking for. To know who I was.

There is still the sound from the river, as of a perpetual, festive brawl, but this will quieten as the evening draws on. The darkness will fall. And then that vengeful lout who haunts the febrile dreams of us begowned and pampered pedants will start to prowl. So you think you are special? (No, I don't.) Well I am special too. You can put mind over matter? Well, I can put matter over mind. Turn the one into the other. Easy. With the toe of a boot, or a broken bottle. Or a bullet. Or a bottle of pills.

What can Darwin tell me that is new? That nothing in this world is fixed, that everything is mutable? But poets have been saying this for centuries. Isn't that the very theme of poetry? "Even such is time . . ." That over millions of years by a process of infinitesimal variation an ape will turn into a man—though, as things go, that is nothing, a mere recent innovation. That Nature is a veritable graveyard littered with failed prototypes, in which Man, who is not the point of the plan, since there is no plan, will surely find his place. But he cannot tell me why what was here yesterday is gone today, or why, when so much has been brought about over so long and so much life has sprung from so much life, a person can become, in an instant, a thing.

It is beyond belief. Beyond belief. In the greyness of that winter morning (the glib punctuality of daylight), I wanted, a grown man in the full maturity of some fifty years, to ask that other, naïvest of questions: and if, in an instant, a person can become a thing, why cannot a thing become a person? I wanted her body to know I was there. I wanted her body to hear me speak. To answer. I wanted to say, just like people do in cheap dramas: "Don't! Please! Come back!" I wanted to say—as if it really were some (convincing) death scene—"Ruth, stop acting! Please. Stop acting."

21

So let me tell you (with special benefit of hindsight) about what might have been, what very nearly was, my last day on this earth.

The scene: a June afternoon; this college; my venerable Fellow's chambers. Outside, rain is sluicing down—one of those vertical, seemingly immovable midsummer downpours which fall from a swollen sky and fill even covered spaces with a damp, sticky breath. The light is leaden. The lamps of study are lit. I sit reading (Darwin: the chapter on Instinct) by my venerable Fellow's fireplace. Beside me, on the coffee table, my working copy of the Notebooks and scattered notes thereon. The gas fire is on, not because its warmth is needed, but to dry a pair of socks that dangle, pinned by a glass ashtray, from the mantelpiece, just to one side of John Pearce's implacably ticking clock. I have just been out (my last mortal errand—cigarettes and coffee) and been caught, in leaky shoes, in the onset of the deluge. To counteract the heat of the fire, a window is half open, so that the room is full of the not unpleasing orchestration of the rain.

A quarter to four by John Pearce's clock. When you are sitting at home by the fire . . . A knock on the door. I open it, in bare feet, a cigarette in one hand, a pencil behind one ear: the perfect picture of incommoded scholarship.

"I was just passing. Shelter from the storm?"

Now I think of it (this hindsight), that climb up my spiral

staircase (ah yes, the stealthy chatelaine) cannot have failed to remind her of that earlier foray, years ago, to Potter's office. Why else, on this wet and lethal afternoon, should she have described to me that very episode—given me the full, sorry saga of her and Potter? So the whole exercise (if that is the word) was a sort of re-rehearsal of that former, ostensibly scholarly assignation—with me in the role of the plausible tutor.

Ah—Katherine, isn't it? Do come in. Now, what was it? Of course—Arthurianism in Tennyson. Well, you have come to the right place, my dear. Spiral staircases and genuine Gothic features. And the fireplace, you notice, a genuine piece of neo-Gothic pastiche, dating from Tennyson's own time. Who shall we pretend to be? Lancelot and Guinevere? Perhaps not. Merlin and Vivien? Yes, I fancy myself as a beguiled wizard. . . .

Seduction by a female agent. The thing is obvious. No one "just passes" my corner of the College: there are gateways, courts, medieval intricacy. And, beneath her rain-spattered raincoat, there is a dress that no one casually wears at four o'clock on a wet afternoon: downy-soft, charcoal cashmere; well above the knee, figure-hugging; a row of winking buttons from nape to small of back. The legs are black and sheer (this is Gabriella's sable costume upgraded). There is a single, thin silver chain round her neck. There are high-heeled shoes—damp and flecked with grit (should I suggest she kick them off?). The legs (I notice) are good legs, but without verve, as if she is not used to showing them. But this gives them a certain—appeal.

"You're working—I can see. I'm disturbing you."

"No, no. Please . . ."

I take her coat. She has left an umbrella weeping on the stone landing, but strands of her hair are wet; there is a drop or two on one cheek (it might have been arranged, this rain). She enters my room with an air of simultaneous premeditation and precipitateness, as if someone, perhaps, has gently pushed her, as if she is stepping on to the stage of some bizarre and potentially disastrous initiative test. And I am meant to guess, perhaps, that it's all a performance, that it isn't *her* idea; and therefore—out of sympathy—co-operate? But perhaps she is intent on not failing this—audition. Perhaps this wouldn't be happening if Ruth hadn't been an actress.

"Katherine— I wasn't expecting— I— What can I get you? Tea? Coffee? Hot soup? A towel?"

She gives the room a long, prying, but distinctly hesitant glance. I have ushered her in, my initiative: she is the inveigled innocent—play it that way round. I think what she takes in first are the notes and the photocopy on the coffee table. Then that there are no obvious mementos, photographs (they are all in my bedroom). Then what she takes in are my socks.

"Ah—I'm sorry—"

But the socks seem to rescue her from incipient loss of nerve. The socks—limp, grey flags of discouragement though they must be to anyone bent on erotic manoeuvring—are in fact the unenvisaged trigger to the afternoon's proceedings. It occurs to me now that if I had not removed my socks and hung them to dry on the mantelpiece, I might not be sitting here, in this quasi-afterlife, trying to recognise my former self.

"It's all right," she says, moving towards the fire. "I need to dry off myself." She gives the skirt of her dress a little pluck and shake, though it doesn't look wet to me. "Besides—I like a man with bare feet."

She reaches out and fingers the socks—a strange combination of the sensual and the housewifely.

"They're dry, you know."

***

And it's at this point, as she turns (catching me, perhaps, eyeing her from behind), that our eyes truly meet for the first time. And I can see in hers that she suddenly realises that the chemistry she is trying to induce might just, after all, be *there*. The gaze sharpens, brightens. Perhaps she won't have to force it, feign it; perhaps she isn't beyond it, past it. And certain things are on her side: this gushing veil of rain; the little orange hint of the gas fire; this innocuous man, all by himself, caught drying his socks.

Ah, yes, my dear—the *Idylls of the King*. Published, as you no doubt know, in the year that Darwin published his *Origin of Species*. At one and the same time these hapless Victorians had flung before them the spectre of their derivation from monkeys and Tennyson's misty and moated chivalric nostalgia. But the latter, as you doubtless also know, was only a wistful cloak for a study of the perils of sexual freedom. . . .

She takes the socks from beneath the ashtray and toys with them, running a hand inside one and spreading her fingers.

"This is awful of me, isn't it, butting in like this?"

She smiles. Then makes her move.

"Are those your notes on the Pearce manuscripts?"

"Yes."

"And that's a copy of the original?"

"Yes."

"May I—?"

She picks up the photocopy, my socks still twined round her fingers. This is the first time I've allowed anyone—excluding Potter—to look at the Notebooks. I don't know what portion of Matthew's agony she briefly alights on.

"Michael is pretty upset that you won't let him help you. You know that, don't you?"

I say nothing.

"Pretty upset. You know what he's like."

There's a sort of plea for corroboration in her eyes.

"I know what he's like."

"But you're determined, aren't you? You've made up your mind."

She flicks through the photocopy as if riffling through a magazine. It seems somehow sacrilegious. I experience a passing urge to grasp it back—as if she means simply to appropriate it and make off with it. I have a sudden, bleak vision of what my life might be like without these—distracting—notebooks.

"I have," I say.

She puts the photocopy back on the coffee table.

"And there's nothing that would persuade you?" She seems to take a deep breath.

She holds up the socks fastidiously, one dangling from each thumb and forefinger, like incriminating articles.

"Nothing?"

I go to take them. I know it's the wrong move.

"Nothing?" she repeats as I grasp them, and she doesn't let go. Her face is transformed by a strange, unlovely effort. It's as though, out of sudden, reckless confidence or out of sheer nervous impatience, she has decided to dispense with whatever further preliminary manoeuvres she may have planned and go full-tilt at the thing.

She pulls me, by the socks, towards her. I am not going to play tug-of-war. But before I can disengage, she lets go of one sock, grabs my free hand with her free hand and jams it against her left breast. My crumpled sock is inadvertently trapped between my palm and her dress. Beneath both, I can feel something lacy, scratchy. The breast is soft and warm.

"You know why I came here, don't you? It's not the manuscripts, it's—"

I pull my hand away. Perhaps I even take a virtuous step backwards. Her face seems about to undergo some further extraordinary transformation. To fall apart, perhaps. She spreads a hand (no longer possessed of a sock) across it, as if to hold it together.

"Oh God, I'm sorry. I'm sorry, Bill. I—"

Her throat is suddenly clogged with wordless gulps. She peers helplessly through her fingers.

"I'm truly sorry. Oh God. I wouldn't have done it if— I mean—I mean—I wouldn't have done it, anyway, if— if—"

But then tears start coming in great wrenching eruptions. She leans towards me. I drop my socks (I have them both now, one in each hand). Quite possibly, the pencil is still behind my ear. I step forward, put my arms around her. I feel her palm pressing on my back, her breasts on my ribs. A wet cheek on my cheek.

It's strange, we are doing now, almost involuntarily, what a moment ago had been the object of intense, abortive machination. What's more, I have this erection, a stiff, indomitable erection, and, though I try to be careful, she must feel it.

It's her turn to pull away. "I think—I think I need that towel you were offering."

And, trying to prevent me from seeing her face, she blunders first into my bedroom, then into the bathroom.

I don't know what to do while she's in the bathroom. I should make tea? Pour brandy? (I haven't any brandy.) Say soothing things through the door, like some penitent seducer? I don't know what will happen when she emerges. She will have regained a fragile composure and wish to leave? She will be minus her dress?

I pick up my socks, think of putting them on; then, as if putting them on would signal some sort of insensitivity, drop them again. I look at my notes strewn on the coffee table. I look at my bare, white feet. To be honest, for much of the preceding encounter, I have felt oddly like a mere manipulated dummy. Now I have the sensation (it's not comfortable—it's like some anaesthetic wearing off) of being dragged out of a state of suspended animation.

And I have this obstinate, towering erection. My body seems constructed around it.

A full minute passes. The plumbing (not medieval, but not up-to-the-minute) sings. I think: what state is my bathroom in? What horrors of male squalor? What scum in the bath?

But I quite forget one thing. When she comes out, she is neither composed nor naked. Her eyes are dry and puffed; but, rather than softened by a look of contrite, mustered dignity, the face is alert, suspicious, vaguely vindictive. It conveys a new sort of bewilderment, as if she, now, is the victim of some trick.

I smile imbecilically. What now?

"Well, you're a sly one, aren't you, Bill? But your visitors should be more careful—leaving their perfume in the bathroom."

This takes me wholly by surprise. But, in the circumstances, it is absurdly proprietorial, absurdly accusatory—not to say wildly imaginative.

I think she realises this too, for she suddenly bites her lower lip, half closes her eyes, and her face is all an ominous quiver again.

What to say? I am bereft of inventiveness. It seems to me that the best thing to say is the truth. Perhaps it will be a way of getting me neatly, honourably out of all this.

(How wrong can you be?)

"Shall I tell you who that perfume belongs to? It belongs to Michael's research student. Gabriella."

She gives me a fierce, astonished, even more accusatory look.

"*Her!*"

"I can explain," I say (feeling surprisingly guilty).

So I tell her about the events of that morning when I found myself a coerced passenger in Potter's car. How I pocketed the perfume. Though I don't tell her how I stalked the corridors of the Library, on a spring day, looking for a girl less than half my age (dressed in kittenish black), with ideas in my head as fantastical and concocted as the scent in my pocket.

All of which produces another convulsion of forgiveness-seeking, another welter of tears.

"Oh, I'm sorry, I'm sorry. I'm sorry. And you did it because of *me*. You're— But I know about Gabriella. Of course I know about her. I know about them bloody *all*, don't I?"

And then, as the tears subside, she begins to tell me, without announcing it, the full story of her life and hard times with Michael Potter (M.A., Ph.D.), beginning at the beginning, with that encounter, long ago, in a room in a university.

I listen. I fetch Kleenex. I make tea. We switch to something stronger. Dry sherry. College reserve. The academic tipple. The rain still thrums. My sitting-room is not furnished for intimacy—commiserative or otherwise. No sofa; two huge and dumpy armchairs which engirdle and engulf their occupants. A room meant, presumably, for learned, man-to-man debate, with much puffing and waving of pipes. We sit islanded from each other, Matthew's Notebooks, like an impotent arbitrator, between us.

And it was her fault, you see. She thinks it was all her fault. (She has this way of being at fault.) It was even her job, at the BBC, that gave Potter his eventual entrée into real-live mediadom. But it would never have happened the way it did—she is sure of it—if they'd had a kid. Or two kids. She used to see famous names pass through the studio doors—more than once, it seems, she saw Ruth Vaughan passing through the studio doors—but what she wanted most then was a child. It wasn't his fault. His machinery wasn't faulty. (Or underused.) It was something wrong with her. Several tries. Several tests. Then, at last, by a fluke, it happens. She gives up her job to be a mother. But the thing is born prematurely and dies within hours, and it seems there won't be a second chance. And within months Potter is messing around with a former colleague of hers, a TV producer called Lena ("Legs-up Lena")—his new career is about to begin.

And she is left only with years of pretend marriage; of feeling that if she hadn't walked through Potter's door all that time ago with her notes for her long essay (chivalric nostalgia!), her life would have been a different thing; and of feeling, all the same, that it's her fault, she is the one to blame—so much so that she even submits to this mad and self-recriminatory degree of ignominy, this exorcistic climbing of my staircase, as if she is returning full circle, to walk through the door again, to try to put it right.

The gas fire fizzes. John Pearce's clock chimes—five, six o'clock. Her face is a smudged, reddened mess—she has first sobbed, then leaked tears. It makes a pitiable contrast with her dressed-to-kill outfit, as if one part of her is a discarded doll, the other an unmasked human being.

But something is happening as she speaks. Her face seems slowly to reassemble. Or rather, a new face, a face I have never seen before, seems to appear, as if something, some layer, some sad accretion, has been rinsed away. It is an extraordinary thing this, like watching some rare natural event, to see another person loom out of themselves.

She folds her legs beneath her on the chair (I'm not sure now that they don't have verve), one hand clasping her ankles. She has abandoned her shoes. Her high heels, my grey socks, lie like the litter from some previous intimate encounter on the worn carpet. We are like young people. Provisional people. These college rooms. These conversations that have no end. As if we have gone back in time and this is us now, beginning.

It could have been her. It could have been us.

And now she has stopped. Now she wants to know about me, how it was with me. She wants to know about Ruth.

But how do you begin? I can't find words. Something is happening. Something is stuck, struggling inside me. Something is turning completely around, inside-out—and she, now, is the calm, re-embodied one, watching me dissolve.

She gets up. She comes and stands by my chair and takes my hand. I don't know if her intention is to lead me, there and then, into my bedroom or merely to kiss me sweetly, briefly, and say something sad, wise and conclusive. But I resist the tug of her hand. I don't know if this hurts her, but she draws her hand away as quickly as I draw mine, as if it's her mistake—all her fault again—then she moves away to the window, her back towards me. She says nothing, but her back—her whole person—is eloquent.

I get up. I go to the window. I stand beside her. It is possible, by an effort, not to touch. There flashes through my mind a whole course of events—a whole fairy-tale prognosis—that I will only institute later (though, tell me, was it necessary to have been jerked back from the gates of death first? Do only ghosts have initiative?). I will give her the Notebooks. I will send her back to her husband. Oh, the true, chaste knight, a true Sir Galahad! She is Potter's wife; Potter is her husband. Potter, with the Notebooks, will become the happy scholar again (happy researching other people's spiritual crises). And when Potter becomes the happy scholar again, the man she once married will be given back to her. Hey presto! The wizard Merlin—ha!

The rain still teems down, but there is a faint gleam in one corner of the sky. The cobbles in the court and the tiles on the rooftops opposite have a pewtery glaze.

And children? Children can be adopted. Substitutes can be arranged. What is so important about this flesh-and-blood thing? This damn flesh-and-blood thing?

"It's going to stop," she says. The air from the open window is cool on our hot faces. "Then I won't have any excuse, will I?"

I try not to look at her. I still have this mutinous erection.

"But I'll go now if you want me to."

Someone, hooded by a raincoat, dashes, feet slapping, across the court.

"Life goes on, Bill," she says. That old trite truism.

"Go when it stops," I say.

But maybe it won't stop. Maybe the gleam is a false gleam, and the rain will go on all night. All night! Yet, even as I think this, the gleam spreads and brightens, the rooftops glisten and, as if someone has closed a tap, the full pelt of the skies becomes a sprinkle.

"Bill—?"

It's a full, hard embrace with nothing restrained or disguised about it. It lasts maybe fifteen seconds, and it's she who breaks off first.

She walks across the room. She retrieves her shoes. She

doesn't glance at the papers on the coffee table. She looks so different from the woman who walked in. She takes her coat from the hook on the door, opens the door. She pauses, her mouth half open as if to say something, but the door is already shut when I say, "It hasn't stopped yet."

I hear the cautious click of her high heels descending the worn and uneven spiral stairs—it's not easy, you have to be careful. I think of her dressing, preparing for this. I look down on to the court. It seems amazing that these buildings have been here for centuries. It seems amazing they should be here at all. I watch her cross to the main gate, but she is all but hidden by her umbrella. A black, man's umbrella. She doesn't look up.

I stand by the window, waiting for the rain to stop. It takes longer than I expected. There is a moment when the sky seems partially to darken again and the deluge makes a temporary come-back. But after a while—I'm not paying attention, and it's as if I awake to the fact rather than observe it—a weak, lemony light floods the court and there is a sudden assertion of routine, incidental noise: footsteps, drips, birdsong.

I go to the bathroom. I need to have a prodigious pee. Tea, followed by sherry, and all this rain—and only now does my erection yield to my bladder. I feel as if I am emptying out my being. I feel as if I am pissing out my soul. The sun shines on the tiles. On one of the glass shelves is Gabriella's unclaimed perfume. On another is an old bottle of pills that a doctor gave me to "help" after Ruth died. Doctors must be short-sighted people.

I take it down, shake it to see how many pills are left. (Apparently, not enough.)

Then I go back into my sitting-room, and with the aid of what's left in the sherry bottle, swallow the lot.

22

It's not the end of the world. It is. Life goes on. It doesn't.

Why seems it so particular with thee?

When the first Aldermaston marchers set out in the late 1950s on their pilgrimage of protest, what were Ruth and I doing? We were sharing our now found love-nest (having slipped the clutches of despotic landladies), a top-floor flat at number twenty-seven, Mayflower Road, Camden. And she was enamoured of the stage, and I was enamoured of poetry, and we were both enamoured of each other. Too happy, too busy being happy, to worry about the Bomb.

But what sort of a plea, what sort of an excuse, is happiness? Perhaps it's the only plea. Why march with banners of protest unless to save a world in which happiness can exist? It is a rare and endangered enough creature, after all, happiness, worthy of special protection. True, among the denizens of this world it has no privileged place ("Why should a dog, a horse, a rat have life, and thou no breath at all . . . ?"). But who, sitting on the Grand Jury of Extinction, would not suffer the eclipse of a thousand drab species (such is nature's way) but wish to spare the birds of paradise?

And what are these things: the theatre, poetry? Bubbles, toys. It doesn't take a bomb to shatter them. They only tell us what is in our hearts. They are only mirrors for our lost, discredited souls.

O Mayflower Road! O garrets under the stars! O *vie Bohème*! O Mimi! O Rodolfo!

How many taxi rides? How many shillings on the meter? How many journeys, all too quick, through the emptied streets, through the small, shy hours of love, before we even dared to speak the magic words? Perhaps love is more than the sum of two people. Perhaps love is a third thing, mysteriously bestowed, precious and fragile, like some rare, warm egg. We wished and feared to hasten it. We took it into our care like diligent trustees, waiting our charge's coming of age.

The time would come when, by much discreet investigation and counting of pennies, our homeward journeys would take us to a shared address. When the vexed geography of our lives would contract into the ecstatic geography of a shared bed (to be exact, a mattress on the floor). The time would come—O Mayflower Road! O my America, my new-found-land!—when behind the drawn curtains of number twenty-seven, which otherwise gave on to a sea of slates and chimney-pots with, beyond, the fairy-tale pinnacles of St. Pancras Station, Ruth would perform for me what she called her snake-charmer's dance, a sort of dance that Mr Silvester would never have allowed his good girls at the Blue Moon Club to perform. Not that my snake needed charming—it stood up, rigid and ready as a tent pole beneath the sheets. . . .

But meanwhile it is still 1957. When the official language of love was still the language of engagement rings and kisses at front doors, when university-registered landladies exercised their censorious regimes, and sex and sin were still conveniently alliterative synonyms. The taxi would drop her first at Pickford Street—our good-night clinches behind the cabbie's back would be swift and muddled—then take me on to Winterton Road, where in my solitary bed I would think of Ruth in her solitary bed, thinking of me in mine.

And I didn't know I loved her till I'd dreamt of her. I didn't know it was the real thing until an illusion had signalled it. Until she'd stepped out of her real existence into this other existence of which only I knew . . .

I still remember that dream: its simple but panic-ridden formula, its tides of anguish and relief. How there was this train to catch. How we were going on this long, momentous journey (oh yes, I know—the symbolism of trains). How we had arranged to meet at the station, a big London terminus. And how, despite careful planning, everything —London Transport, my own flustered brain, the perils of the street, a bulging suitcase—conspired to stop me arriving on time. A taxi broke down. There were crowds that wouldn't part. I was late, irrevocably late. The train would be gone and so would she.

But as I crossed the station concourse, there she was, waiting, waving, by the barrier. And there, still, was the train. It was all right, you see: she had spoken to the driver (she had spoken to the driver!). Didn't I know this was a special train: it couldn't possibly leave without us?

We fell into an embrace, an intimate and swooning embrace, there and then on the crowded concourse. And when I woke up, the embrace, the whole dream, still clung to me, I still existed within it, as in some warm envelope. What's more, I was convinced that she must *know* she had been in my dream—that she too must have had a dream, a parallel dream, in which she had waited for me at the station, stricken by the fear (but she had this obliging engine driver) that I might never turn up.

So I never dared tell her—never in thirty years—for fear

of breaking some beautiful, tacit conspiracy: "I had this dream . . ."

But the dream gave me the courage (that very day) to say the words I had not uttered before. You see, it was I who said them first, though she echoed them soon afterwards, as if to prove my (our) dream had been mutual. And all that afternoon, of course (they are truly magic words), was like a dream. A dream.

Where did this happen? It happened in, of all places, the Reptile House of the London Zoo in Regent's Park. Where do you go, what do you do, on a cool, grey Sunday afternoon in August, when the pubs have closed and everywhere else is shut? We clanked through turnstiles. We drifted into the sheltering darkness of this home for exiled toads and vipers. It was not the first time, I suppose, that lovers had availed themselves of its dim-lit sanctuary. And there, under the unimpressed gaze of comatose pythons, disgruntled alligators and forlorn tortoises, we whispered into each other's ears the words that my (our) dream had endorsed, and nuzzled and pressed against each other and behaved as the human species will behave under such circumstances as ours. And, of course, now the words had been spoken, there was no denying that further question, asked by our bodies if not our lips (hadn't our souls already eloped—by special train?): When? Where? How?

How strange the contrast between the dazzle, the display of the Blue Moon Club and these furtive but intrepid creatures, plotting with reptilian stealth their happiness. Love makes of its initiates bold undercover agents in the hostile territory of mundanity and propriety. We resolved, that same afternoon, that nothing less was our due than a whole night in each other's arms. Which meant, given the rigours of our situation, the expedient of some cheap hotel. I was to make the arrangements. Next Sunday. Could we afford it? We'd have to. Could we wait that long? Just about. We walked over Primrose Hill. Sweet Primrose Hill. A primrose sun, hiding behind grey, watery clouds. We parted, to go our separate ways in Camden, my flat feet floating on air. . . .

That moment when the performance begins! That magic moment when the lights go down and the curtain trembles; when the pretend thing, the made-up thing becomes the real thing and the audience, in their dark rows, turn to ghosts. How can it be? Why should it be? What's Hecuba to him? That moment when things come alive.

It doesn't always happen. There is good acting and bad acting (I know this). We sit in our seats and think of a thousand things. But she could do it, that simple, marvellous thing: she could bring things to life.

Who was she, this sorceress? A little girl with a bee in her bonnet about becoming an actress; the only child of a doting father and a disapproving mother; a night-club dancer who in the cold-blooded gloom of the London Zoo Reptile House indulged with me in hot-blooded but as yet unconsummated passion; a woman who for nineteen years of her life inhabited the undiscovered country of my complete ignorance of her. Then loomed into my view. And the world's. Ruth.

They say I should write her biography. It has been put to me more than once—by friends, by a publisher or two, even, on that last visit, by a well-meaning Sam ("You know the book I think you should write, pal. What's with this Pearce guy, anyway?"). The life of Ruth Vaughan, actress. Each time, it has come with the tacit, the soft-toned hint that this might be, as it were, a cure for grief. But it seems to me it would be an impossibility, a falsehood, a sham. It's not the life, is it, but the *life*? The *life*.

How was it done? What was the trick? I don't know. I couldn't act for toffee, but I know what it's like, sitting here in this dimming garden, not to be sure who you are. They say that actors and actresses are really shadowy, half-formed, insubstantial people. Dogged by a poor sense of their own identity and a lack of personality, they make up for it by striving to become—these other people. But why not start with the other premise? That actors have an excess of personality: more to spread around. And why not start from the premise—it would be logical and fair and neat, wouldn't it, even if it's patently not so—that nature has given each one of us an equal, definitive and sufficient personality?

And let me be clear, in any case, of one thing: these other people that she became and at whom, with other people, I marvelled—they didn't matter to me. It didn't matter to me whether she became them or not, so long as she was, also, herself. Herself. And it wouldn't have mattered to me if we had never had all those things, never known all those things—the tours, the great days: the stuff of biographies—if not to have had them would have meant to have her still, here, now.

But then what I ask is this: could there have been a Ruth Vaughan who did not do all those things, who never became an actress?

Of course.

Of course not.

And could there have been a Ruth Vaughan who did or did not do all those things, who was or was not all those things, without ever entering my life or my entering hers?

Of course.

Of course not. Of course not.

And can I really believe that in all this turning into other people, in all this promiscuity of personae, up there before the lights, she never ever—?

Not the life but the life. I used to watch her pacing up and down at the end of the garden at the cottage, addressing the air. For me the most wonderful thing was always this act of rehearsal, this straining of life after life: ballet dancers, on a frosty morning, at the *barre*. I remember once when she was in full flow, complete with her running commentary of interjections, expletives and self-exhortations and her battery of cigarettes, a man came to fix a TV aerial to the chimney. From which, of course, he had a grandstand view. Did she stop? No. She knew he was there. Did she abate her voice or her pungent asides? No. From his perch, the aerial man would have beheld Ruth talking volubly to people who weren't there, not to mention rattling away to herself. The classic signs. I remember his look of suppressed bewilderment as, the job done, his ladder removed, I at last enlightened him (having joined in the game): "My wife is an actress." Which didn't prevent him, I'm sure, from going away with the conviction that my wife was mad.

I think now of that aerial man, with his ladder and van. His faltering nonchalance. Perhaps it wasn't just that he thought Ruth was crazy. Perhaps he might have been happy to stay up there longer by the chimney. I see Ruth turning to me, after he'd gone, to share in the joke, her eyes beating her lips to it as always, the sun on the field, a hand in her hair, the wide mock-pity of her laugh: "Poor man! Poor man!" And I think how the aerial man might have been *me*, how it might have been my lot only to view for half an hour in the course of my day's work this strangely behaved, this extraordinary, this adorable creature.

You see, nothing else will do. No simulations, fabrications, biographical conjurations. Slowly, yes, slowly you abandon the wilder delusions, the ruses, subterfuges, superstitions of grief. The days of eating meals for one but set for two, of clothes still hanging untouched on hangers exactly as they were left. The moments of indescribable mental concentration when you try to summon out of some recess of reality the exact sound of her footstep, the exact way in which she would turn the key in the lock. The bouts of talking out loud and alone, but not to yourself (*my* rehearsal sessions), to the thin, cheating air. The days of signs, traces—dreams. Oh yes, the dreams. Now she has stepped for ever out of her own existence, doesn't she enter, even more readily, even more lovably, the existence of your dreams?

Yes. Though, tell me, which would be crueller: not to have or to have these dreams?

And what of the other images, the undreamt images? Surely you are lucky—lucky. The films, the videotapes, the hundreds and hundreds of photographs—publicity shots, rehearsal shots. You can turn a page, push a button, press a cassette into its slot, and there will be Ruth—moving, talking, breathing—before you.

But how can I explain it? The pictures mock me. They are, they are not Ruth. I can't bear to look at them.

And nothing is left but this impossible absence. This space at your side the size of a woman, the size of a life, the size—of the world. Ah yes, the monstrosity, the iniquity of love—that another person should *be* the world. What does it matter if the world (out there) is lost, doomed, if there is no sense, purpose, rhyme or reason to the scheme-less scheme of things, so long as— But when she is gone, you indict the universe.

I would believe or not believe anything, swallow any old make-belief, in order to have Ruth back. Whereas Matthew— Whereas this Pearce guy—

Nothing else. Only the exact filling of the exact space. Only the actual reversal of nature. And now you see the little joke nature has played on me. She has granted me my wish—after a fashion. She has brought *me* back to life.

And what should I expect now: that I should live for ever?

But the lights are dimming. There is a hush in the auditorium. The curtain is lifting. It is 1957. The marchers are not yet marching, to save the world, along the road to where, once upon a time, I spotted trains, took tea with my mother and, conceivably, was conceived; and the two young people who command our attention still have a quaint, residual feeling that the world has already been saved, that the great cosmic battle for good and evil has already been fought and won—even for their sakes—when they were small. And it is only four years since a new queen rode in a fairy-tale coach to her coronation; and some bright spark has named this age the New Elizabethan Age, as if the mere name of a queen imparted some historical magic and the world were once more waiting to be discovered and explored.

What does he do, this young hero of ours, charged with the task of providing for a first night of bliss? There are no hotels in Camden, and, besides, that is too close to home. His thoughts and his steps take him to the vicinity of Paddington Station, where he eyes from outside, with an intensity of circumspection (he should have worn a hat with the brim pulled down and turned up the collar of his coat), the ranks of plausible hotels that accost the traveller hying to and from the West Country.

It was here, of course, that he first alighted in the capital, in the classic guise of the indigent waif, scorned by his elders, come to find his future in the big city. (Now he has found his future.) And it was from Paddington Station, which still reeks of coal and steam though the Great Western Railway is no more, that the trains that once thrilled him in his younger days set forth. And it has already occurred to our young hotel-assessor that the station in his dream, so blessedly adapted to the needs of two very important travellers, was Paddington.

He selects a hotel. Are names significant? It is called the Denmark Hotel. The white stucco seems newly painted. It has stone steps, leading up to its fanlighted front entrance, and, so far as he can see through the glass-panelled door, what lies within is not outrightly forbidding (he imagines the fearsome business of signing the register) nor blatantly at odds with its outer pretensions. There are three hotels in the terrace, and it is the only one to have its front steps thoughtfully whitewashed at the edges. There is, of course, the thorny question of the price.

He doesn't go in. Later that day he telephones, not from his Camden quarters, where Mrs Nesbitt generously allows her lodgers to make use of the phone—while stationing herself squarely within earshot—but from a call-box in the street. He thinks he has prepared a casual and credible style of inquiry. He is even ready, if needs be, to spin some yarn about how they will have travelled down—he and his wife, that is—from the north that day and will be getting a train to Somerset the next morning (he has in mind Weston Super Mare: it is August, after all, the holiday season).

But he is caught by surprise by the female voice at the other end, which is not so far removed from Mrs Nesbitt's, though with a practised smarminess that Mrs Nesbitt cannot muster: a voice that seems to go with a certain length of earring, a certain weight of bosom and a certain adroitness at sizing people up. And he is tripped up by the perfectly feasible "For one night only?" and by the abrupt "And whom is this speaking, sir?" Up to this point he has thought: what is wrong with his own name? But, suddenly panicked, he plucks out of the air the name Nesbitt. "Nesbitt. Mr Nesbitt."

Yet the thing is done. He establishes that the price is three pounds ten shillings. A small fortune. A room is booked for the following Sunday. And that night, at the Blue Moon Club, he tells her (she giggles; he feels a little stupid) that she will have to remember that she is Mrs Nesbitt.

It is 1957. All this stealthiness is not unwarranted, if perhaps overdone. But what true lovers were they who never learnt to speak in whispers or tread on tiptoe? They arrange to meet in a café on Camden High Street, from where they will take a taxi to Paddington. He tells Mrs Nesbitt (this is getting confusing) that he is going to his mother's and stepfather's for the night, and packs a medium-sized suitcase with redundant clothing. No doubt Mrs Nesbitt will think this excessive for a journey of one night and that a Sunday evening is a strange time to be beginning a journey home. But there is nothing he can do about this: on Sunday nights the Blue Moon is closed; and his baggage has to fit more than one alibi. He takes to the street, suitcase in hand, anxiously eyeing his watch, and it occurs to him, again, that he is re-enacting his dream.

It is a wet evening, shot with interludes of silky, brassy light. She is first at their meeting place, carrying a small travelling bag and wearing a borrowed ring. He is, by this time, in a fair fever of nerves, but her presence calms him, rallies him, instructs him. He realises that what this is is simply an exercise in acting (one of the few of his life). Tonight they will have to pretend—and not pretend—to be other people. Her smile imparts a spirit of mischief and audacity he has quite overlooked. Let us give this night its due.

"So—Mr Nesbitt."

They dine on cod and chips and strong tea, by a steamed-up window that seems, in its veiled opacity, somehow appropriate. Beneath her raincoat, she wears a blue, white-dotted summer frock that buttons down the front. He re-alises that in just a little while— It is strange to think that only the night before, in the Blue Moon Club, she was all satin and egrets' feathers, but this dress, with its polka-dots and buttons, which is neither too modest nor too flaunting—the sort of dress a young wife might wear when setting out with her husband on her holiday—excites him more than he can say.

They linger in the fish and chip parlour. Though neither of them utters the thought, it is understood they are waiting for darkness to descend. This too seems appropriate. When you are out on an adventure . . .

When they can see their faces in the misty window, they leave.

Nothing is meant to be. Everything is meant to be.

They hail a taxi. They are used to taxis. (There are no problems: it doesn't break down.)

"The Denmark Hotel, Norfolk Square." Can the taxi-driver guess?

The woman at the desk has neither pendulous earrings nor ramparts of bosom. She is thin, toothy and angular

---

and has an air of veiled boredom. He signs the register. A good, a commendable performance. There are no trick questions. Only the momentarily disarming "Will you be wanting a call in the morning?"

"No, that's all right—we'll manage."

"Only we don't like our guests"—a piano-key smile—"to miss any trains."

She holds out, dangling from a wooden bobble, the key to number thirty-two (ever afterwards a magic number). And before any smirking porter can intervene (but there is no porter, it's not that sort of place), they turn with their bogus bags to mount the stairs—where with each flight, the carpet and paintwork get progressively dingier, while, as if to compensate, excitement flares between them.

You have to picture the scene. How it was then, on a wet August night in 1957, in the days before she was famous. The room looks over the street. The backcloth, beyond the window, is the inky shimmer of London under rain. But the curtains are soon drawn, and almost as soon, it seems, clothes are removed, plucked, pulled, yanked from impatient flesh. He had not expected it quite, this frenzy and breathlessness to be unclad, as if some off-stage voice, some prompter's whisper, should have gently enjoined: take your time, you have all night. Nor was he prepared for the arresting candour, the simplicity and amazement, of nakedness. And this, you see, is me. And this is me.

He was not prepared, either, for the tender and inspired fluency (as if to complete the candour) with which each one of them offers the other on this indelible night the complete and unabridged story of their lives up until this point. His is a strangely dramatic tale (though he doesn't know the half of it yet), full of comedy and tragedy in the romantic streets of Paris, and hers is a tale of the obscure London suburbs. But it is she who will be the actress, who will be the Queen of the Nile.

And so it is that he tells her, what he has never told anyone before, about his—father. That he took his life.

Rain patters on the window (tomorrow will be bright and new). There is faded, flowery wallpaper, a rickety wardrobe, a wash-stand that gurgles shamelessly in the dark.

How strange, how incomprehensible, that whispered phrase. How unreal, even as he speaks it. How impossible that either of these young people, whose lives, this night, have never been so richly possessed, so richly embraced, will ever come to such a pass. He took his life, he took his life.

A Note on the Type

———————

The text of this book was set in Walbaum, a type face designed by Justus Erich Walbaum in 1810. Walbaum was active as a type founder in Goslar and Weimar from 1799 to 1836. Though letterforms in this face are patterned closely on the "modern" cuts then being made by Giambattista Bodoni and the Didot family, they are of a far less rigid cut. Indeed, it is the slight but pleasing irregularities in the cut that give this face its human quality and account for its wide appeal. Even in appearance, Walbaum jumps boundaries, having a more French than German look.

Composed by PennSet, Inc., Bloomsburg, Pennsylvania
Printed and bound by Fairfield Graphics, Fairfield, Pennsylvania
Designed by Anthea Lingeman